An excerpt from Odalisque

Kai pushed his plate away. "Well, thanks for the most arousing and utterly ridiculous conversation of my life. If nothing else, this would make a great movie plot, this whole odalisque thing. You should pitch it to your director friends."

"You want the guy's card? The odalisque agent? I forcibly removed it from Jess."

"No, I really don't."

"It's right in my wallet." Mason reached for his back pocket and somehow Kai couldn't summon the impulse to shake his head. Mason fished out the embossed ivory rectangle and held it across the table.

"I'm not taking it."

"Take it. I don't want to argue with Jess about it anymore."

Kai swiped it from his fingers and looked down at the card's tasteful, subtle design. *Maison Odalisque*, *Agt. Sebastien Gaudet*, and a phone number. "He doesn't have email? A website?"

Mason chuckled. "These kinds of arrangements don't take place over the Internet. If you aren't rich enough to get on your personal jet and fly to see Monsieur Gaudet face-to-face, you aren't rich enough for one of these odalisques."

Kai tried to bite his tongue, but the question burst forth anyway. "How much? How much did your sheik pay?"

"The math is straightforward, my friend. One flat mil a year. One million for a willing, horny, erotically trained cockslave at your beck and call for three hundred and sixty-five days."

Kai smiled. "A bargain."

"I think so," said Mason, looking down at his phone. Kai could see his friend's sex-siren wife on the phone's display background. "I happen to think there's no price too high to pay for sexual contentment. Sexual adventure, even." Mason looked back up with a grin. "Life is short, don't you think?"

Odalisque

By

Annabel Joseph

Other erotic romance by Annabel Joseph

Mercy
Cait and the Devil
Firebird
Deep in the Woods
Fortune
Owning Wednesday
Lily Mine
Comfort Object
Caressa's Knees

Erotica by Annabel Joseph

Club Mephisto

Coming soon:

Cirque du Minuit
The Edge of the Earth

To Leslie, Elaine, Karen, Janine, Heather, Kati, Linda,
Adrienne Wilder and James R. Tuck,
for their help and support.

May our stories always out-spice the salsa.

And to Brandy G., for offering a valuable perspective I
didn't have.

Chapter One:
The Code

Kai Chandler closed his eyes and tried to tune out all the soft chattering around him. He was the only one lingering over his plate in the corner of the ballroom. He should have been up on his feet, swilling wine, working the room, but he couldn't get in the mood. Across the white-and-silver-gilt decorated space, a small orchestral ensemble played Barber's *Adagio for Strings*, a song that used to move him to tears. Now he listened in a kind of anesthetized stupor. He appreciated the wistful beauty of the piece, but seemed unable to feel anything deeper.

He was here at least. His movie-star friends Mason and Jessamine had managed, after much hounding, to drag him out. Oh, he'd never stopped his patronage of the L.A. Philharmonic, but he hadn't felt any joy in it for a while. He hadn't felt much joy in anything, but that was his own fault. For God's sake, it had been a year now since his marriage disintegrated.

As Barber's piece reached its maudlin climax, Kai stared down at the gourmet chocolate cake on his plate and started smashing it to shreds. Why couldn't he climb out of this funk? He was wealthy and healthy. He owned a thriving tech company which allowed him to throw money at causes he believed in, like the Philharmonic and their inner city music mentoring program. He ought to be happy. He ought to be ecstatic.

Ah, Fauré's *Pavane*. Much more bearable, if still somewhat mournful. Was this a charity bash or a wake? Kai looked from under dark lashes at Caressa Gallo, the visiting cellist who elevated the already-glittering gala to the must-attend charity event of the season. He had noticed earlier that she was heavily pregnant. Pregnant bellies taunted him, made him wonder what his own children might have looked like, with his dark half-Indian coloring and Veronica's blonde-haired, blue-eyed perfection. He would never know now.

"Kaivalyan, you whore!" Kai cringed as Mason Cooke, one of his oldest and closest friends, leaned down and slapped him none too gently on the back. Kai's fork went skittering from his plate, sending splotches of hundred-dollar cake across the pristine tablecloth.

"Hi, Mace," Kai said, glancing up with a grimace. Mason was tall, rugged, all-American beefcake, with dark, perfectly tousled hair and blue eyes that had melted a million women's hearts—on screen and off. Kai never really thought of his friend as a celebrity, but at these events Mason truly played the part, as did the striking woman beside him— Jessamine Jackson, the other half of Hollywood's premier uber-couple.

Mason pulled up a chair. "What are you doing lurking back here in the corner? You're the organizer of this gala."

"They don't want to see me." Kai gestured to Jessamine in her glittering scarlet gown. "Plenty of luminaries here for the star-gazing crowd."

"Ah, but you're the chairperson for the foundation." Jessamine, sex starlet extraordinaire, seated her curvaceous frame squarely in his lap. "And you might not be a celebrity, but you're certainly the sexiest bachelor in the room."

Kai rolled his eyes and exchanged a glance with Mason, who was all too used to his wife hitting on other men. Mason was badass enough to be amused by it, rather than threatened.

"Success is an aphrodisiac," Jess purred, running her fingers through Kai's hair. "And I think you are the hottest fucking man on the planet. Aside from Mason, of course."

Kai laughed despite his mood. It was impossible to feel down with Jessamine cooing in your ear. "Are you going to let your wife seduce me?" he asked Mason.

"Yep. Anything for the cause."

Kai dumped Jess off his lap, more for self-preservation than any comedic purpose. With her glossy honey-colored hair, luminous eyes, and banging body, she was irresistible in normal circumstances. In close quarters she was excruciating, especially considering she wasn't his.

Kai stood and took Jessamine's hand, bringing it to his lips. "You're a vision, Ms. Jackson. I can't tell you how much I appreciate you being here. You and Mason both."

"It was our pleasure to attend," said Mason. "And it was great to hear Caressa Gallo play. She's something."

"I'll say." Jess, an unrepentant bisexual, gave the pretty cellist a lascivious look.

"Jesus," teased her husband. "Give it up. She's not available."

"How do you know?" Jess pouted.

"Well, the first hint is the big pregnant stomach she's sporting behind that cello. I also happen to know she's married to Jeremy's former assistant."

"Really?" Jessamine looked shocked.

As if on cue, the string ensemble took a break and a tall, handsome man materialized at Caressa's side. The couple exchanged sickeningly infatuated looks, resulting in a snort of derision from Jessamine. "Well, would you look at that. She *is* taken. God, why does everyone hook up with everyone else in our little circle? It's like...inbreeding."

Mason rolled his eyes and headed to the bar as Jessamine sashayed over to join the cellist and her husband, along with movie star Jeremy Gray and his wife. Kai tried to place her name. Belle or Nell or something. He had seen the Grays now and again at LoveSlave, the highly private and exclusive BDSM club hidden away under the streets of West Hollywood, and they undoubtedly had seen him too. What Jessamine said was true. Los Angeles was a huge town, but their wealthy, often hedonistic clique was small. Small enough that all of them knew his business. Knew that Veronica had used him and left him feeling like a fool. As much as he would have enjoyed speaking with the talented cellist and his other acquaintances, he still felt compelled to hang on the outskirts and hide. The group was laughing, probably over something Jess had blurted out. Caressa's lovestruck husband placed one hand casually on his wife's bulging waistline.

Kai scrutinized her face. Did she love him? They seemed so easy together, and so disgustingly in love. But was she acting? Was he? The man used to work as a personal assistant. It stood to reason that Caressa Gallo was the wealthier of the two.

Did they have a prenuptial agreement?

It was none of his business. It really didn't matter how lovingly and happily they interacted, or how much that reminded him of his own glaring mistakes. From the start, his marriage had gone downhill. Like a chump, he'd continued to work at things. He'd blamed himself. He felt guilty for working long hours. He analyzed his personality for flaws and constantly worried about what he was doing wrong in the relationship. When Veronica asked for a divorce, Kai had felt it like a physical blow. Failure, after everything he'd tried to do to save them. It was his lawyer who pointed out that she'd filed for divorce on the exact day she became eligible for full benefits under the prenuptial agreement. Their fifth wedding anniversary, to be exact.

His lawyer had built in the five-year requirement to discourage gold digging, but Kai supposed five years wasn't much time to put in for a 35 million dollar payout. He'd advised Kai to hire an investigator to look for evidence of adultery, which would have negated the agreement. They didn't find any evidence of adultery, only three secret abortions his wife had undergone. He was father to three ghost children who haunted him even now, years after they'd ceased to exist at his wife's hand. He'd been so stupid, *so* stupid. He dreamed of them sometimes. In his dreams, his non-children gazed at him accusingly, as if to say, *this is your fault.*

Mason returned from the bar with a couple drinks and collapsed into the seat beside Kai. He glanced across the room, following Kai's gaze. "Yikes. Happy couple alert. How are you holding up?"

Kai grimaced and made some vague, noncommittal noise. Mason kept staring at him, a technique Kai knew was intended to draw him out, but there was really nothing to say.

Mason's face registered disappointment. "So, reconciliation with Veronica is totally out? There's nothing left? Nothing you can build on?"

Kai stabbed at the cake congealing on his plate. "Reconciliation would be fucking impossible. As far as my feelings for her, she can burn in eternal agony and hellfire and it still won't be enough."

Mason raised one dark brow. "Okay."

His friend didn't know about the ghost babies, or the vicious things Kai and Veronica had said to one another at the very end. Kai and Mason generally talked about everything. They'd come from the same quiet lower-class suburb south of the city, and had been through a lot together as they clawed and fought to make better lives for themselves. But Kai found himself unable—or unwilling—to share the darkest events of the breakup of his marriage. He didn't believe anyone else could ever understand all the guilt and loss he felt.

"Anyway," Kai said with a dismissive wave, "she's already seeing someone else."

Mason frowned. "You pretend you're over her." He imitated Kai's careless gesture. "But you're really not. What's happened to you?"

I lost faith in love. I lost faith in trust. I lost faith in...faith. "Nothing happened to me. I'm here, aren't I?"

"Yeah, but you look like you'd rather be anywhere else. You used to live for this shit. For the arts, for making a difference. You used to glow at these shindigs."

Kai gave him a raw smile. "What? I'm not rah-rah-save-the-world chipper enough for your liking? I'm more into the cancer charity this month."

Mason shook his head. "You have a great job, a great life, these causes you believe in. You've improved a lot of people's lives. On top of that, every single woman in the room is checking you out, wondering how to get into your pants."

"Or my wallet."

"So one woman took you for a ride. Live and learn. Look around at what you've done. A lot of kids have a chance, a lot of musicians have a livelihood thanks to you. So your marriage didn't work out. My first marriage didn't work out either. It might be time to move on."

Kai momentarily considered clocking Mason right between his famous blue eyes with his fist, or maybe with the plate of mashed-up chocolate cake. It was easy for Mason to talk about moving on. He couldn't walk five steps without bumping into a woman who wanted to fuck him, and he was married to the sexiest female in the world.

"You know, I don't feel like I'm in a good place to start a new relationship. When things calm down..."

"But are you happy? You should be happy. You're a fucking cinema tech mogul, for fuck's sake. You should be living the high life."

"Let it drop," Kai muttered. "I appreciate your concern, but I can handle my life just fine. I'm a big boy."

"So I hear." Jessamine returned, trailing a swath of expensive perfume. She sized up Kai's surly expression and leaned down to take her husband's arm. "Mason, I just had the most wonderful idea. Why don't we invite Kai to come along with us to the sheik's house? It might cheer him up."

Mason looked like that was the least wonderful idea he'd ever heard. Kai looked between him and Jessamine.

"The 'sheik'? Is he really a sheik?"

"Oh God, no." Jessamine laughed. "We just call him the sheik because—"

"Jessamine." Mason's voice was a warning. Kai had never seen Mason try to rein Jessamine in, and as expected, Jessamine didn't fall into line. She waved a hand at her husband and leaned closer to whisper in Kai's ear.

"We call him the sheik because he recently purchased an *odalisque*. Can you believe it? So depraved."

"What the hell is an odalisque?"

Mason tugged on a lock of her hair. "Jess, that's supposed to be a secret."

"I won't tell him the guy's real name." She turned back to Kai. "He's nobody you'd know anyway. Some spectacularly rich textile magnate. He bought a se—"

Mason pulled his wife down into his lap and clapped a hand over her mouth. "I think you've had a little too much to drink, darling."

Jess wriggled, pressing back against her husband, and whispered something behind her hand. Whatever she said, it must have been potent. Only Jessamine could make a hardened playboy like Mason Cooke blush.

"So, you never answered my question," said Kai. "What's an odalisque?"

Jessamine exploded in ribald peals of laughter. Mason pushed her to her feet and steered her toward the door.

"Google it!" she yelled over her shoulder. "Odalisque. O-D-A—" Again, Mason muffled her voice and waved farewell to Kai with his other hand.

Kai watched them go, jotting a note on his napkin as the string ensemble sat down to play another set.

* * * * *

It was almost a week before Mason was free to meet for lunch. Kai glowered at him over Mexican and margaritas.

"I searched for the word 'odalisque' and all that came up was a bunch of crap about slaves and harems. Tell me you and Jess haven't entered the slave trade. This 'sheik' friend of yours isn't involved in human trafficking, is he?"

Mason made a face. "I knew you'd suspect that."

"My sister works for Amnesty International, for God's sake. You don't want her in your face about it. If this 'sheik' friend of yours is holding a human being against his or her will—"

His friend silenced him with a look. "Do you really think we'd get involved in human trafficking? Really? Jess is a thoughtless and maniacal pervert, but I doubt even she would stoop so low." Mason almost said more, then busied himself rearranging the nachos in front of him.

"Spill it," Kai ordered.

Mason swirled a broken chip in a bowl of salsa, thought a moment, then started to talk.

"Okay, you know my wife somehow finds the weirdest, most freakass people in Hollywood. Without fail."

Kai nodded in agreement.

"So a couple weeks ago she got invited to this guy's house for a party. We'll continue to call him the sheik, shall we?"

"Why not?"

"So this 'sheik' is a single guy, dirty dirty rich. More money than he knows what to do with, but lonely as the day is long. He's not a sheik at all, he's from Indonesia. He owns a company that manufactures luxury fabric for designers and fashion houses. Velvet, silk, cashmere, high quality wool for gentlemen's bespoke suits. This is all he does. No social skills, no polish. No skills at picking up girls or protecting himself from women who are out to take advantage of him. But he wants someone, you know, to fulfill his...needs."

"Of course he does."

"So he took his fistfuls of money to France and acquired something called an odalisque." Mason paused, frowning. "Not some*thing*. Some*one*. A woman."

"Like a mail-order bride?"

"No. Nothing like a mail-order bride. Not a wife or girlfriend or escort or whore, not anything like that. He told Jess about this *Code d'Odalisque*, this lifestyle these women adhere to, which basically amounts to being a sexual slave to a man. Not for play scenes or kink. As a divine calling type of thing."

Kai snorted. "A divine calling? I see."

"Yeah, I know. I showed up expecting some brassy fake-boobed slut from the Valley, you know, some kooky kinky sex thing. But it was..."

Mason stopped and looked away, took a drink from his margarita and put it down, then leaned closer, suddenly animated.

"Kai, I can't even explain this shit to you. We got to the party. There were maybe five other people there besides me and Jess. All guys. And there was this girl, this odalisque. I don't even know her name, but I will tell you, my friend—she knocked me dead."

"Beautiful?"

"Beautiful doesn't cover it." Mason waved a hand. "Beautiful, graceful, all that, but so much more. She was like some...otherworldly creature. When you touched her, she reacted, and if it was acting, it was really, really good acting. She took on the whole room, all the men and Jess too." He stopped and looked around, lowering his voice. "I'm talking blowjobs, ass, pussy, face shots, double and triple teaming. She was fucked and fucked and then fucking fucked again and she took all of it with this incredible sensual poise. I can't explain it. It was like...we were the ones doing the fucking, but she was the one in control. We all left that night completely in love with her. No, not in love. We were in *adoration*."

Kai watched Mason, surprised. His friend wasn't normally given to exaggeration and flowery speech. The odalisque must really have been something. "I'm sorry now you didn't invite me along."

"You know, if I'd known, I would have. But I expected a typical gangbang scene."

"A *typical gangbang scene*? Jesus, what do you and Jess get up to after hours? I've never participated in any gangbang scenes, typical or not."

"Are you judging us, Mr. Whips-and-Chains? Because everyone knows you're heavy into the kinky stuff."

Kai choked on a mouthful of refried beans. "Everyone who?"

"Jessamine knows. Which means everyone knows. But who cares? This is L.A."

"Well, there's kinky stuff, and then there's gangbang scenes with a sheik and his exotic French sex slave. So you said there's some code?"

"Yeah, the *Code d'Odalisque*. You can find it online. It's pages and pages long and so fucking hot it'll burn you. I got halfway through and had to stop because I was getting lightheaded from nonstop jacking off."

"Too much information."

"Sorry. But seriously, it's fucking hot. These women literally exist to accommodate cock. They live for it. They do whatever their owner desires sexually. Whatever. Nothing of a sexual nature is off limits."

Kai was going to start masturbating himself in a moment. "Really? Nothing? What about stuff like..."

Mason smirked knowingly. "Your kinky stuff? Hell yeah. Whatever you like. They are purely sexual. They shimmer with it. Like Jess, only submissive and open to whatever you wanted. This girl at the sheik's...she was there to be used, and she *wanted* to be used. She *craved* to be used. That was the hottest thing. They're pleasure slaves. They're...specialized." Mason imbued the word *specialized* with so much lewd, lascivious emphasis that Kai started to laugh.

"So when do you and Jess get your own odalisque?"

"Oh, Jesus Christ. She'd already booked the fucking tickets to France when they told her odalisques only served men. They said I would have to be the one to acquire one, and I don't particularly care to. Oh, Jess was spitting nails, but I don't want the responsibility. I already have Jess to wrangle, you know? I told her she had to be content playing with the sheik's odalisque." He smiled at Kai. "And yours, when you've picked her out."

Kai shook his head. "I don't think so."

"Didn't the whole thing start in your part of the world? Didn't they have slaves and harems in India?"

"They had slaves and harems everywhere once upon a time. And I'm only half-Indian."

"You're Indian enough, you handsome motherfucker. And rich enough too."

Kai held up a hand. "Don't try to talk me into it. I'll fucking do it, and I shouldn't."

"Why not?"

"First of all, this is not legal or realistic. People cannot actually own sex slaves—"

"No, it's an arrangement. A rental. Year-to-year, in the sheik's case."

"Literally? Year-to-year?"

"Apparently, half the money goes to an account for the odalisque to utilize upon her retirement, a quarter goes to the agency that places them, and a quarter goes to charities dedicated to the obliteration of human sex trafficking."

"Okay, now you're making this shit up."

"I'm not making it up. This is all on the level. Consensual, monitored, legitimized, more or less. Sort of like taking on an au pair or a foreign exchange student."

"Except you don't use your au pair or foreign exchange student as a no-holes-barred gangbang sex slave."

Mason got a glazed look in his eyes. "I've always wanted an au pair."

"You don't have kids."

"Yeah, that's the problem."

Kai pushed his plate away. "Well, thanks for the most arousing and utterly ridiculous conversation of my life. If nothing else, this would make a great movie plot, this whole odalisque thing. You should pitch it to your director friends."

"You want the guy's card? The odalisque agent? I forcibly removed it from Jess."

"No, I really don't."

"It's right in my wallet." Mason reached for his back pocket and somehow Kai couldn't summon the impulse to shake his head. Mason fished out the embossed ivory rectangle and held it across the table.

"I'm not taking it."

"Take it. I don't want to argue with Jess about it anymore."

Kai swiped it from his fingers and looked down at the card's tasteful, subtle design. *Maison Odalisque*, *Agt. Sebastien Gaudet*, and a phone number. "He doesn't have email? A website?"

Mason chuckled. "These kinds of arrangements don't take place over the Internet. If you aren't rich enough to get on your personal jet and fly to see Monsieur Gaudet face-to-face, you aren't rich enough for one of these odalisques."

Kai tried to bite his tongue, but the question burst forth anyway. "How much? How much did your sheik pay?"

"The math is straightforward, my friend. One flat mil a year. One million for a willing, horny, erotically trained cockslave at your beck and call for three hundred and sixty-five days."

Kai smiled. "A bargain."

"I think so," said Mason, looking down at his phone. Kai could see his friend's sex-siren wife on the phone's display background. "I happen to think there's no price too high to pay for sexual contentment. Sexual adventure, even." Mason looked back up with a grin. "Life is short, don't you think?"

Chapter Two:
Maison Odalisque

Kai didn't take a private jet. He didn't actually have a private jet, but he did have a lot of money, enough to manage a million if it came to that. *If.* He was on a fact-finding mission, though, that was all. He'd phoned Sebastien Gaudet and found him personable and well-spoken. The man had reassured Kai that it was perfectly fine to fly over just to look around and ask questions.

And Kai had a lot of questions. First and foremost, what the hell he was doing flying to the French countryside to visit a manor where they trained odalisques.

Odalisques. The unfamiliar, grandiloquent word sounded almost as silly as the idea of buying a woman's favors for a year. He didn't know whether to be alarmed or excited by the fact that he was pretty much living out the plot of some contrived porn novel.

He hadn't told Mason anything about this trip. Or Jessamine, or Satya, his women's-rights-crusading sister who would bite off his head and chew it to pieces if she knew he was even considering acquiring a sex slave.

No, Kai hadn't told anyone the specifics, only that he was taking a much-needed vacation to France for a week. God, he had shitloads of work to do. Why was he doing this?

Odalisque

Because all you do is work. And you're lonely. Your wife gutted you and you're not capable of surviving another relationship anytime soon. Why let a woman in, why try to get to know her when it would inevitably end up where his marriage had ended up? Betrayal, bitter accusations, humiliation.

An odalisque might be the answer to all his problems. If things worked out, what a wonderful lifestyle it would be. Sex—hot, willing sex— whenever he wanted it. However he wanted it. Quick, slow, raunchy, affectionate, nasty, endless, kinky or vanilla, upside down or up in a tree or rolling down the side of the mountain he lived on. Kai would lead and she would follow obediently, because that was her code, according to what he'd read. Submissive, available, enslaved to his cock by choice.

He would buy—or rent—her services, and bask in her loyalty and patience, her subservience and admiration, all sandwiched in between marathon sessions of depraved sex. Best of all, there wouldn't be a lot of emotional minefields to tiptoe across to get to what he wanted. He could lay her down and lose himself and not waste what little free time he had on relationship issues.

By the time he got in his rental car in Paris and started on the hour-long trip to Maison Odalisque, he'd gone from feeling embarrassed and skeptical to feeling almost jubilant. He'd made an embarrassing amount of money for someone in his mid-thirties, and in this one thing, he would spoil himself. If he found the right girl, if he found the whole odalisque thing to his liking, he would plunk down a cool million without a second thought. If even half his lustful daydreams came true, a million would be a small price to pay.

In this state of hopeful elation, Kai arrived at the Maison. He shook off creeping jet lag and produced his passport in order to be buzzed through an arching iron gate by a stone-faced security goon. The house certainly gave an appearance of respectability. He'd half expected to arrive at a ramshackle dive and be robbed and left for dead, but the impressive edifice of Maison Odalisque communicated wealth and fastidiousness, not danger.

It was more than a house, actually, but not quite a mansion. There were twenty or so windows just on the front, and six imposing columns. Around him, rural fields and forests glowed with the gold of a late winter sunset. A long cobblestone drive circled to the front of the house.

A valet took his rental car and luggage and directed him politely up the stairs to the massive front door. He undoubtedly knew why Kai was here, but his expression gave away no opinion. He had the deferent manner of someone accustomed to serving the rich. It was something Kai was only starting to get used to in the years since he'd started his digital technology firm as a poor, ambitious twenty-something with visionary dreams.

But none of those dreams had ever involved French manors and odalisques.

As soon as Kai dropped the ornate brass knocker onto its base, the door swung open. He was guided into a soaring foyer by another impeccably proper employee. The third one now, and all three were nearly as wide as they were tall. Their strength was emphasized by the fitted, understated suits they wore. It occurred to him that a country house full of sex slaves would require some pretty heavy security.

As polite as the man was, Kai had no doubt the giant could have him in a headlock on the floor at the first threatening word or gesture. That didn't worry him at all. It was one more sign that this Monsieur Gaudet had his shit together. One more sign that this crazy stuff was for real.

As if on cue, a well-dressed man strode around the corner, his hand already extended in a gesture of greeting. "Mr. Kaivalyan Chandler, I presume? I am Sebastien Gaudet."

Kai sized up the man. He was impressed that he'd pronounced his full Indian name without tripping over the syllables. That Gaudet was Indian himself was not remotely possible. Kai had never seen such a pale, white-blond man. His short hair framed an aristocratically angular face, and his eyes were a piercing blue. His smile was warmly disarming as he shook Kai's hand. Kai immediately felt at ease in his company. "Hello. My friends call me Kai."

"Well, let's not stand on formalities. My friends call me Bastien. It's very nice to meet you. I trust your trip went well?" Mr. Gaudet's— Bastien's—English was flawless. Kai nodded in response.

"It's gone smoothly thus far."

"And hopefully will continue on so. Would you like to take some time upstairs to rest before dinner? Or perhaps there are some questions you would like answered first?"

Kai looked around the foyer, to the winding marble staircase, to the gleaming tile floor. More chateau than dungeon, really. The building was welcoming and cheerfully lit. Artwork and sculpture covered many of the surfaces. He smiled at his host.

"I'm kind of relieved you aren't in black leather, holding a whip."

Bastien laughed. "I assure you, the feeling is mutual. Fortunately, we manage to head off most of those types before they make the trip."

"Am I the only, uh, gentleman here at the moment?"

"The only one seeking, yes. A few friends may come and go during your stay, but only because I deem them utterly discreet and trustworthy. On that count, you must feel at ease. We are a respectful society here, and we value discretion above all."

Kai got the message loud and clear, although Bastien never lost his easy, genial tone. It was the same easy tone he remembered from chatting on the phone, the same easy tone that convinced him to fly over just to chat, just to have a tour and ask some questions about the *Code d'Odalisque*. Kai looked around once more, as if he might glimpse one of the mysterious odalisques he'd come to see. But no, they were kept in *occlusion*, Bastien had explained. Odalisques were trained to live in confinement, wet and waiting for Master and whomever Master chose to share them with.

"I think I will take a few minutes to rest before dinner," said Kai, clasping his hands in front of his pants to hide his burgeoning arousal. *A few minutes to rest, or masturbate furiously. Probably the latter.*

"As you wish." Sebastien Gaudet inclined his head with a smile.

Kai was shown to his second-floor room by the same gentleman who'd let him in the door. He found his luggage neatly arranged beside the bed. Kai reached in his pocket for a tip and was waved off with a low, obsequious bow. "I am at your service, monsieur," said the servant with a pronounced French accent. "If you need anything, simply call." He indicated a red button beside the light switch, and then melted out the door.

Kai lay back on the full size bed. The ivory padded headboard was silk and absolutely pristine. The whole room oozed propriety, from the crisply pleated drapes to the dark, heavy, polished wood furniture. There was no way in hell he could possibly jack off in this stately space.

If not for Bastien's easy, relaxed manner, Kai might have felt threatened by the strangeness of the whole situation, but instead he was able to lay back and close his eyes. His mind drifted to thoughts of undulating sex goddesses and willing, wanton women. Was there one in the room above him? One on either side?

Next thing he knew, a sharp knock awakened him. The manservant had brought a dinner jacket in the event he needed one, but Kai had his own after being told it was customary at the Maison to dress for dinner. Less than an hour later, Kai was escorted downstairs to a cavernous dining room.

Even with Bastien's considerable social skills, Kai found the formal dinner uncomfortable. As wealthy as he was, he didn't usually dine on bone china with real silver utensils, at a twenty-foot table lit by shimmering candelabra. Each course was brought in by yet another grimly respectable and all-too-masculine servant. For a house that boasted scores of submissive slave women, men did a lot of the work around here. Bastien caught him looking around the dining room after the third course, and grinned at him.

"You are wondering when you will see one of the lovely ladies of our house."

Kai raised an eyebrow. "Perhaps they'll bring the dessert course..."

His host chuckled. "I'm afraid not. Odalisques are not servants, not in a household sense. This is what separates them from their BDSM-lifestyle sisters. A slave in a Master and slave relationship might be expected to perform any manner of drudge tasks or chores in the name of 'service.' The Master perhaps sees this as a way to test her devotion and submission, or exert power over her. With an odalisque no such tests are needed. A lifestyle slave might endure humiliation, degradation, even contempt at the foot of her Master, but an odalisque is treasured, never tested. She is a slave of sensuality, not drudgery."

"So I understand. But what if they enjoy being degraded or set to unpleasant tasks? None of them are masochists?"

"That surprises you?"

"I just thought a woman willing to give up everything to live for the pleasure of a man—"

"Would have masochistic tendencies? Many do. But they are trained to pair self-respect with submission. The owner of an odalisque desires a beautiful, admirable woman, not a cringing vessel to be defiled and abused. When a masochistic woman wants to live as an odalisque, we encourage those tendencies to be satisfied in the course of sexual interactions. For instance, a woman may like to be whipped as foreplay, or have her nipples tortured to reach orgasm. This type of masochism relates directly to sensuality and sexual craving, and excites both Master and odalisque. But if a woman wishes to live as an abject creature,

22

humiliated and hurt and denied pleasure, she does not really have the air of erotic majesty we seek."

"*Erotic majesty.* I like that. But doesn't that make the slave pretty much an equal to her Master? Or perhaps even more powerful?"

"Not at all. The odalisque submits—always. But only sexually. She submits her body to her Master's use. Her mind, her self-respect, her personality remain her own. I assure you, many men find it more alluring than the self-effacement of the typical BDSM slave. You get all of the sexual submission you desire, with none of the need to micromanage your slave or develop tedious protocols. You may enact all the *sexual* protocols you wish, but afterward, you can walk away knowing your slave is self-possessed enough to manage herself until you wish to make use of her again."

"And you can take her out, right? You don't have to keep an odalisque hidden?"

"Yes, you can take her out as a companion, or share her favors with discreet friends. You can take her to work if you might have sexual need of her there."

Kai grinned. "Time to tint the office windows."

"Precisely," said Bastien. "But of course, an odalisque must never be compelled to make money in the outside world. When you acquire an odalisque, you sign an agreement to keep her in comfort, and to not require any work above and beyond that of sexual service. It goes without saying you would not accept money from others for her use."

"That would make her a whore."

Bastien nodded curtly. "Exactly so. That is not a word we like here. People often misunderstand. We are not in the business of exploiting or degrading women. If that is your desire, I hope you will choose not to take an odalisque into your care."

"I don't want a woman to abuse, I can assure you of that. I just want a woman who can give me sex without all the extra baggage. I don't have time to deal with the baggage."

Bastien smiled, then gestured to the servant at the door to bring the final course. His gaze returned to Kai. "You have no idea how common that is among those of your set. Some rich, powerful men enjoy lives of leisure, but most work remarkably long and grueling hours, hours that preclude deep interpersonal relationships. At the same time, they do not wish to forego the pleasures of the flesh. If anyone is deserving of endless pleasure, it is a man who works as hard as you."

"Ah, endless pleasure." Kai accepted a sinful-looking torte from the servant's tray and grinned at his host. "You know all the right words to say."

"Let's be honest. The modern woman is expected to be strong and fiercely independent. The modern male, by contrast, is expected to be much more submissive than men in eras past. Dominant male sexuality is criticized as inappropriate and exploitative. *Code d'Odalisque* rejects these modern values and celebrates, rather than despises, the intensity of male sexuality. The code invites a woman—without shame or coercion—to live as a submissive servant to a man's voracious sexual desire. Of course, the man she serves must be deemed worthy of this submission."

Bastien paused for a sip of his after-dinner coffee, then continued in a franker tone. "The odalisques understand their fortune in fulfilling that need for gentlemen such as you. Most of these women could not afford the luxuries their owners provide them. It is pleasure given for pleasure. In fact, many develop almost worshipful feelings for their Master."

Kai frowned. "But then...what happens when the year is up?"

"Odalisques can be in service to the same man for up to six years, if both parties wish it."

"No, what I mean is, what happens at the end of the term, if the odalisque has become emotionally attached?"

"I never said anything about emotion," Bastien corrected him. "I meant worshipful in a sense of sexual worship. Craving, desire. We have a word for it, a coarse word perhaps: cockslavery. It is a state to which all odalisques aspire. But for an odalisque to make emotional demands on her Master—this would be an utter desecration of the code. They are trained to sublimate such feelings, funnel them into a more heightened sexuality, for the fulfillment of Master, of course. But I go on and on. Perhaps it would be best if we paid a visit to the odalisques' quarters. I'm sure you will find that much more illuminating than my words."

Kai pushed his plate away. "I would very much love to visit the odalisques' quarters." God, he hoped he hadn't sounded as horny and eager as he felt.

Chapter Three:
The Tour

Bastien led Kai down a long, silent corridor. On either side, erotic sculptures graced Italianate grottos. Kai looked down at the black and gold diamond-patterned tile beneath his feet and imagined a girl writhing beneath him as he took her there on the spotless floor. He was feeling ridiculously worked up. Perhaps that was Bastien's aim—to have him whipping out the checkbook before he even retired for the night.

His own home was nearly as large as the Maison, but decorated in a modern style. If he acquired an odalisque—which seemed more and more likely by the moment—he would be expected to provide her with "quarters." He'd read that online, in the code, and had immediately started imagining the love nest he would create. He would buy all the velvet pillows in L.A., all the filmy curtains and overstuffed sofas that could be had. Endless pleasure. *Cockslavery.* He barely suppressed the groan that rose in his throat. When was the last time he'd enjoyed a woman without anxiety? Without guilt? Just sunk between a woman's legs and lost himself? He couldn't remember.

"This way." Bastien's hushed voice drew him back from his thoughts.

They turned left at the end of the corridor to find a winding set of carpeted backstairs. As they passed to the second floor, the comfortable warmth of the house became even cozier. Bastien took off his dinner

25

jacket and invited Kai to do the same, leaving them with an attendant stationed at the top of the stairs.

"Serge will return it to your room. We keep the upper floors warmer year round," Bastien explained. "The odalisques are kept naked. A great part of their training is teaching them to feel natural without clothes. You'll find they are charmingly uncomfortable when they're dressed and taken out amongst humanity. And charmingly eager to shed their clothes when you bring them home again."

Bastien stopped in front of the first room on the right. "None of the doors are locked. Ever. It will be the same in your house. An odalisque has no need for privacy." He pushed open the door, revealing a mid-sized, neat, uncluttered room. In the center of the room, a girl with short chestnut hair was reading on her bed. She was, as Bastien had led him to expect, quite naked. Still, it was a shock. She made no movement to cover herself, nor did she look the least bit embarrassed. She simply regarded both men through assessing, trusting eyes over the top of her book.

"Good evening, Fiona," Bastien said, nodding to her. "I am showing Monsieur Chandler around."

"Hello, Monsieur Chandler," Fiona replied with a flirtatious smile. Her twanging Southern accent sounded strangely out of place in the posh surroundings.

"Fiona came to us from Georgia," Bastien explained. "A peach in every sense of the word. We presently have girls from eleven different countries here at the Maison. Sometimes more, sometimes less. The desire to serve has no nationality. The visas and paperwork keep our lawyer busy, but it all works out."

He shut the door on Fiona and took Kai to the next room, this one on the left. Again, the lovely occupant was sprawled on the bed naked; however, she was not reading. Her legs were splayed open and she was masturbating with one hand and squeezing her breasts with the other. Again, not the slightest hint of embarrassment. Kai, however, was glad his skin tone hid the flush in his cheeks.

"Good girl, Cecile," murmured Bastien, before backing out and closing the door. He turned to Kai. "We teach them nothing sexual is shameful. It requires deprogramming in some cases, where women have been taught from a young age that sexuality is sinful or shameful. We use every method at our disposal to reverse that belief." Bastien smiled. "As

26

you can see, girls like Cecile have learned to embrace their sexual urges without any modicum of reserve."

Kai could see all right. He'd wanted to fall on Cecile, with her bountiful breasts and her glistening pussy. Bastien, however, continued down the hall. "Something you may want to consider, Kai, is what type of woman would best be a match for you. Here at Maison Odalisque, we have all body types, all hair and eye colors, and a great many ethnicities. And while language is not a necessity between Master and odalisque, you may prefer one with a good command of English. Or—pardon me—Hindi?"

Kai shook his head. "I'm afraid I'm totally Americanized. My mother tried to teach me, but..." *But I was a bad son. I had no time for her wants, her needs.* He could have conquered the Bollywood digital film industry if he'd made half an effort to pick up the language and culture. His father hadn't been any help, encouraging him to embrace everything American while belittling his mother's Indian habits and customs. Only once had they flown to India to meet his mother's family. It was a short, overwhelming experience in culture shock. When Kai lost his mother, he realized too late that he'd lost all chance of knowing that side of himself. "It would probably be better to choose an American girl," Kai said. "I'll be keeping her in Malibu."

Bastien took him to three or four more rooms. All the girls were friendly and as openly assessing of Kai as he was of them. "Do they have a choice?" Kai asked. "I mean, in who acquires them? Veto power?"

"Of course. Everything here is one hundred percent consensual. If a woman has misgivings about a man who wants to take her, we work with both parties to find consensus. If, after a period of consideration, it's still a no—for whatever reason—we respect that. It would be a disaster to send a woman off to sexually serve a man she feels antipathy for."

"But what if she gets where she's going and realizes afterward they're not compatible? Or what if the man decides he doesn't want her after all?"

"Good questions. I suppose I must start by explaining that the odalisque is protected by someone called an overmistress. We don't send them off to the far corners of the world without a safety net. For the first month, the overmistress meets with the odalisque weekly. After that, she meets with her once a month, or sooner if an issue presents itself. The overmistress is empowered to remove any odalisque who is in emotional distress over her situation. In that case, the owner is reimbursed for the cost of the odalisque and, if the issue was not caused by his mistreatment, permitted to choose a replacement at the Maison."

"That sounds smart. And fair."

"In the second case—if the man changes his mind—he is permitted to return the odalisque to the Maison and choose a new one. However, only one exchange per year is permitted. We are not a short term rental service, if you catch my meaning."

"I catch it completely."

"The best outcome is for the odalisque and Master to bond into a cohesive, satisfying sexual unit. This can only be done with interaction and use. A Master who neglects or ignores his odalisque is likely to find himself alone. Or, to put it more directly, a cockslave must have cock." Bastien paused. "In some cases, a secondary relationship develops with a favored friend of the Master, one with whom he frequently shares. This is permissible, particularly if the Master is traveling or busy at certain times of the year. I have even known Masters to hire 'toys' for their odalisques to play with in their absence." He smiled. "I suppose it all depends on how possessive or magnanimous you are."

Kai fiddled with one of his shirt cuffs, remembering Mason holding out an ivory card. "I can think of a few friends who wouldn't be averse to helping me out. One of whom is a woman."

Bastien shrugged. "A woman now and again can be a welcome adventure for an odalisque. But they are only trained for the pleasuring of males."

Only trained for cock. So refined, and yet so nasty. Kai's cock throbbed, bursting for release. It was actually getting kind of hard to walk. They looked in on another girl with gorgeous auburn curls, lazily primping in front of a mirror.

"Some of them are very intellectual," Bastien said with a grin as he closed the door. "Some of them are rather more...shallow. Airheads, even. Is that not what you Americans say? Again, this is a personal preference. Some gentlemen prefer an empty head."

Kai grimaced. "I'm not one of them."

"What type of woman do you like?"

Kai felt put on the spot, so he just came out with the basics. "I like longish hair. I like creative women. I like nice tits but nothing fake. I like large features—big mouths, big noses. Expressive eyes. I like normal bodies, not too thin, not too fat. Maybe a little fat. I like curves. I love curves," he amended a moment later. "I love curves a lot."

"Come then." Bastien led him up another stairwell to the top floor, to the last door on the left. The room was slightly smaller, but no less comfortable. The ceiling slanted down, with a window seat set back in the wall. A woman was curled up there on tufted cushions. She was in her early to mid-20s, if Kai had to guess, and she scribbled in a notebook with great concentration. As Bastien approached, she abruptly left off. "Good evening, Constance. This is Mr. Chandler."

Constance was a fair approximation of everything Kai had just spouted off. She had long curly hair—tons of hair. Magnificent. It was hard to tell the color of her eyes in the soft light, but she had the same openness and relaxation in her face and mouth that he recognized in the other girls. But this one was too exotic looking to be pretty. She did have a big nose, and gorgeous big lips. She exuded as much sweetness as sex. She put her notebook and pen to the side, still gazing at him.

She didn't speak. She seemed shy. She was so beautiful, so mysteriously beautiful. Why? Because of the way she looked at him in that shy, curious way? Kai forgot Bastien was even standing there until the man shifted and gestured toward her.

"If you wish it, Constance will be happy to grant you relief."

Kai turned the words over in his head a few times before he caught the meaning. *Relief.* Of course, his raging hard-on wouldn't go unnoticed in a house like this, especially as it now strained toward the top of his waistband. Dress pants hid some things, but not a cock like his. Constance crossed the room and knelt before him expectantly, her hands in her lap. *Cockslavery.* Without another thought Kai's hands were at his pants, working at button and zipper, releasing himself.

Bastien handed him a condom, as if the scene taking place was expected and normal, and Kai rolled on the condom as if it was. It didn't bother him that Bastien obviously had no intention of leaving. With all the security around, it stood to reason that an odalisque would never be surrendered to a stranger. And Kai was a stranger to this world, this amazing world where beautiful, shy women came to kneel before him and suck him off on a word. But Bastien's silent presence communicated that she was only being lent, under her protector's careful supervision.

Constance reached for his cock, cupping its length and weight, kissing the tip through flavored latex. Her lips were red, not garish, but lovely soft red contrasted with her pale complexion. He imagined her clasped against his darker skin, a silhouette of womanly desire. He twisted a hand in her curls, marveling at their softness, just as she opened her mouth wide.

It was torture to let her guide him. He wanted to take over, thrust into her throat so the lust and excitement that had been building over the entire evening could finally explode. But he regained his control. Her skill was such that he had to pause and appreciate it. She wasn't sloppy, but focused and mindful of his reactions.

He guided her with the pressure of his fingers against her scalp, and shudders and moans when he was most pleased with her. She licked up the front of his glans, flicking, teasing, and then around the crown, then she took him so deep he almost lost it again. She hummed softly as she sucked him, so the sensation of it resonated down his cock to his balls. His fingers tightened in her hair, pulling her closer, not wanting to be too rough, but needing her closer, closer...

She took him deep until her lovely nose was pressed against the wiry kinks of his thatch. "Oh, God—" he gasped. It was as much hysteria as it was prayer. He tried to hold off, tried to make the blowjob last, but her avid skill, her focus on pleasing him—it was a completely new experience. This was no grudging, lackluster blowjob. This was cock worship. He finally understood that term.

She was taking him deep now, over and over, adding pressure and teasing with her tongue, sending tremors down the backs of his thighs. The orgasm, when it came, nearly brought him to his knees. He still held her hair, grasped and fisted it, trying not to pull. Only that concentration, that warning bell that he might hurt her, kept him from collapsing where he stood. He hunched over her as his balls contracted and waves of release swept his entire core.

She gripped him with her lips as he rode out the climax, then went still when he untensed, and waited. He didn't want to leave her mouth—ever—but after a moment or two he eased back, caressing her face as she slid her tongue across the barrier between them.

He'd learned one thing for sure. This was for real. These women really did have a hunger to please sexually. Constance smiled up at him from her knees. It wasn't a brassy smile, or a vixenish one. Just a pleased, content smile that touched some primal part of him, the part that wanted to be *wanted*. To be desired. Unconditionally and totally.

"Thank you," he said. It sounded silly, to thank her so formally, but he would have been embarrassed to yell out what he really wanted to say: *That was the best fucking blowjob of my life!*

"There's a bathroom over there," Sebastien said. Kai took the hint to go dispose of the condom and put himself to rights. He looked in the mirror, wondering if Constance had truly enjoyed sucking his cock as much as she'd seemed to. He felt himself changed in some way. He felt more masculine, having availed himself of the *erotic majesty* of an odalisque.

And yet, her little bathroom was reassuringly normal. An old fashioned wooden hairbrush lay beside neatly arranged baskets of cosmetics. He could imagine her pulling the brush through her long hair as she stood naked and damp from the shower. He could also imagine bending her over the counter and spanking her with it on her heart-shaped ass just before he eased forward and positioned himself at her hot, wet entrance— *Down, boy. Reel it in.*

When he returned to the room, Bastien and Constance were sitting on the edge of her bed, deep in conversation. At Kai's reappearance, Bastien patted Constance's knee and stood. "I'm afraid it's getting late, even for an odalisque. They tend to stay up late, and lay in bed long past dawn. The privilege of the kept," he said, winking at Constance. Again, she smiled that guileless, contented smile. At the door, Kai turned to say goodbye, feeling foolish. What was the protocol for taking your leave of a woman you didn't know who'd just sucked you off? Bastien also bid Constance good night and shut the door behind them.

Kai walked a moment in silence, at a loss for words, and Bastien seemed content to let him think. Finally Kai said, "Thank you. That was a nice surprise."

"I gathered you needed it. It's no fun to be in a house of sex slaves and not have a means of release. Tomorrow, I'll show you around the training facilities and you can take a good look at all the women. Constance is lovely, and doubtless a very good match for you, but there are others who are similar to her in temperament and appearance. Often, in these circumstances, it's best to rely on a combination of reason and impulse in making your choice. When you find the one, you'll know, but it's best to look at all of them before you make a final decision. In your room, you'll notice a binder with profiles and photos of all the currently available odalisques."

"How many are there?"

"I'd say it's in the realm of thirty-six or thirty-eight at the moment. Forty is our cap, but throughout the year, that number fluctuates. Spring is by far our busiest time, so we try to have a full house of women trained and available. By fall, we might be down to fifteen or twenty, and then there is the pre-holiday rush. We are always canvassing for new candidates to keep our numbers at a sustainable level."

"Where do you find them? How do you know which women to approach?"

Bastien looked coy. "That's an industry secret, but suffice it to say, we have our proven strategies. And a surprising number of women find us, through lore or word of mouth. The Internet has been a great help in distributing the *Code d'Odalisque* along certain receptive channels. You'll often find 'Code d'Ode' groups on mainstream sex and fetish sites."

"You don't advertise, do you?"

"There is no need. Word of mouth seems sufficient in bringing us both the candidates and prospective owners we need."

"Are there ever girls who don't find an owner?"

"Of course, although it happens rarely. After six years, an odalisque leaves service whether she's found an owner or not. At that time, if she has never been acquired by a Master, she receives a sum equal to the amount she would have earned during two years of ownership. One million dollars. Hopefully it soothes any sting."

"I imagine it does." They were outside Kai's room now. Bastien extended his hand.

"Here I will wish you good night. In your room, you should find the portfolio of profiles, as well as a tray with some snacks and a nightcap. If there is anything further you require, do not hesitate to summon the staff. As far as discussing the available women, we will plan to do that on the morrow if you would be so kind as to take notes on the ones that most interest you. We rise late here. If I do not see you at breakfast, I shall expect you at lunch."

Again Kai found himself alone in his opulent ivory guest room. At the desk was a leather binder about two inches thick, along with a silver tray of shortbread, fresh fruit, and excellent brandy. He was tired, but not too tired to settle down with the book. He would keep odalisque hours; stay up late and laze around in the morning.

He leafed through the profiles, which were alphabetized by first name. Wonderful for Abby and Artemis, not so great for Yolanda and Zenaida. The profiles contained all the applicable data. Height, weight, age, nationality, languages spoken, even allergies and religious preferences in some cases. It listed each woman's interests, favorites and turnoffs. It was noted whether a woman had been an odalisque before, or whether she was a "novice." Some of the women were listed as *fellatrices*, or oral sex specialists, or *sodomellas*, anal sex enthusiasts. Some categorized themselves as *orgophons*, odalisques who were skilled at orgies. Some specialized in Tantra, others in sado-masochistic play. All offered the full slate of services, no matter their specialty.

Kai hovered over Constance's page longer than any of the others. Something about her had drawn him in, more so than the other girls they'd visited. But he couldn't remember if he'd felt that strong reaction before the blowjob, or after. *When you find the one, you'll know.* Constance listed yoga, writing poetry, and etymology as interests above and beyond sexual slavery. She didn't list a hometown. Interesting.

As far as sexual specialties, he was happy to find her in the sado-masochism camp. He thought again of the wooden hairbrush and her spectacular ass cheeks. So what if she was into the study of insects? He could deal with that.

Was she the one? He would probably know by tomorrow. He forced himself to leaf through the book and pick out a few alternates. After he ruthlessly eliminated various women for being too tall or too short, having fake boobs, not speaking English, and just generally not being attractive to him, he further eliminated those who were not interested in sado-masochistic play, those whose interests seemed boring, or who didn't have any creative endeavors listed on their hobby sheet. After that, he was left with a pretty manageable pool of five candidates, including Constance.

So what did this mean? Was he really, really going to do this? He tried to picture himself at home with Constance, using her whenever it pleased him, in whatever ways pleased him. Having her walk around nude, a sexual creature at his beck and call, relaxed and content in the opulent nest he'd build for her. Writing poetry in her notebook with her legs pulled up under her, then putting it away so he could cover her with his body and empty himself in her again and again...

Oh, yes, he would do this. If any part of his mind still questioned, his body was absolutely certain. In fact, his body was far too excited again. This time he couldn't restrain himself, pristine bed sheets or not. If anyone watched via hidden camera, they got an eyeful. He sprawled naked on top of the covers and masturbated to orgasm three times before he could manage to fall asleep.

Chapter Four:
The Training

Kai woke up as conflicted as he'd been horny the night before. This was all so casual, so perverse. A woman he didn't even know had dropped to her knees the night before and given him a blowjob. Another had masturbated in front of him while he'd stared at her like some visitor at the zoo.

How could he even consider buying a woman for the sole purpose of using her body? Well, he wouldn't be buying her, he reminded himself. This was not human trafficking, that ugly world. This was anti-human trafficking, where the women actually became richer and more powerful than before. What could Constance do for herself with five hundred thousand dollars of his money? And a quarter million would also be donated to anti-trafficking charities.

So why did he feel so horribly guilty about it all?

Because you're buying a woman. You're paying for sex.

But it wasn't so different from a man throwing money and apartments and jewels at a mistress or a girl-on-the-side. Was it? He went back and forth over the moral conundrum of the situation until his head hurt so badly he couldn't fall back to sleep. He got up instead and went for a run, directed by a new, fresh-faced young butler to a lake behind the house surrounded by a trail. The familiar *thump thump* of his gait along the shaded path dispelled both his headache and his dithering.

Life was short, and frustrating and complicated. This thing, for one year, could be simple. Simple pleasure, simple enjoyment. The worst that would happen is that it wouldn't work out, and then he'd just release her. He'd be out a million, but so what?

With this refreshed and calm mindset, he returned to the house to shower, shave, and sift through a mountain of emails as he ate an early lunch in his room. Afterward, Bastien took him to visit the "training facilities" as promised. These facilities turned out to be a series of similarly opulent rooms on the opposite side of the house. But unlike the tasteful parlors, dining rooms, and bedrooms, these rooms were designed and decorated for the business of sex.

The first room Bastien showed him was, predictably, a gym. It was empty at the moment. "This is usually the ladies' last stop of the day," his host explained. "After they complete their schedule of sexual training, many of them can be found here, winding down with a short workout before they head out to the grotto."

"The grotto?"

"Follow me."

Bastien led him through a side door and into a garden that was green even in winter. A low stone building sprawled at the end of a path. They ducked beneath the lintel into a dimly lit, humid and fragrant space. It was a swimming pool, manmade but cleverly designed to look like some kind of ancient spring with boulders, flowers, and overgrown shrubs.

"I bet the water is warm as a bath tub, even when it's snowing outside," guessed Kai.

Bastien grinned. "You can test that hypothesis later when you take a dip with the women. I've been known to do so myself after an especially stressful day. For now, let's continue on our tour. There are many provocative sights to see."

They made their way from the grotto back to the building. The next room was large and airy, brightly lit from picture windows on the side wall. The room was equipped with three wide, white padded tables, although only two were in use. A man attended to the two women tied face up to the tables, arms over their heads and legs spread wide. The man had no air of menace or even sexuality, aside from the toned, muscular body under his pristine lab coat.

"Is he a doctor?" Kai asked.

"He's what we call a trainer. All these women are on a personal voyage of sensual development. What we seek from them can't be taught, only teased from inside with encouragement and reassurance. And of course, our trainers are all male, since our ultimate goal is for an odalisque to be at ease and sexually open around men."

"So the men—the trainers—all have sex with the women?"

"Occasionally they do. Not in a sordid, abuse-of-power type way. There are some things that are just better understood when a trainee is interacting with a real flesh-and-blood man. But the majority of the training is related to sexual sensitivity, and loss of inhibition and self-protectiveness. A little touch goes a long way."

Bastien nodded at the tables, where the man was fingering one of the restrained women. She moaned and pulled at her bonds, her legs clenching. The trainer murmured to her quietly, seeming to urge her along. Kai wished he could walk closer to hear what he was saying—and get a closer look at the enraptured face of his pupil. Her cries rose in volume and Kai was looking forward to witnessing her climax when the lab-coated man drew away. He ignored her disappointed groans and turned to touch and stroke the other woman's smooth pussy lips.

"Why did he only tease her?" Kai asked. "Aren't odalisques allowed to come?"

"Actually, we hope for them to become quite orgasmic. This is only a technique in acquainting them with their hot spots. Each woman has a different physical makeup, different nerve bundles here and there. Gerard is helping them identify what feels best to them, and how to seek it from their partner's touch. They'll be allowed to come." Bastien smiled as the other woman's cries rose in volume and intensity. "Eventually."

"Why are they tied down?" Kai chuckled softly. "Neither one looks like she wants to get away."

"Bondage is part of the odalisque experience. We recommend that new owners restrain their odalisques often. It is all very tied up in the idea of surrender. Pardon the pun."

Bastien led Kai from that room into another room, this one dark rather than light. The sensual cries of the two women were replaced by absolute silence and stillness. Kai looked around the peaceful space furnished with tufted sofas, upholstered chairs, and floor pillows. Three women were "training" here, each arranged in erotic positions with varying degrees of bondage. One was bent forward over a sofa with her legs in a spreader bar and her hands cinched behind her in leather cuffs. Another was lounging back on a pillow with her legs drawn up and held open by some creative rope work. Another was bound into a kneeling position, her head bowed. She might have been sleeping, she seemed so relaxed. Another white-coated male attendant sat at a desk, ostensibly monitoring the bound odalisques while going over paperwork of some kind.

When Bastien spoke, it was in hushed tones. "You see, they are most at ease this way. Bound, subjugated, waiting. You could blindfold or hood them and their state of relaxation would remain the same. We do sometimes blindfold or hood them as part of their training. They enjoy it, for the most part."

Kai stared at the immobilized women. "What if I'm not into hoods? What if I don't know how to do all those intricate rope ties?"

"You are certainly not obligated to use rope or hood your odalisque if it doesn't please you to do so. The type and flavor of restraint is up to you, but most owners find bondage improves the submission of their slave."

Kai looked around at the women. Although two of them were not his preferred physical type, they were all truly beautiful. Their silent acquiescence, the peaceful, trusting way they waited for...what? Whatever. A man's *voracious sexuality*.

Bastien led him down the hall to the next room. This one had no furniture of any kind aside from several bolsters and beanbags. "We call this the penetration room."

"I can see why." Kai couldn't help but gawk at the nude, moaning women reclining in various positions around the room. Each of the women had one or more dildos protruding from her orifices. "That looks like an effective means of training."

"It sounds strange, but it really does require training to take any manner of cock with grace and ease. Pardon me for noticing last night, but you are above average in size. It is for men such as you that this training takes place. The odalisques learn their limits, and in some cases, how to stretch those limits. We also work with them on developing the elusive 'penetrative orgasm.' It is untrue that women can only orgasm from clitoral stimulation. With proper conditioning, many learn to climax solely from penetration and thrusting. Bigger, more functional orgasms are the ultimate reward."

"Certainly a worthy goal, and thanks for the flattery about my size. Although it made me slightly uncomfortable."

Bastien laughed. "We harbor no uneasiness about sexual openness here. But perhaps we'll skip the fellatio room and head right to the sado-masochism space. I seem to remember Constance and Sandra being on the schedule with Stephen."

Before Bastien even opened the door, Kai heard the repetitive crack of disciplinary impact. Once inside, Kai took in the fetish equipment—spanking benches, crosses, racks—before his gaze fell on the restrained victim on the far side of the room.

Constance. He had already developed an avid fascination with her.

She was kneeling on a padded platform. A white-coated trainer was spanking her ass and spread inner thighs with a leather paddle. She cried out with each blow, but at the same time ground her pubis against an upstanding dildo strapped to the table beneath her. Her reactions were gorgeous, purely wanton and needful. Her bottom was scarlet and absolutely perfect in shape. Kai felt an intense urge to grab the paddle from the trainer and take over himself.

She was clearly aroused, wildly aroused, which aroused Kai almost painfully. When she tried to sink down and penetrate herself with the toy, she received an especially sharp crack from the trainer—a warning to obey. Kai watched as this teasing sequence played itself out again and again. He wanted nothing more than to grasp her weaving hips and bury his cock inside her to the hilt.

"You see," said Bastien, "the goal is for them to learn to equate pleasure and pain. For someone like Constance, the wiring is already there. There is only a refinement of the connection. A little more pain eventually triggers a little more pleasure. It's a wonderful process." Some of the strain Kai was feeling must have shown on his face, because Bastien said, "Perhaps you would like to test the method out yourself."

Kai's erection was throbbing. He looked at Constance, his hands opening and closing, craving to touch her. "I'd love to test it out. Yeah."

Bastien approached the table and ran a hand down Constance's back. She lifted her head to look at her caretaker, her eyes hazy with pleasure. "Stephen, give Mr. Chandler an appropriate pair of nipple clamps for the girl."

The sober-faced trainer walked to the wall and returned with a pair of clamps connected by a chain. "Put them on her," Bastien said to Kai, "and then please avail yourself of her pussy if you wish. Or have her ride the dildo for you. Whatever you would most enjoy."

Constance looked over at him, her gaze alert and yet deliciously sultry. Her expression communicated what Bastien said—that anything Kai chose to do to her would be perfectly acceptable. And God, of course he was going to fuck her. Stephen removed the dildo from the table and rearranged his charge, having her brace herself on her arms. She spread her thighs a little wider until she was at the perfect level for him to fuck. Intercourse logistics. Was that another class taught here?

It occurred to him that in this house of forty or so odalisques, he was putting his dick in the same one for a second time, and happy to do so. He walked around the front of her with the clamps and pinched her dark pink nipples. She was cock-twitchingly responsive, throwing her head back and staring up at him with striking light green eyes. She was a stranger to him, and yet familiar. She was the girl he'd always fantasized about but had never had: the girl who would do anything he asked and seek nothing in return, only more and more pleasure.

As horny as he was to get to the fucking, he took his time applying the clamps, teasing and playing with her nipples, enjoying her quick hissing intakes of breath. He didn't feel any need or pressure to talk to her, to reassure her. To procure her consent. By now, he knew that wasn't the way things were done at Maison Odalisque.

Bastien handed him a condom, and then faded back into the corner of the room along with the trainer. With one last tweak of the clamps— *beautiful moan*—Kai returned to stand behind Constance, unfastening his pants. He unbuttoned but didn't remove his shirt. It was kind of thrilling, undressing just enough to make use of her. Kai rolled on the condom and positioned himself. She threw another hot, hungry look over her shoulder, causing his cock to buck in his hand. He felt desire and lust like a fire building in his groin, his shoulders, his thighs, his face. He was burning.

Jesus, what was it about her? He ran his hands over her body, caressing and exploring her. Her skin was smooth and warm, and her hips had the perfect proportion of roundness for his taste. He curled his fingers around her waist, then slid a hand up her back. She arched her spine and made a needful sound that hit him in his tightening balls. God, it wasn't a fake porno sound, or anything forced. It was the sound of honest, excited feminine arousal. At any other time, that would have been his signal to drive deep, but somehow he wanted to draw out this moment, to really bask in this possession of her.

"My God, you're beautiful," he said. Not his fanciest line ever, but there wasn't much blood left in his brain for composing sonnets. He was aching to be inside her, to feel her from within. She gave another low moan as he teased her pussy lips with the head of his cock. He could see the glistening proof of her excitement and smell her scent. He drove his fingers through the slickness, pressing his thumb against her clit. Her whole body seemed to tense; she looked back at him again. Her lips were parted, the extent of her need for him clearly written on her face.

It was all he could bear. He closed his hands hard on her hips and drove into her. He didn't just want to fuck her...he wanted to cover her with his body and become one with her. *We strongly discourage emotional attachment. It complicates what can otherwise be a beautifully simple thing.*

Simple. Simple. Keep it simple.

It was so simple to him. She was a goddess, and he was her god. Her cunt was a portal to the mysteries of life that had so frustrated him lately. Why? It was so simple. Male. Female. His cock inside her and her pussy driving back against him, clenching and wreaking the last vestige of nobility from his mind. "Ah, Constance..."

She made some small plaintive sound, and he remembered the clamps. The chain swung each time he thrust in her, doubtless tormenting her. He reached beneath her and took the chain between two fingers. He tugged it and her noises grew louder. Her breath was coming harsh and fast like his own. He linked his thumb over the chain and drew it down, down, his fingers opening against velvet skin. Her abs clenched, her whole body working to contain him as he lengthened his strokes.

She was starting to shudder. The harder he pulled the chain, the wetter she got and the more her pussy gripped his cock. She was ridiculously tight around him. He imagined other classes. Wetness 101. Pussy Gymnastics. Where did women learn such skill? He didn't care, as long as he got to enjoy it.

He tugged the chain down again and snaked his other hand forward to cup her pussy. He touched a finger to her clit and was rewarded by a guttural cry. Her ass cheeks were still scarlet, hot against his pelvis. He stroked her clit and she let out her breath with a shiver. She twisted her hips violently and came, squeezing so hard around him that his own orgasm exploded and rolled over him. Cock, balls, taint, thighs, and his clenching abs pressed against her back. His arms tightened as he pulled her closer, closer. He would squeeze the life out of her.

Remembering himself, he drew back and let her go. For now. Stephen and Bastien were in the room, watching and waiting. *We strongly discourage emotional attachment.*

But appreciation was surely okay. Admiration, even. He admired the hell out of her, that was for sure. Kai disposed of the condom, buttoned his shirt and did up his pants before he went back to stand in front of her. She dropped her head against his arm as he reached to release the nipple clamps. Her hair felt like silk.

She whined softly. Kai knew she was enduring the painful sensation of blood flooding back to her nipples, a pain surely as brutal as that of the actual clamps. She peered up at him, so submissive even in her distress. He stroked her face, pushing back a few curls, feeling deeply tender now.

He helped her kneel up and sit back on her heels. Even now, with her breasts most likely aching, she presented them to him willingly, not quailing or turning her shoulders in. He couldn't resist pinching each sore tip. Constance didn't seem to mind—in fact, she got that glazed, horny look again. He wanted to kiss her. He wanted to take her to bed and stay there a week.

But then Bastien and Stephen reappeared at his elbow. Bastien pinched her nipples as well, even harder than Kai had. "She is a very good girl, isn't she?"

"She is...superlative." Kai hoped she realized he meant it. She met Kai's eyes with a half-smile, shy again now. Jesus God, she was so fucking sweet. And yet so basely and unashamedly sexual. It was a potent cocktail, one that was making him feel slightly drunk.

"You'll be seeing more of Constance this evening at dinner," said Bastien. "I've arranged a little party with the five girls you're most interested in, and some gentlemen respected by the house. It should be a very enjoyable event. But for the moment, would you care to continue on our tour?"

With some regret, Kai turned from Constance and let Bastien lead him to a few more rooms. There was a flexibility room where odalisques perfected various exotic positions—intercourse logistics after all. There was also a waxing salon, and yes, a room where women did various exercises devoted to strengthening their pelvic floor muscles. Constance's cock-pleasing vaginal power explained. None of it shocked him anymore. He only wished Mason was here to see it, because Kai would never be able to do justice to it when he told him about it later. And what would Jessamine have made of all this? She would have been wildly excited, climbing Mason and probably Kai too. As he was considering that arousing imagery, Bastien drew him to a stop in the hall.

"If you have a moment, I feel there's something I should tell you about Constance. Something rather important."

Kai felt clanging alarm at Bastien's sober expression. "Don't tell me she has some fatal disease."

"Nothing so dire as that. But there is something you must know about her before you make your final decision. Constance was born with a congenital auditory disorder. She is profoundly deaf."

Kai shook his head, frowning in confusion. Bastien had to be mistaken, or joking. Kai had spoken to her and she'd responded. Hadn't she? Bastien had given orders and she'd obeyed.

"Constance is adept at reading lips," Bastien explained. "She is even more adept at reading body language and expressions. It's part of what makes her so good at what she does."

"But...but..." Kai could have sworn she'd spoken to him, responded to his words. But thinking back, he realized she hadn't spoken to him once. Only looked at him with those attentive, alert eyes. "She can't hear anything?"

"Very little, and then only at certain frequencies. Constance hears with her eyes. That's why blindfolding her or otherwise obscuring her sight is not permitted in her case. I'm sure you understand."

"I— God— Of course I understand. I just— I had no idea." Kai thought a moment, questions crowding his mind. How could he have felt so close, so connected to her and not even realized she wasn't hearing his words? He tried to mask his unbalance in practical questions. "How do you communicate with her? I mean, how does she talk back? Can she talk at all?"

"She prefers not to talk, although she can say a few words. Yes. No. Please. Stop. She can say her own name and undoubtedly could master the name Kai, although Kaivalyan might present a challenge for her. Otherwise, she prefers to write or sign. One of our overmistresses knows ASL. American Sign Language," he clarified.

"Yeah, I got it."

Bastien grimaced. "You're annoyed. You believe I should have told you sooner. Does it alter your attraction to her? Shall I un-invite her tonight?"

"Of course not. I'm just wondering how a relationship like this would go down without the means to communicate clearly."

"She can communicate as well as you or me. She can read your lips with pretty good accuracy, and write down any responses or questions she has. You need only provide her with paper and pen, and be patient as she writes. She can write fast, I assure you. We have had some arguments on paper. It's quite similar to the real thing."

"What did you argue about?"

"We argued because she wanted her disability listed in the book I gave you. I told her no. I wanted her to be considered on the grounds of her copious merits, not her one shortcoming."

"Why did you take me to her first?"

"I didn't take you to her first. She was the fifth or sixth girl if I recall—"

"You know what I mean. The blowjob. Do you throw her at everyone first?"

"I don't like what you're insinuating. I took you to her because I sensed a possible match between you. And my senses were right. You're deeply attracted to her. So deeply I daresay you had already made your choice. I actually offer her to very few prospective owners because she appeals to a very rare taste. Do you really think I throw her at everyone first in some effort to be rid of her? She is, to my mind, one of the most desirable and fascinating women here."

Kai stood tense, feeling ashamed that he wasn't dealing with this more calmly. Why was he really upset? Because Bastien hadn't told him from the outset that Constance was deaf? Or because the perfect girl he'd built up in his mind wasn't so perfect? It didn't change his desire for her, he was sure of that. But he was disappointed. He was equally sure of that, and guilty for feeling that way.

"She is a complex and vastly intelligent woman," Bastien said. "Hearing or not."

"I'm sorry I reacted badly. It just surprised me. And I guess I'm worried about what kind of accommodations I'll have to make in order to take her on."

Bastien looked at him a long moment. "You know, she wouldn't like for you to be thinking that way. She likes to believe no one has to make accommodations for her."

A couple of girls sashayed by, and the men moved back against the wall to let them pass. Kai no longer found the nudity the least bit jarring. The odalisques whispered to one another, and the taller one threw a flirtatious glance back at Kai. Bastien led him in the other direction, toward the main house.

"When Constance came here a few months ago, we argued. I told her it would be too difficult for her to perform as an odalisque without a voice, without hearing. We fought, angry words with pen and paper." Bastien led Kai into his office. He went to one of the shelves and lifted a piece of paper from beneath a crystal weight. He handed it to Kai. In a dark, scrawled script she'd written, *I can do anything any of these other women are doing. Anything! And I can do it BETTER.* Kai could see her anger, her frustration, right there on the page. He handed it back to Bastien.

"I have no problem with her being deaf. But now I feel sorry for her. I can't help it, I do. I don't know how I can honestly choose now, how I can measure her against the others without factoring that pity into the mix."

Bastien frowned and squared his shoulders. "Well, then. That isn't workable. Pity in any form would not be acceptable to her. We'll go on as planned tonight with the other four women, but I think it best to shelve Constance as a candidate for now."

Kai wanted to rip Bastien's head off. Didn't he understand? "That's not what I meant—"

Bastien cut him off with a raised hand. "As I said, she reads expressions and body language with far too much acuity. She will not agree to go with you anyway, if she senses you feel that way about her. She won't want deference and pity. But this is fine, she will understand. Between the four other women, you're sure to find a workable match. All the ones you selected are lovely, and every bit as sexually talented as Constance herself."

"You say she will understand. You won't tell her what I said?"

"I will simply tell her that you have struck her from your list. It won't seem cruel to her. It's a fact of life here. Each visitor considers several women on average, but only ever takes one. Now, if you will forgive me, I have another engagement. Perhaps you will return to your room for some refreshment and rest. Tonight will most likely be a late night."

Kai found himself in his room moments later, feeling irate and admonished, for all Bastien's polite gloss. He knew he ought to go through emails again and check in with his business manager, but he was too agitated to do any good communicating. He considered—just for a moment—packing his bags and walking out the door. He decided to take a nap instead. There were still four more girls he'd earmarked as interesting that he hadn't even met. At the very least, he owed them a look, the same consideration he'd given Constance.

But he found he couldn't sleep at all, imagining her face when Bastien told her she wasn't coming to the "party" after all.

Chapter Five:
The Choice

Constance cycled between elation and panic.

When she'd first met Mr. Chandler the evening before, she'd found him attractive, yes. Way attractive. His eyes were so soulful, and his face so expressive when he spoke. She imagined he had a beautiful voice, and she was jealous of the other girls who got to hear it. But she was the only girl who had gotten to *feel* Kai Chandler. His body was quite an instrument. He'd made her senses sing.

He was tall, about six two or six three, with a commanding physical presence. Of course, he was a rich, successful person like all the men who visited here. He'd probably banked on that raw charisma to get ahead in his career. He was muscular, solidly built, with bronze burnished skin and beautiful exotic features. Full lips, an interesting nose, a strong jaw, and wavy black hair pushed back from his face.

It was his eyes, though, that were a revelation. Being deaf, she looked at eyes for meaning as much as lips, and his eyes were deep emotional pools. Intelligent and observant. You expected rich men to be self-involved and narcissistic, but no. Not Kai Chandler.

She'd wanted to converse with him and learn more about him as much as she wanted him to fuck her. She'd gotten the latter finally in the S & M room, a nice rough domineering fuck, tempered by surprisingly gentle caresses. Even though she'd already worked out and showered since then, she still remembered the feel of his girth and hardness. She still remembered the sensation of his cock stretching her, sliding into her while his fingers gripped her waist.

To be perfectly honest, Constance wasn't here at Maison Odalisque for the sexual perks. She liked them, sure, but ultimately she was here to make a lot of money and gain independence—financial, emotional, and otherwise. That was mission number one, a goal that had driven her for the last ten years, since she'd packed her bags at age fifteen and left home. The sexual side of what she did...that was a means to an end. Usually.

But Kai had made her forget her ulterior motives for a few magic moments and just revel in the sex. The seduction, the thrill. Powerful and intense lust, and Kai's infinite ability to hurt her or arouse her. He had wanted her, truly wanted her. She'd seen it in his amber brown eyes that seemed to hide nothing. If *he* was what she had to endure to make the money she needed, it was a pretty good trade in her view.

But Constance was still nervous. It was obvious from the way he'd interacted with her that Bastien hadn't told him yet she was deaf. She'd always considered the quietness of her communication would lend itself perfectly to this lifestyle, but the two men who'd been taken with her so far had withdrawn their interest when they learned she couldn't hear. She was thankful for that now. She hadn't felt anything with either of them like the connection she'd felt with Kai Chandler.

So maybe it was all meant to be. Bastien often spoke of seeking that special chemistry, being attuned to finding your other "sexual half." He prided himself on pairing his clients with the most compatible odalisques, and Constance had come to realize he truly had a knack for it. In the last year, Bastien proudly pointed out, only one odalisque had been returned to the Maison for "issues." Constance knew Bastien had brought her and Kai together because he sensed promise there. What if... *What if...*

What would it be like to be his odalisque? To live in service to him, to his needs and his powerful sensuality? She could make money and yet receive even more. His dominance and sexual skill.

Constance sensed Bastien in her room then, although she wasn't facing the door. The vibration of movement, an infinitesimal inkling of sound. As soon as she turned to him, the nerves downgraded to disappointment. His face said it all.

"Constance, love. Just rest tonight. There's no need for you to come to dinner with Mr. Chandler."

She watched his lips form the words, disbelieving. Devastated. Translation: He doesn't want you. He changed his mind. Bastien came to sit beside her, already dressed for dinner. She wanted him to go. She wanted to cry in private, but he handed her the notebook they used to communicate.

She wrote, *You told him.*

"Yes. It was time to let him know."

He wanted me, didn't he? Before you told him.

Bastien looked down at her words, his face reflecting his own disappointment. "I think so."

But not enough, she wrote bitterly. She put down the pen to wipe away a tear. She hated that she was crying. She hadn't cried the other times. To be honest, she'd felt anger the first time, relief the second. But this time she felt rejected. It hurt. Bastien tilted her face up so she could see what he was saying.

"There now. I told him you wouldn't get upset. You know this is all part of the process. You need to find the right man. Not just the man you want the most."

She frowned and flipped the pen around in her fingers. Then she wrote, *Why would a man like him need an odalisque anyway? He's so hot. He can't find it without paying for it?*

Bastien laughed and she laughed too, spewing tears and snot. He handed her a tissue and held her while she cried for a while. She was careful not to get any tears on his dinner jacket. Not only because it was undoubtedly an expensive jacket, but because she didn't want Kai to know she'd cried over him. It was pointless in the end. Maybe all of this was pointless. She took up her pen again, bit the end of it, then wrote, *Do you only keep me here out of kindness? Because if there's no place in the world for a deaf odalisque, I'll go.*

Bastien shook his head, his face darkening. "Of course you're free to go at any time, but no, I don't keep you here out of kindness. I keep you here because I believe you'll make a spectacular odalisque for some fortunate gentleman. But let me turn the questioning back on you. Are you here because you think you're not capable of doing anything else with your life?"

Constance thought a moment before she scrawled her reply. *No. I'm here because scribbling poetry and masturbating doesn't pay the bills.*

Bastien laughed again. "Ah, yes. Your poetry. It's true that very few poetesses make five hundred thousand a year. As for your masturbatrix qualities, these will undoubtedly stand you in good stead."

They chuckled together, and Constance felt grateful for Bastien's unwavering support. All of them sort of idolized Bastien, although he rarely used them sexually. He was father, best friend, and bodyguard all rolled into one. He would always look out for her. So what if Kai didn't want her? Constance would get over it. At the very least, she'd gotten some very arousing memories out of the whole debacle. She looked into Bastien's eyes and mustered up a smile.

He seemed relieved. "You'll be okay, *ma chère?*"

She nodded and wrote, *Thank you for everything. I know you only want what's best for me, and I appreciate that.* She paused, and then added, *May I serve you? Please?*

Bastien studied her with his trademark assessing gaze. "Are you offering in some attempt to move past Mr. Chandler? Or because you truly wish to serve me?"

She thought a moment. *I always wish to serve you,* she wrote. *But maybe I'm a little lonely at the moment. And sad.*

He ruffled her hair, brushing it back over her shoulder. "You know what I say about emotion. It can be a danger in this lifestyle. I want you, but I think it would be better to let you work through this sadness in some other way than with your lips around my cock. Rest a while, and set your mind to things. Perhaps later you might visit the grotto for a swim. That always cheers you up."

After one last hug, he stood and went to the door, then winked back at her. "Save those cocksucking skills for next week. We've got a pretty high profile head of state coming in."

* * * * *

Kai brooded during dinner. The lights were low and the whole production was faultlessly elegant, as elegant as possible when half the guests were in evening jackets and half the guests were nude. The other men were cordial and easygoing. Over a light repast and wine, they politely questioned Kai on his travels, his philanthropies, and his experiences with his tech company. To his relief, none of the guests showed up in weird masks or costumes. The women were lovely, all four of them. Madeline, Camille, Gwyneth, and...oh...the other one. He couldn't recall her name.

He also couldn't get over the feeling that one woman was missing.

After dinner and another round of drinks, they retired to an adjoining room. The only light came from a fire burning in the large fireplace. Exquisite champagne flowed from bottles stashed in various locations. The men began to shed their clothes and the women took up alluring stances around the room. Lounging on a couch, leaning back against a pile of pillows. One of them—Camille?—cleared the long low coffee table and lay right on top. Bastien seemed to engineer all of it like some perverse concierge. He led Kai over to Gwyneth, who deftly helped him undress. Kai's clothes disappeared, he knew not where.

A couple of the men sat on the couch, speaking loudly in French as women knelt before them and started sucking them off. It was erotic, deviant. It was like something out of a French porn film. God, if only Jessamine could see this.

Gwyneth was having her way with Kai, drawing his growing erection to its fullest degree in order to sheathe him. Meanwhile, Camille was masturbating on the table, legs spread wide, head thrown back in carefree pleasure. It wasn't long before the other two men descended on her, stroking and encouraging her. There was no contempt or belittlement, no gangbang vibe to the proceedings. It was sensual and beautiful, not ugly. Kai gave credit to Bastien for that.

Kai finally relaxed and gave himself up to Gwyneth's skilled ministrations. She licked and toyed with his cock—yes, with every bit as much skill as Constance. But she wasn't Constance. She was thinner, blonde rather than brunette, and much more flirtatious. She teased and chatted and cooed. She smiled more than Constance and almost obsessively batted her eyes. Kai looked around the room rather than at her, pretending Gwyneth's mouth was that of another woman he preferred.

What if it was Constance on the table being used? Would he have cared? His mind shied away from thinking about it. One of the men was now fucking Camille enthusiastically, while the other buried himself in her throat. A third man was milling around, fresh from his own blowjob, squeezing Camille's tits. The other two girls were double teaming the other gentleman, their faces buried in his crotch. The lucky libertine drew his legs up with a desultory smile at Kai. One of the girls—what the hell was her name?—took the opportunity to shove her face into his taint. Kai's cock throbbed in Gwyneth's mouth. Kai wanted that, exactly that. He stopped Gwyneth with a hand on her head. "Come here."

He led her to the sofa where the other man was finishing up. Soon three tongues and three mouths were licking, sucking, lapping. His balls, his cock, his taint, the crease of his thighs and the muscles that ran up in a 'v' on either side. He couldn't remember any of the odalisques' names now, only thinking of them as Big Boobs, Soft Hair, and Full Lips. God, they were all beautiful, all of them, but none of them intrigued him like Constance. Maybe that was for the best. He hadn't come here looking for intrigue or the dire emotional connection Bastien had warned him about.

No. He'd come looking for sexual relief, depravity without guilt. He stopped the girls with a grunt and grabbed the one in the middle, pressing her back against the floor. He had to be inside one of them, any one of them. He'd fuck this one, it would be fine.

He entered her without preliminaries, finding her copiously wet. He drove her against the floor with his thrusts, drove deep and slow inside her, enjoying the warmth of her cunt. This one had brown hair like Constance, only straighter and softer. She sighed against his ear. Across the room he heard the other men egging on Camille, heard groans and moans and a feminine wail of pleasure peaking.

It sounded fake.

Constance. *Constance...*

The coos and sighs of the girl he was fucking sounded fake too. He emptied himself inside her, not caring about his partner's pleasure for the first time in his life. There were four other men in the room, not including Bastien. One of them could bring her off. His heart wasn't in it.

He pulled away from her, leaned back against the couch and peeled the condom off his dick. The rush of his orgasm dissipated, leaving him feeling empty and more than a little dirty. He watched the other participants fucking, banging, laughing and feeling each other up. One of the girls was going down on another one and doing a respectable job of it. He observed the scene with almost clinical detachment, the same way he viewed porn at his house.

His orgiastic impulses had fled with his climax. He looked around for his clothes and found them draped over a stand in the corner. The girls sent him a few glances while he dressed. *Yes, you're lovely. Not for me though. For someone else.*

Bastien drifted over, still fully dressed, still in host mode. "Leaving us so soon?"

"Forgive me. It's been a long day. But thank you. The hospitality at Maison Odalisque is"—he swept a hand around at the various fornicating couples—"legendary. It was an enjoyable dinner." He refrained from giving any critique of the four candidates, and Bastien didn't press as he escorted him to the door.

"Before you retire, perhaps you'd enjoy a late night swim at the grotto," Bastien suggested. "It should be near empty at this hour. The water is fine, very warm and relaxing. And of course, there's no need for a bathing suit."

A refusal was on the tip of Kai's tongue, but then he thought about relaxing in the humid, secluded pool, and found the idea really suited his mood. He went straight from the dinner party, not even putting his jacket back on.

The grotto, too, was lit by the light of a recessed fireplace. Faint lights shimmered beneath the water of the man-made pool, creating an almost eerie glow. Mist danced on top of the water in little wisps. Kai threw his clothes over a nearby rock, and was about to slip into the water when he realized he wasn't alone. A woman was sitting across the pool from him, twenty or thirty feet away. She was hunched over on a rock, her shapely pale legs dangling into the water. She turned her head to look at him and stared.

Constance.

She didn't smile, didn't even acknowledge his presence. Instead, she sank into the water and began to swim—away from him. He called out to her before he realized the stupidity of it. He dove under the water instead and used the faint filtered lights to find her. When he grabbed her legs, she struggled. He surfaced to the sound of her hoarse scream. "Stop!" she said, perfectly clearly. "No!" Those two words seemed to exhaust her available vocabulary. He tried to soothe her but she responded by pushing him away.

"Constance, relax," he said. "Calm down." *She has to see your lips to hear you.* He took her chin in his fingers and stilled her shaking head. "Look at me. Listen. Calm down."

She subsided under his gaze. He saw, now, how her eyes fixed on his lips. Then she raised her eyes to his and gave him a look that felt a lot like a hot knife twisting in his chest. He shook his head, denying the reproach he saw there.

"It wasn't me. It was Bastien. All I said was that...that I wasn't sure..." Kai paused, trying to think of words that wouldn't sound like excuses, but she was off again, slipping from his arms like a mermaid. She slid under the water and took off like a shot, but he was taller, stronger. Faster. When she came up for air, he was waiting for her.

"Constance!"

His expression must have arrested her, if not the pleading note in his voice.

"Give me a minute to explain. You have to understand—" He drew her close, not wanting her to flit away again. His fingertips traced her curves under the water. He made sure she was looking before he spoke. "It scared me at first, okay? The responsibility of communicating with you. I wasn't sure I could do it. It has nothing to do with you and everything to do with me. Bastien misunderstood..." Or maybe he had understood all along. "Wait. Did Bastien tell you to come here tonight?"

Constance thought a moment, and then rolled her eyes in a perfect approximation of Kai's own feelings.

"That manipulative bastard," Kai said with a laugh.

Constance pulled away from him. She didn't swim away, but bobbed in the water at arms' length, dissecting him with an astute gaze.

Kai drifted beside her, moving his legs slowly to stay afloat. "Listen, I know now... Now that I've thought about it... Look, I want you, and you're the only one I want. Everything else is secondary, and I'm sorry—so sorry—if your feelings were hurt." He looked down in the water, where her hand floated next to his. He took it, lacing his fingers with hers. "I'll learn sign language. Whatever. We'll figure it out as we go along. I can even live with your insect thing."

She looked confused. He said it again, more slowly. "Your insect thing. It said on your profile that you were interested in etymology."

The most amazing thing happened then. She laughed. She threw back her head and laughed out loud. The melodic sound echoed off the rocks around them while Kai watched in wonder. Obviously, she was laughing at him, but he didn't care. He thought to himself, *she can't even hear how beautiful her laughter sounds.*

She swam to the edge of the pool near the fire, and he followed her. She pulled herself half out of the water and picked up a little notebook and pen. She wrote two lines while he floated in the water beside her, and then thrust the page under his face.

Etymology—the study of the origins of words
Entomology—the study of insects

He looked back over at her. "I see. Well. That's actually a relief."

Odalisque

She laughed again, her face alight with happiness, and tossed the notebook down. He picked it up and drew her close, handing it back to her. "Tell me. Write for me. How do you feel? Do you want to come with me to the U.S.? Be with me for a year? My odalisque?"

She didn't even glance at the notebook, nor did she write a word. Instead she put her arms around his neck. She laid her cheek beside his, trailing fingers through his hair. "Yes," she whispered against his ear. "Yes. Yes. *Yes.*"

He caught the last *yes* in a kiss. He took her mouth with all the pent up frustration—and now relief—of his desires. Yes, she would come with him. She pressed closer, and it was all he could do not to spear her on the head of his cock and drive all the way in. If only he had protection, he would have. But there would be plenty of time for that.

Instead, they spent an hour swimming together, exploring one another's bodies and getting one another painfully aroused. The shadows danced around them, lending an air of unreality and timelessness to their play. In the absence of condoms they resorted to hand jobs. She rode his fingers under the water, braced against him with her arms clutching his neck. He bit and sucked her nipples, hard and cold in the air above the water, and thrilled to each jerky twitch of her hips. By the time she came, he was nearly bursting himself. She reached eagerly to grasp his cock, running her fingers over it in breathless exploration. It felt naughty and secret. Kai had no doubt they weren't alone here in this deserted place. He hadn't attempted to locate the camera, but assumed it was there. But it couldn't see under the water, to their grasping fingers. It couldn't hear her sigh in his ear, or his low answering moan as she caressed his balls.

When he came with a growl, spent his cum in the currents of the murky water, she watched with her hyper-observant gaze. He knew she could never just be some mindless, inert body for his usage. Again, he felt the specter of awesome responsibility he was taking on. But it would be worth it. He was one hundred percent convinced of that.

So, the next morning, when they sat across the table from Bastien and Maison Odalisque's elderly lawyer, Kai didn't feel one iota of doubt. Only impatience—it would be a full month before Constance could come stay with him. Of course, that made sense. Such involved arrangements couldn't be undertaken in one night. Odalisques weren't a cash-and-carry kind of thing.

Kai signed releases for background checks and credit inquiries. He agreed to present medical tests and physicians' references so he wouldn't have to use condoms while she was in his care. He signed agreements to require barriers for any others who shared her, agreements to provide needed medical and dental care, and a "privileged" level of keeping and shelter. He agreed to allow her freedom from any menial obligations.

He learned some things too. That odalisques were guaranteed one day a week free of sexual use by their Master, unless they voluntarily granted him rights. He learned that odalisques were given respite during the days of their period. That odalisques were, by agreement, to be allowed "adequate" time to sleep, to the tune of a required eight hours a night. Kai mentally added it up. All that time he *wouldn't* be allowed to fuck her. He chuckled inwardly at the anxiety that provoked. It would never be enough time, never. In the event a year *wasn't* enough, the contract allowed for a renewal, up to five times. Six years. After six years of service, all odalisques retired with the small fortunes they had accrued.

It was all very fascinating. Kai slid a look at Constance perched on the edge of her chair beside him. For the first time since he'd made her acquaintance, she was wearing clothes—and she looked very fetching in her long black jacket and pencil skirt. In negotiations and the signing of documents, odalisques were equals, not slaves, and so clothes were a necessity. Her hair was pulled back in a chignon—a loosely elegant one his fingers itched to bring down. Her legs were primly crossed. Somehow he knew those stockinged legs ended in a garter belt and nothing more.

A month. It's not possible.

But he had a lot to accomplish in that month. He had to take a crash course in sign language—that was task number one. He had to give her a method of communicating with him besides the pen and paper she clutched in her lap. He wanted her to be able to look at him and speak to him without fumbling for a pen.

He also had to outfit her personal dwelling rooms, explicitly described within the pages of the code. An *odella*—sleeping quarters— and an adjoining *saray* outfitted for many lustful hours of pleasure. Sofas, beds, cushions, curtains, lush and plentiful plants, and maybe a spanking bench or two. He would give her the rooms near the rooftop garden and the infinity pool. She would be a naked, willing captive in his tower.

So involved was he in all his excited fantasies that when the meeting came to a close, he was caught off guard. Constance was gone too soon—he only had time for a soft kiss and a quick grope beneath her skirt. Yes, stockings, garters, no panties. *Sigh.* One month. *One month.* He'd just authorized a one million dollar bank transfer. The least he was owed was a see-you-in-a-month sendoff fuck!

"The month will pass quickly," said Bastien, watching Kai's crestfallen gaze follow Constance's legs from the room. "If I might have a moment to speak privately with you…"

The lawyer left, and for the first time, Kai picked up on a confrontational vibe from Bastien.

"First of all, I'd like to thank you for visiting Maison Odalisque. I'm very happy that we were able to accommodate your needs."

"And I'd like to thank you for suggesting a swim in the grotto last night." Kai gave him an accusing look. "You really are very good at what you do."

Bastien chuckled. "I've been doing it a long time. I've developed a sense for good matches. I've developed a sense for a lot of things." He leaned forward on his elbows, sobering. "I just want to caution you, as I caution all our candidates for ownership, that the *Code d'Odalisque* does not outline or delineate, in any way, a binding emotional attachment between owner and odalisque. Sometimes the newness and excitement of the relationship carries the risk of a romantic misunderstanding, from both sides. This is, in fact, something we advise you to avoid."

"Yes, you've mentioned this before. But as I said, I don't have time in my life for 'romantic misunderstandings.' There's no need to worry on that account."

"Of course. I'm only telling you to be on guard. A woman who enters odalisque slavery is not, how do you say, girlfriend material. She expects—and very much needs—to be used sexually, and not led to expect relationship-type things. Your cock should remain the center of Constance's concern from day one, and as her keeper, the burden of responsibility in this falls on you. Odalisques are naturally submissive and given to worship. Just be certain, from the start, that she is worshipping the right thing."

Kai shifted and shrugged. "I can assure you Constance is going to have my cock in her face and in her holes plenty of the time she's with me. *Constance*-ly, if you know what I mean." Kai thought he was hilarious. Bastien didn't crack a smile.

Kai tried again. "I've grown quite cynical in these matters. Honestly, it's a relief to me to know what my financial loss will be at the outset, and to know that the woman in question is not going to pretend to love me. No playacting. Everything on the table."

Bastien studied him. "I sense some bitterness in your words. Please tell me you are not a hater of women."

"Only some women. Well, one. My ex-wife to be exact." Kai gave Bastien a rueful smile. "You know the age-old story. Conniving bitch pretends to love very rich man. Keeps up her side of the act just long enough to fulfill the terms of the prenuptial agreement. Waltzes off with millions of his dollars into the arms of her new lover."

"I'm sorry to hear you were victimized in that way."

Victimized. The word startled Kai. No one had ever said it to his face, that he was a victim, although that was exactly what he'd felt while it was going down. "I'll try very hard not to let my bitterness over my ex-wife color my interactions with Constance. I really do like her very much. I can't claim to be the best judge when it comes to women's character, but she doesn't seem to me like the scheming, soul-crushing type."

"No. Odalisques don't scheme or crush souls. There's no need. The simple beauty of the whole thing is that there need be no emotional manipulation. No power plays. I think Constance may be exactly what you need at this point in your life. I hope you will find great fulfillment in your ownership of her."

Kai thought about the month to come, about all the things he had to get ready. About how eager he was to have her at his beck and call, constantly available and willing. "I very much hope so too."

For so long, Kai had been in a haze, choking on distrust, loneliness and betrayal. Now he felt like he could breathe again. Constance would be his much needed breath of fresh air.

Just one more month.

Chapter Six:
Finally Here

Kai was getting nothing done. He didn't know why he was even trying to work from home on this day of all days. He clicked off the Chandler Systems website and over to the airline site to check the flight times for the twentieth time. Stupid, since he knew her plane had landed about an hour before, and that his driver had long since been dispatched to pick her up. She was here. On her way.

He wandered from his office out to the living room and up the staircase to the patio and pool. Taut white awnings stretched above him in geometric opulence. He lived high up in the Malibu hills, next to movie stars and billionaires, with all the security and privacy anyone could want. The crystalline infinity pool could only be reached via the second floor, and dropped off the hillside. You could swim right up to the edge and look down over the cliff, watch the water trickle over and disappear. It was an illusion of course, like so many things about him. Illusion of success. Illusion of having his shit together. God, when was the last time he'd taken a swim?

He sat in one of the chairs under the shade of the awnings. His house was like a mausoleum. He'd sold the last house, the one he'd shared with Veronica, and bought this one, which suited his mood at the time. Contemporary lines, sharp corners, hard and severe. Everything neutral. He'd never felt compelled to change it—until he'd gone shopping for Constance the week he got back from France.

Her room at the Maison hadn't been particularly colorful or overly decorated. In fact it had been decorated very much like his house, in neutral and understated tones. But he'd wanted color. Garish floral cushions tossed on a bright crimson sofa. A mahogany canopy bed with deep vermilion sheers shot through with gold threads, sheers he'd imported from India. He hadn't consulted any interior decorators, any outside stylists. He'd done it on his own and found his tastes stuck somewhere back in the wonder of his great-grandmother's squat, odoriferous home on the outskirts of Mumbai, the home he'd only visited once during his childhood. He couldn't imagine why he wanted that for her, but he did.

Then he'd stopped at an antique shop and picked out an armoire and dresser inlaid with tile in a kaleidoscope of bright colors. The shop clerk had run a finger over the uneven surface and whistled. "Wow. This is loud."

And then Kai had understood. He was furnishing her room *loudly*. It was the interior decorating equivalent of yelling at someone who couldn't hear. Had he really meant it that way? He'd recalled the addendum to her odalisque contract, protecting her from blindfolding. *Constance hears with her eyes.* Would she take one look at her surroundings and get a headache?

When she arrived, he would ask her whether she liked it or not. He practiced the signs with half-conscious nervousness. *Do. You. Like. This. Room?* The sign for "room" was simple, his hands delineating a squarish space. A lot of the sign language was obvious. He'd worked at it every day until he got conversational, and fingerspelled until he got fast and smooth with the letters. The fingerspelling was the hardest thing by far. His teacher had gripped his wrist so he didn't bounce his hand while he tried to spell in his mind and translate the letters into signs. He was a pretty smart person usually, but language had never been his strong suit.

Fortunately, being able to make the signs wasn't important. Constance could read lips. What would be important would be decoding *her* signs. He hoped he didn't end up looking like a complete ass.

Kai went back into the house and drifted to her bedroom. Her *odella*, in odalisque vocabulary. He'd practiced that too, all things odalisque, embracing the silliness and perversity of it. He'd studied the full body of the code lying in bed with his cock in his hand. It was certainly arousing reading. He couldn't wait to fuck his beautiful sex slave, to lie her right down on the cushions and bury himself inside her...

But he hadn't told anyone she was coming. Not Mason, not Jessamine, not any of the people he worked with. Not even his sister, who made it her business to know everything about him, no matter how personal it was. When he'd met her for lunch downtown, Satya had picked up on his mounting anxiety over Constance's arrival. He'd explained it away as work problems. To his co-workers he explained away his anxiety as sister problems. It all worked out. He figured he would tell everyone later that Constance was his girlfriend. Maybe, eventually, he'd tell a few trusted friends the truth, but not right away.

In the beginning, he wanted her all to himself.

It was ten after four already. Where was she? Kai was about to call his driver when he saw the black sedan pull around the front. He walked out, and realized he was actually holding his breath. He let it out in a long slow gust and drew in air again. The door opened and a middle-aged woman got out. Close cropped dark hair, a smart business suit. For a moment he thought they'd sent the wrong odalisque, and then he realized this must be the overmistress.

The older woman turned, leaned down and gestured, and then Constance stepped out of the car. She was also dressed in sedate black business attire. She looked remarkably put together for someone who'd just gotten off a transatlantic flight. Her glossy dark curls fell forward over her shoulder. She flipped them back and turned to him, and broke out in a shimmering smile.

She wanted to be here. It was written all over her face. He'd bought her and she was here, clearly happy, clearly excited. He'd planned to greet her in sign language and surprise her. *Hello. Welcome.* It seemed stupid now, not enough. Kai strode to her instead, took her hand and drew her close. She melted against him. He was vaguely aware of the overmistress standing beside them, but not aware enough to care. He kissed Constance's soft lips, and she parted them and responded in kind. She was so warm and real in his arms. So present.

He drew away from her and drank in her pleased expression. He squared his shoulders, raised his hands and signed, "You're finally here."

She looked taken aback for a moment, so he thought he'd signed the wrong thing. She raised her own hands and formed slow words. "You learned to sign?"

He smiled sheepishly. "I'm going to try. I'm a beginner. Be patient with me."

She was blinking now, her fingers against her lips. He watched her, not knowing what to do. The overmistress tapped her shoulder, and when Constance was looking at her, signed "Let's go inside."

Kai turned, leading them to the door. "Of course. Let's go inside." *Look at her when you talk.* He turned back and said it again. "Come inside. Your room's all ready. I hope you like it. And I am so, so happy you're here."

*   *   *   *   *

Constance followed him, staring at his broad back, his impeccably tailored clothing...or maybe it was his physique that made the clothes fit so well. So Kai had learned to sign for her. It touched her deeply—and put her on guard. He would be so easy to fall for.

And that wasn't in the plan.

He led her through his house, past a gleaming grand piano, past a sunken sitting room furnished in modern lines. A wide hallway stretched in two directions, with numerous doors. He ushered her and Ms. Dresden up a carpeted, open stairwell to the second floor. Her suite of rooms was on the right. He opened the door.

"I'll give you the full tour, of course, but this is where you'll stay. If you hate it—"

Constance didn't hear any more because she had to look away from him. The room was a wonderland. It was a huge open space, larger than most people's apartments. Much larger than the military housing she'd grown up in. Everything was big in scale—the sofas, the furniture. A wide archway framed a sleeping space with an inviting, curtained bed. There was a massive closet. Overkill really, since she'd only brought one suitcase of clothes. There were cushions on the floor, cushions on the chairs, cushions piled on the bed. There were vases of flowers on the side tables and dressers, and beautiful tree-sized potted plants. A large desk graced one corner of the room. Stacks of notebooks were arranged next to a cup of pens.

And everything—everything—was vividly, brightly colored.

She turned back to Kai and Ms. Dresden to find them talking. They faced one another so she couldn't listen. From Ms. Dresden's gestures she gathered they were talking about the room. They turned to her and she was sure she wore the goofiest smile in the history of smiling.

"I want to jump on the bed."

She watched Kai to see if he understood her signing. She tried again, slower. "Jump." She pointed. "Bed."

"Oh, jump on the bed," he said. "Be my guest."

She took off the high heeled pumps she was unaccustomed to wearing, and did a flying leap. She sank into a fluffy embroidered counterpane while cushions and pillows spilled around her. She hunched herself to her feet and jumped a few times, ducking the filmy orange canopy over her head. Ms. Dresden cocked her head to one side and signed, "Not very dignified."

Constance laughed and collapsed down on the pillows. She looked at Kai and saw approval, and something else that made a pulse start to thrum in her veins. Male hunger. She could read it on his face like the title of a book.

This would be their book. This was the first page. Ms. Dresden silently left the room and shut the door behind her.

He walked toward the bed with a seductive smile. She'd forgotten how large and imposing he was. "You're a long way from home, little odalisque."

He didn't bother to sign; she was staring right at him, at his handsome face, his full sexy lips. She laid back on the cushions, running her fingertips over the embroidery and lace. This was the life of an odalisque. He was her Master, and she craved to please him more than she'd expected to. He stopped beside the bed and she signed, slowly, so he could decode it, "This is my home now."

He looked pleased by that. "You like it?"

She knew he was talking about the room, but she was thinking about him. "Yes, I like it. It's beautiful." *You're beautiful. Let me serve you.* Her fingers went to the buttons of her jacket. She meant to undress, a slow seductive striptease, peeling away layers until she was as she should be: nude and open to his gaze.

But her new owner had other ideas. He fell on her and undressed her himself, with a rash impatience that thrilled her. He tossed her jacket over the headboard, undid her blouse's buttons and pushed the front open to reveal a sheer bra. He toyed with it a moment before clicking open the front clasp to fondle her breasts. His fingertips felt so rough—a curt, demanding touch that made her feel instantly submissive to him.

He pushed her fitted skirt up to her hips and hooked a finger in the elastic of her garter belt. She wasn't wearing panties. He traced the top of her stockings and then slid his fingers down her pussy cleft. She arched, opening herself to his skilled probing. His lips were at her neck, her shoulders, nibbling on her clavicle. He was clean-shaven but still his cheek felt rough against her skin.

He smelled divine.

Aftershave, soap, and his own natural smell. She twined her fingers in his hair and felt the jerky movements of his hands pulling at his pants. She ached for him, needed him to fill her. This was what she'd wanted, what she'd dreamed of having someday when she'd begun her training at Maison Odalisque. She was with a handsome, strong man in a beautifully furnished home on a blissfully cozy bed.

He pushed inside her, spreading her open for his possession, and consolidated her dreams into reality. His cock within her was hard, unyielding. Hot acute friction, with no latex barrier needed between them now. She clamped her legs around him and grasped his ass cheeks, feeling them clench and unclench through the fabric of his pants as he moved in and out of her. She almost closed her eyes, let herself be borne away merely on sensation.

But no, she was too curious. She wanted to see her Master. As he arched over her, she stared at his muscular arms braced on either side of her, his lightly furred chest bearing down on her. She watched him open his mouth over one breast and then the other, making her shudder with hot licks of pleasure. She felt his breath against her skin and looked up to meet his gaze.

His eyes were fixed on hers, communicating deep, overpowering desire. They were magnificent, a light amber-gold color she was certain she'd never encountered before—and she remembered people's eyes. The way he looked at her stimulated her as much as his thick cock between her legs. The hint of a smile played across his lips. He was happy.

Kai, Kai, Kai, Kai... She knew his name in her head, felt it on her tongue, although she was too embarrassed to attempt to say it. She'd practiced it in her room the last month, touching her lips, trying to form the right sounds, which wasn't easy when you couldn't hear them. She touched him now, utterly fascinated with the feel of his skin, the hardness of his body. His cock stroked her in the perfect spot, with the perfect rhythm. She was suffused by pleasure and enthralled by his confident possession of her. She had worried a little, that things might be awkward when she arrived here. Or that, God, he might change his mind about wanting her.

But he seemed very pleased to have her. His movements were controlled and yet some thread of wildness snaked and grew between them. He squeezed her breasts, hurting her, making her moan and arch toward him for more of the shocking ache. She ground her clit against the wiry hair at the base of his cock, sparking singing sensation. Ironic, that her independence would come to her through this subjugation. Through being *his*. His to use, his to possess. More ironic still that she basked in every moment of it.

She gasped for breath and clung to him, thrusting wildly in answer to his own roughness. She tensed her thighs just at the edge of the precipice, and then tumbled into orgasm in a shattering rush. Pleasure washed over her, rendering her helpless. He dug his knees into the bed and bore her down, down, down, impaling her without mercy. She could feel him clutching the fabric of her skirt, not letting her move one centimeter beneath him. He shuddered over her and came to rest, his hands moving up to her shoulders. He pressed his face against hers and laid still, his cock pulsing inside her.

Kai. She almost whispered it, but words had such power. *Be on guard.* A moment later he pulled away, lounged back to rest on the pillows beside her. From the sudden rise and fall of his chest, she thought perhaps he sighed. He licked his lips and looked over at her with an expression she couldn't place, and then he kissed her so she couldn't keep thinking about it. When he pulled away, he ran his long, tapered fingers over the buttons of her blouse.

"So...do the clothes come off now?"

"Whatever you want," she signed. "Always."

"Except on your day off. When is your day off?"

She shrugged and signed again. "Whichever day you prefer."

"So I'm in charge from here on out. Is that what you're saying?"

Her gaze left his lips to meet his eyes and smile. She knew he didn't really expect an answer. He dipped his head and kissed her again, undressing her slowly, taking a while to stroke and trace her stockings before he finally drew them off. He gathered her close then, so close. She basked in his warmth, his gentleness, his leashed strength and the comforting breadth of his chest. He tipped her face up to his.

"I can hardly believe you're finally here."

My God, his eyes. They were like the earth and sea in one. Constance wanted to snuggle with him, skin to skin. She wanted him to fuck her again, to take her with the same raw need he'd just shown. She reached for his shirt, wishing to pull it off him, but he stilled her hands.

"Not now. She's still out there, isn't she? Your overmistress? I don't even know her name."

Constance spelled it out for him, twice, because she spelled too fast the first time.

"Ms. Dresden." Kai nodded. "I think Bastien told me that. We'll have plenty of time—a year—to fuck like bunnies, but I hate to think of her standing out there waiting in the hall." He gave Constance one last kiss and squeeze and stood to fasten his pants.

"My God," he said, leaning down to be sure she was listening. "You have no idea how happy I am about that disappointed look on your face. Or that smile," he added as she burst into laughter. "Now get your little odalisque ass out of bed."

* * * * *

They dined together on takeout, Constance, Kai, and Ms. Dresden. Kai was relieved to learn the overmistress had no expectation of being put up in the house. He didn't want to be looking after a guest at the moment.

No, Ms. Dresden would stay at a hotel nearby for a month in order to check in with Constance weekly, and then continue to check in with his odalisque—in person—once a month until the end of her sojourn with him. It was a lot of flying, and he told her so.

"Can't you just video conference with her or something?"

Ms. Dresden shook her head and shot that down in her clipped New England accent. "You can't always gauge someone's well-being over webcam, or telephone. We want to be in the presence of our charges, to touch them and look in their eyes to reassure ourselves everything is okay."

Kai paused, digging through his Lo Mein. "Have there been times things weren't okay? Odalisques who had to be...removed?"

He could feel Constance's eyes on him, listening. Ms. Dresden stopped with her fork lifted halfway to her mouth, and put it down again.

"Yes, there have been a few instances. Very few. Our owners know from the outset they'll be monitored, and that scares away the majority of the bad-intentioned. Background checks and our own freak radar shake out the rest. But in our twenty-three year history, there have been a few unfortunate situations. A couple of women who were actually harmed. There are always those wealthy men who feel the rules don't apply to them."

Ms. Dresden continued eating, although both she and Kai were watching Constance. The silent woman seemed particularly vulnerable, nude as she was, while the other two of them were clothed. Ms. Dresden took a sip of wine and asked in a casual tone, "How do you feel, Constance? About your new home?"

Constance thought a moment and then let loose in a stream of sign language that left Kai utterly stumped. He caught words here and there, and her smiling expression reassured him the overall tone was positive, but he also realized how much he still had to learn. What would he do when Ms. Dresden left?

Well, it wasn't like they'd be hanging out all day chatting. He'd have to go back to work in a day or two, when he was sure she was settled in. When he'd completely spent his pent-up erotic yearnings on her. All over her.

He fidgeted in his chair. Even the way Constance signed was a turn on. Or maybe it was her gorgeous, perky breasts. Either way...

"I'm glad to hear it," Ms. Dresden said, still trying to include him in the conversation. "Did you get all that, Mr. Chandler?"

His befuddled look made Constance laugh. Kai loved her laugh so much. He shot her a crooked smile and Ms. Dresden grinned at them both like a flustered chaperone.

"It is only my opinion, but I believe the two of you will suit just fine. Mr. Chandler, I'll contact you with the approximate dates of my visits."

"What will you do in the meantime?" Kai asked. "Hang around L.A.?"

"There are other odalisques in the area to look in on, and women who've expressed an interest in the program. We visit them personally before we invite them over to France. There's always work to do to keep the program running. But your work is at an end, Mr. Chandler. Now is your time for enjoyment."

"You can call me Kai if you like."

"I'll call you Mr. Chandler, because ours will be a formal and necessarily distant relationship. I am here for her, you see. Not for you."

Domme, he thought to himself. Not long afterward, Ms. Dresden took her leave, bidding them both good-bye at the front door. Kai's driver would take her to the Maison's Los Angeles residence. She promised to return to check on Constance in about a week.

Constance turned to Kai as the door closed, looking for the first time slightly nervous. What should he do? He could help her unpack, perhaps. Give her the extended tour. Show her the swimming pool and rooftop garden. But he didn't really want to do any of those things.

"Constance," he said instead. "God help me. I need you again."

Chapter Seven:
Settling In

Kai fucked Constance twice more in the saray adjoining the bedroom. The first time he draped her over a pile of cushions and took her right on the floor, doggie style, slamming his hips against her gorgeous heart-shaped ass and driving deep. He chose not to let her come. He didn't issue any commands on the subject; she wouldn't have heard him anyway. No, he simply took his pleasure, and she was well trained enough to understand that her role at the moment was to act as a vessel for his lust.

Afterward he turned her over and nuzzled her and gazed into her wide eyes. He said "Good girl," and her smile told him she understood. He turned her back around and pushed the cushions away, making her kneel on all fours while he ran his hands all over her, squeezing and measuring her feminine curves. She endured his coarse investigation, spreading her thighs wider when he nudged them and arching her back when he ran a firm palm up her spine.

He could tell she was still simmering, still aching for satisfaction. She had also been driven deep into submission by his quick, selfish fuck. Her pussy was wet, glistening, and her eyes continuously searched his out, looking back over her shoulder at him for some signal of what would come next.

Kai thought she wouldn't like what was coming next. Or perhaps she would. Her shapely, round ass cheeks were due to be marked. Past due. Poor thing. He knew she was tired from her journey and probably terribly sensitive from missing out on the previous orgasm.

Too bad.

Kai lifted her by the arm and walked her over to the platform in the center of the room which might have passed for an ornate iron bed. It wasn't a bed though—her bed was in the other room, piled with soft pillows.

No, this was a stage designed for fucking, bondage, and other delicious pastimes. Each of the four solid posts was fixed with eye hooks at various heights. The headboard was a broad lattice of criss crossing bars so that he could affix her to it in any way he wished. The footboard was shorter and padded on top. It had been designed to be high enough that when he bent her over it, her feet would dangle off the floor. All in all, it was a wonderful place to torment a horny sex slave.

It also had an extra-firm mattress since it would be used for fucking, not sleeping. Rather than bright colors, this bed had taut white sheets. When he tied her there to await his pleasure, he didn't want it to feel so comfortable she fell asleep.

Yes, he was a bit of a sadist.

She stared at the iron frame now, and her look of nervous arousal sparked new lust flaring in his veins. He had to urge her forward toward the padded footboard. A moment later, she was arranged in a position he liked very much, her hips draped gracefully over the black vinyl surface. Her bottom was forced up on display, and her legs hung below, trembling slightly. Every so often she would kick one leg as if testing how far it was to the floor. Even on her tip toes she couldn't have reached the carpet.

Kai stood and watched her for a while, enjoying her tiny fidgets and noting the shiny succulence of her cleft. Then Kai crossed the room and opened a tall mahogany cabinet. He drew the doors wide so Constance would be able to see all the torturous instruments inside. She made a soft groaning sound.

There were clamps, paddles, whips, straps, cuffs, and other novelties he'd use to play with her. Straight sex would have been enough—quite enough—to sustain him. Her talents were just that good when it came to fucking and sucking. But he also got to play with her in the kinky ways he liked, which was the proverbial icing on the cake.

69

But God, where to start? He finally decided on some leather cuffs and a whippy long-handled strap. He strolled over to the bed with them, going half hard already from her look of dread. He placed the strap in front of her flushing face, then stood behind her and drew her hands to the small of her back. He fixed a leather cuff to each wrist and then hooked them together. She was so horny she tried to scoot back against his cock as he worked the buckles. She was rewarded with a sharp slap to the side of her thigh. His cock surged again at the sound of impact and the sight of scarlet blooming over her unmarked skin. He reached for the strap—

Then he stopped. Damn. They hadn't negotiated any type of play limits or safe words, and he'd already cuffed her hands. Signing wouldn't work anyway, not for an important discussion like this. He didn't fully trust his decoding skills yet.

With a sigh, he went back into her bedroom to the desk. He grabbed a notebook off the top of the stack, and a pen. He returned to the saray, writing as he went. He placed the notebook in front of her face.

We need to talk about limits and a way for you to safe out if you need to.

She looked up at him and shook her head firmly. "No."

No. It was one of the few words she could say. It sounded slightly forlorn when she said it. She drew it out more than a hearing person might. *Nooo...*

He picked up the pen and wrote *Yes. And I want to have this conversation in writing, so I'm going to release you.*

She pouted as he undid the cuffs. Without changing position, she grabbed the notebook and started to write.

I don't want a safe word. I don't want to put any limits on you. I'm yours to use as you wish. I'm your odalisque.

Kai frowned as she pushed it across to him. He wrote in his neat script just below her swirly hand.

I don't know how much pain to give you. I have no idea how much pain you like.

She looked at him like he had taken leave of his senses. Without pause, she wrote *I like whatever pleases you.*

Kai levered himself off the bed, stood over her and crossed his arms over his chest, shaking his head. She was skilled in body language, and surely understood his meaning. They wouldn't play if she didn't give him some kind of guidelines. With a scowl, she grabbed the notebook and scrawled out a long passage.

I trust you to read my body language. I trust you to tell when I'm nearing my limits. I trust you not to truly injure me. I trust you to know when it ceases to be pleasure/pain, and just turns into pain. I TRUST YOU.

She showed it to him with a raised brow. He had to admit she had a point. As a dominant, he had learned to use his partner's reactions to choose the intensity at which he played. But in past scenes, there had always been a backup plan. A word that meant stop.

He circled the words *I TRUST YOU* and wrote *Thank you.* Then he wrote, *Your safe word will be 'no.' Don't say 'no' unless you want me to stop what I'm doing. Okay?*

For a moment it looked like she might argue, but then she nodded. Kai whisked away the notebook and placed it on the floor under the bed. His mind was already back on track, and his body was itching to follow. He was going to strap her butt cheeks scarlet and then he was going to fuck her right over the footboard. He was going to take her ass while her legs kicked and dangled helplessly, and he was going to keep on fucking her tight hole until she came.

He thought about telling her that—making her look right at his lips and read the words there. *I'm going to beat your ass and then fuck it.* But then he thought it would be hotter to just do it and have her accommodate him. Cockslavery in action. All her holes were his to use at will.

He was so wrought up his fingers fumbled with the buckles. When he finally had her restrained again, he stood back to admire her. This time, the two-foot-long strap dangled from his fingertips. He swung the black leather in an arc and caught her across both cheeks. She jerked and made a lovely sound of distress. Why did he imagine she would be quiet? You didn't need fluent speech to whine, moan, or scream. She wouldn't be able to do much begging, true, but that suited him fine.

He brought the strap down again with a satisfying crack. She clenched her ass cheeks and struggled a little in her cuffs. With the third blow, he hit her a bit harder and she squealed through her teeth and reached down to cover her ass with her cuffed hands. His answer to that little attempt at respite was to bring the strap down lower, across the tops of her thighs. She almost rose off the bed, she jerked so hard, but the footboard had her pretty well stranded with her reddening ass up in the air.

Poor little odalisque.

He squeezed her ass for a moment, giving her time to calm down. He grabbed a handful of her lovely hair and tilted her head back to check her expression. Half-panicked. Half-horny. *Oh, I like you like this.*

His cock was raging for her, practically bursting, but he wasn't quite through with her yet. He placed a firm hand over her cuffed wrists, pinning them securely to her back, and with the other hand, swung the strap down on her ass several times in quick succession. She cried out, kicking her legs in earnest now. All that did was make her ass an even more enticing target. He gave her maybe ten more licks, reddening each cheek evenly. She was beautiful in her distress, crying out and moaning, making plaintive, begging sounds.

So she could beg after all.

And she had been correct. Kai could tell, just from looking at her, where she was on the pain scale. He had a pretty good sense already of taking her far enough, but not too far. He gave her three more solid cracks, finishing cracks, and then took the strap back to the cabinet and grabbed a bottle of lube. It was his favorite type because it had a little sting to it. Lubricated assfucking didn't come without its drawbacks, at least when he was in charge.

God, he really *was* a sadist.

He grabbed a condom so he wouldn't suffer the same stinging effect as her. Constance watched all this, looking wrung out and breathless. She pressed her mound against the top of the footboard, seeking relief. Well, there was a reason it was padded vinyl. He would make her clean her juices off it later.

For now, he stepped behind her glowing red ass and parted her cheeks, squirting a generous amount of the lube onto his fingers. She tensed a moment as he swirled the slick substance around her hole, and then pressed a couple fingertips inside. She seemed to relax then, and accept that her asshole was about to be filled with his rock solid cock.

Then, after fifteen seconds or so, she started to whine and squeeze her cheeks together. Yes, that was about how long it took to notice the effect of the warming lube. She threw him a reproachful look. He gazed back, her slightly-sadistic lover. *Yes, I know it's uncomfortable. I enjoy watching you squirm.* He positioned the head of his cock against her clenching asshole and moved his hips forward. Her hands made fists in her cuffs. He took them in one hand and held her down hard against the footboard, and used his other hand to press his cock into her resisting passage.

Good God, she was so tight. He pushed slowly and steadily until he felt her body relax. She moaned, a low guttural moan, as he drove all the way balls deep. Her sphincter tensed and pulsed around him as she shifted her hips. She was undoubtedly still feeling the prickly heat of the lube at the same time she had to accommodate the full invasion of his length.

Kai fucked her at a leisurely pace in the beginning. He'd dreamed of fucking her ass for many weeks now. He reveled in his possession of her and the way she responded. She trembled and moaned, behaving as if nothing pleased her more than the ruthless invasion of his cock deep in her hole. He quickened his thrusts, feeling the hot wetness of her pussy against his balls. Her ass clenched him so tightly he almost lost control.

"Come, you hot little slut." She couldn't hear him. He didn't care. He wanted her to come, to pulse and clamp down on his cock and milk him while he pounded against her scarlet cheeks. He wrapped a fist in her hair and pulled, pumping in her faster, watching her shoulders tense as her hands worked in the cuffs. Then, with a high pitched cry, she went rigid and shook through what must have been a powerful orgasm. He held her hips and drove deep, every inch of penetration a wicked pleasure. Pulsating spasms racked his body as he pulled her ass back against his hips.

Constance went languid as he finished inside her. She arched back to him as he rode out the aftershocks, as if she still wished to offer him more of her. More, more, more. He was going to take everything he could get.

For a long time he stayed hard and still inside her, enjoying the tightness of her ass and the beautiful sight of her body sprawled over the footboard beneath him. Now and again she made little plaintive sounds. Now that the crisis had passed and the thrill of her orgasm was waning, the itch of the lube was probably returning full force.

Still, she laid there and put up with the torment. Even now her shapely ass was offered to him. If he was of a mind to do it, he surely could have fucked her again. Most women were so defensive about their asses. He'd had to practically bribe his ex-wife to fuck her there, and when he did, she'd whined and complained through the whole thing as if it were a terrible ordeal.

Maybe it had been, for Veronica. But Constance was *trained*.

Kai leaned down, still inside her, and licked a trail up her spine to her nape. She shivered as he kissed her below one ear. He withdrew from her ass, already looking forward to the next time, the next way he'd take her, the next way he'd make her come.

But not now. She was clearly exhausted, and clearly still suffering from the bothersome lube. He uncuffed her and told her, with a sign, to be still. Kai went to the cabinet to return the cuffs, and then to the bathroom to discard his condom and start running a bath in the large garden tub.

Only then did he lift Constance down from the footboard. He pretty much had to carry her limp body to the bathtub. He might have worried if she hadn't looked up at him with a fuck-happy smile. He grinned back, amazed by this creature he'd brought to live in his house. She was a smutty sex siren one moment, and a sweet darling the next. He'd been balls deep in her ass just a few minutes ago, but now he had the strongest impulse to cuddle her close. She clutched at his shoulder and laid her head against his chest, and he was sad the walk to the bathroom wasn't longer.

He turned off the water and guided her into the tub, climbing in after her. Like everything in his house, the tub was oversized and overblown—and it was only the guest suite bathtub. She bobbed beside him, watching him with her expressive green eyes.

"It's like the grotto, isn't it?" he said. "Just a little smaller."

She laughed at his joke and then picked up the soap, gesturing to ask if she could wash him. He nodded and let her lather him up, her agile fingers tracing his contours and kneading away the last of his stress about this momentous day. She was here. He'd already pretty much fucked her raw and she was still smiling at him. Hell, she was practically devouring him with her eyes, and she was being none too coy about exploring him with her fingers. Her hands slid down to his cock and intimately caressed him. He allowed himself to enjoy it for a few moments, but then he grabbed her wrist.

"Enough. You've had enough for one night. We still have three hundred and sixty four days of bliss remaining."

He watched to see if she understood, especially as tired and spacey as she looked. He was coming to realize she didn't pick up every word, even when she was paying close attention. A lot of the gaps must have been filled in by context and body language. Kai took her hand and pried the soap from her, put it aside and fingerspelled the word in her palm. *B-L-I-S-S*.

She smiled and looked shy, and then she took his hand and kissed his palm. Bliss, fucking bliss. God, he owed Mason big time for this. Kai hauled her against him. He kissed his odalisque, tenderly at first, and then with all the intensity of his happiness. Would every day be as satisfying as this day? Constance was too good to be true, surely. Tomorrow would be a little less exciting, and the next day, maybe she wouldn't even bother to smile.

God, no.

Maybe every day would get better and better. They would come to know one another—one another's bodies and one another's deepest wants and needs. Ah, her kisses tasted like wine and honey. He cupped her round ass in his hands and felt her fingertips curl around his neck and then up into his damp hair. He finally broke away with a sigh, and busied himself washing her in kind. It was either wash her or fuck her again, and he couldn't do that in good conscience, not when she was barely staying awake. The hot water was relaxing them both into a coma.

A few minutes later he had her out of the tub, toweling her off and drying her thick head of hair. How lush and dark and curly it was. For a moment he thought, *our children would have beautiful hair...*

Holy shit, this is what Bastien had been trying to warn him about. *Sometimes the newness and excitement of the relationship carries the risk of a romantic misunderstanding, from both sides.*

Kai took a deep breath, just stopped and held her close. He buried his face in her neck and breathed in the scent of her, soap and the lavender oil he'd added to the water. This time she was the one to pull away. He watched for her to sign something, but she turned from him instead and started opening and closing drawers and bathroom cabinets. She found a toothbrush and clutched it in front of her until he took the hint.

"I guess I'll—"

She moved to see his face, and he remembered at the same time to look at her and talk. He tried again. "I guess I'll let you settle in and get some rest. Let me know if you need anything."

She nodded, and, feeling awkward suddenly, he left. Well, it was her room, not his. Odalisques slept in their odellas. Masters didn't. Kai went down the stairs and across the back hall to his own bedroom suite, bone tired now that he'd left her. He collapsed on the bed, then docked his mp3 player and brought up a Mozart sonata on his sound system. He turned it up so loud he thought the neighbors could probably hear it from a half mile away. But she wouldn't hear it.

After the second movement he stood and wandered back down the hall, back up the stairs to her suite of rooms. The door was open. He could see her lying on the bed, nude, one leg thrown over the comforter and her hair spread across the pillows. Her face was angelic in repose. The sound of violin and piano battered off the walls and vibrated the light fixtures, and yet she slept. Beautiful odalisque.

The next day, she woke with her period. "How many days?" he asked her forlornly.

"Three or four," she signed back.

Kai remembered all too well that her menses was one of her off-limits times. A specific clause in the contract actually forbid using *medical or hormonal methods to deprive the odalisque of this natural monthly function.*

Kai had thought, what kind of sick fuck would want to do such a thing? And now he knew. A sick fuck like him. He wanted to haul her to the gynecologist for some kind of pill or procedure that would make it go away. He wanted to—oh, hell.

Instead he smiled at her and made himself go in to work, mentally counting down the days.

Chapter Eight:
Enslaved

After Kai set off for work, Constance slept in her cozy vermilion bed. She dreamed of burnished berries and desert windstorms. She dreamed of colorful bazaars and swimming in a warm deep ocean. She woke up around noon to the gentle whisper of heated air against her skin. She traced it to one of the furnace registers blowing right at the bed. Kai had obviously set her suite of rooms to be the warmest in the house. But even naked, she didn't need to be *that* warm. She'd have to tell him to reset it.

She got up and took a long bath in the same tub they'd bathed in the night before. Everything in the rooms he'd set aside for her was beautiful and luxe. The towels were soft and the soap had a unique, alluring scent, like lavender and sugar. Muted light filtered in through high windows. Constance could see the blue of the sky as she drifted in the water. She got brave and started pushing the buttons on the bathtub console, and enjoyed a nice bubble-jet massage. Ah, it made her want to masturbate, but she felt almost too lazy to. Almost.

That done, she got out and inserted her menstrual cup, then headed downstairs to the kitchen. His house was like a palace to her. Maison Odalisque had been impressive, but this was even grander. What was she doing here? Constance Flynn, who had grown up in ugly, utilitarian military family housing, surrounded by garage-sale furniture?

She crossed the sunken living room to the white baby grand piano sitting on a raised dais in the corner. Very Liberace, the white piano, she thought with a smile. But then most of Kai's house was white, or neutral. And everything was open wide. She'd been in nightclubs that were smaller than this room, and stripped on stages that were smaller than the piano's platform. Stripping. Now that had been a mistake. Men got unpleasant when they thought they were being ignored. She just hadn't been able to hear them when they called out to her.

Like her mother, Constance had made so many mistakes in her life. Maybe this was another one. But there was only one way to tell, and that was to do it. That had always been her *modus operandi*, but she wasn't sure if it had served her well or made her life worse than it might have been.

Constance sat at the piano and slid her fingers along the polished white and black keys. She lifted the piano's lid down and then back again. He'd had it open. Did that mean he played often? Even if he did, she wouldn't be able to hear any more than muted vibrations. She depressed the keys, one at a time for a while, and then in great groups, smashing and bashing them, knowing she was probably making an awful clamoring sound. She ran her fingers up and down, counting as she went.

Then she felt a touch on her shoulder and screamed.

She turned, her arms clasped to her chest, breath gasping in her throat. Kai smiled back at her, resplendent in his business suit and tie.

"I didn't know you played," he signed.

He was teasing, laughing, but she'd almost passed out. Her heartbeat finally calmed in her chest. "You scared me!" She exaggerated the sign for *scared*, clasping her chest again. "Don't sneak up on me, please."

"I'm sorry. I would have called to let you know to expect me, but... I have to put in a phone you can use. What are they called? TDD phones?"

"You don't have to," she signed.

"If there's ever an emergency, you'll need a phone."

"Deaf people use instant messaging now." She had to spell out the word *instant messaging* twice, and once he got it, he looked sheepish. She hadn't meant to make him feel stupid when he was trying so hard to help her. "It's okay," she signed. "Can you get me a smart phone?" He understood *smart phone* a lot quicker, before she even finished fingerspelling it. He nodded.

"Of course. I'll bring one home for you tonight." He'd reverted back to speaking, which was fine, since she was getting pretty used to reading his lips. When she wasn't distracted by their perfect shape and dark berry color.

She gestured to his well-tailored suit. "I thought you were working today."

"I was, but I wanted to come home and check on you. You were so groggy and tired this morning."

She smiled. "I'm better now. I slept."

"Did you eat breakfast? Or lunch?"

"Not yet."

She could tell he only caught the *no* in her sign, and not the *yet*, because he got all fretful and started pulling her into the kitchen. She'd wanted to ask him if he played the piano, but he seemed stuck in caretaking mode right now, and she found it so sweet she didn't have the heart to distract him from it.

He piled fruit and artisan bread and something called soysages on the counter in front of her. He explained that he didn't eat meat, which Constance found vaguely arousing. She could take meat products or leave them, but vegetarianism just sounded so...healthful.

She turned down the soysages and bread and had some cereal instead. He made his own sandwich of cheese and sprouts and slices of red and yellow peppers and started to eat it, standing across the counter from her.

"Why don't you sit down?" she signed.

"I have to run. I have a lot of work stuff on my mind. But when I get home later I'll make dinner for you, and we can get to know each other a little more. Is that okay?"

Constance was confused. "Is what okay?"

"If we get to know each other."

Constance watched as he flicked a stray bean sprout off the front of his shirt. "Why would that not be okay?" she signed, puzzled.

"Bastien said we should guard against forming an emotional attachment."

Constance gazed at him, at his lips and broad shoulders and amber eyes. "Bastien means not falling in love," she signed slowly. "But we can talk and get to know each other." She thought a moment. "It's not as fun to fuck a stranger." She used the more obscene sign for *fuck* and noticed by his smile that he knew it.

"Sometimes it's exciting to fuck a stranger," he said.

Now she smiled and gave him a lascivious once-over from head to toe. "We can do what pleases you. Always."

He lifted one eyebrow as he took the last bite of his sandwich. "It might be wiser not to make such open-ended offers to perverse gentlemen like myself."

Constance made no answer, only stared at him. She was the one naked and exposed to his gaze, and yet she was the one molesting him with her eyes. He came around the counter and clasped her close, cupping her ass cheeks, which were still faintly bruised from the night before. Then he tilted her head up and gave her a look that made her very sorry she had her period at the moment.

"I'll try to be home early," he said.

* * * * *

Constance wrote a little and then slept again. She didn't dream. Her mind was quiet for the first time in a long time. She felt an unfamiliar sense of comfort and peace in her new situation. Either that, or Kai was having airborne sedatives piped into her odella along with the breezes of warm air from the furnace vents.

It was nearly March. Soon, she would be able to open the large picture window on the far wall and feel spring breezes against her skin. She might even ask Kai if he would help her move the bed over there. Why wouldn't he? He was a wonderful owner. He seemed to want to do whatever would most make her happy.

Constance woke with her notebook still open on her bed. God forbid he would come in and start reading her stuff. He would laugh his ass off. She never showed it to anyone, as much as she felt compelled to continue writing. Why did she bother?

Well, why not? She could do as she liked with her life now. That was the whole point of becoming an odalisque. Well, aside from the endless sexual ecstasy. Just as she was daydreaming about such ecstasy, her owner stuck his head in the door. She smiled at him and pushed her notebook under her pillow.

Wow. There was something about a hot man in a business suit. She sat up a little straighter. Her hands formed the signs that were like second nature to her. "May I serve you?"

He looked confused. "I thought you were off limits right now?"

"I can't receive. But...I can give."

His mouth fell open a little. "Oh, wow. Really? I thought I was in for a three-day dry spell." He was already moving toward her, his hands at the fastenings of his pants.

She looked up at him, laughing. "Three days is not exactly a dry spell," she signed.

He gazed back at her with a rakish smile. "And oral sex is not exactly giving. There's some receiving involved too." He made an obscene gesture, one long, bronze finger poking through the circle of his opposite hand. "Is this an official sign for anything?"

Constance was overcome by a fit of giggles that transformed into full-out laughing at the look of mock disappointment on his face. His expression changed then, and he leaned down to kiss her. He pulled away and ran gentle fingertips down one cheek. "Constance. I wish you could hear what you sound like when you laugh. Or can you? Can you hear it? Inside your head?"

It was a stupid question, but he didn't know. "I can't hear things like you hear them. I pretty much can't hear anything." She exaggerated the sign for *anything* into a sweeping dismissal, feeling peevish all of a sudden.

He was still looking at her with that awful, sympathetic look. "Your laugh sounds so pretty. Like bells."

She shrugged. "I don't know what bells sound like." She dropped her hands to her lap. She was tired of signing. Tired of trying to communicate with him while he watched her with patient forbearance. She reached for his fly and signed again, "May I serve you?"

For a moment he continued to stroke her face, then ran his hand up to touch her hair. She looked back at him, hoping he wouldn't say anything else. *Please, please, just let me do what I'm here for.* Finally he drew her forward, down to her knees. He unbuttoned his shirt as she freed his half-rigid cock from the front of his boxers.

Constance sat back on her knees for a second, taking him in. His cock was thick—even at half mast—and vein-y. The head jutted out toward her, part of a growing, pulsing sculpture. Soon enough she would internalize everything about the shape and scent of him. She would memorize every ridge and vein she explored with her tongue. She would learn which spots made him groan and which movements made him buck in her mouth.

His open shirttails rested against his hips, framing the view, and his hands hung open at each side. His hands, my God. She wanted to kiss them. She wanted to nibble and suck his long, curved fingers as much as his cock. His stance was dominant enough to bring an ache to life between her legs. It was as if time stood still, and she watched herself in this tableau from somewhere across the room, kneeling before him in all his masculine glory. Her subservience flooded her psyche like a drug.

You are a sick, sick puppy, Constance.

She reached out to touch him, to feel the velvet texture of his skin, the heat of his arousal. She brought his cock to her lips and set about memorizing the things he liked best. She hadn't had him this way since the very first evening she'd met him, when Bastien had brought him to her room under the eaves, and she had looked up to see an Indian god. Tall, formidable, and effortlessly sensual, even when he was serious and reserved.

Constance looked up at him now as she slid her tongue from the base to the tip of his cock. He stared back down at her, her immovable Master, and thought about...what? How she felt? How she looked? How she gazed at him like a wanton slut? She moaned softly and he seemed to jump against her mouth. He was fully hard now, hard like stone, like marble.

She teased him for a long while, tracing, sucking, caressing him with her tongue. He stood still, hands open, shirt drawn apart. She reached up to place her palm against his hard, flat abs, against his waist, pulling him closer. She fought not to gag as she drew him all the way deep in her throat. His living flesh stole her breath. This was the epitome of submission and while it made her feel vulnerable, it also made her feel powerful. She reached down to finger herself, helpless to control the impulse. She was drooling all over him, giving a sloppy, reckless blowjob. She would definitely have his boxers wet, but she didn't think he'd care.

Then some resonance changed, and his body tensed under her fingers. She knew he was reaching the height of his arc. She hoped he would climax in her mouth. She wanted to taste him and savor him, and get to know the flavor of him. When she'd gone down on him at the Maison, he'd been wearing a condom, and she'd been left with nothing but the bitterness of latex in her mouth. *Oh, Kai. Kai...* She gazed up at him just a moment. He gritted his teeth and stared back at her from under sultry lids. Constance increased the pace and pressure of the blowjob, and his hands moved from his sides, coming to rest on her head.

Kai didn't grab her. She probably would have been alarmed if he'd grabbed her and jammed his cock deep. No, she only felt his fingers tangling in her curls and clenching slightly. Soon after, with a buck of his hips, he spurted cum into her throat, onto her tongue. She tasted the sweet salty essence of him and loved it from the start.

She loved him.

No. *No.* Of course she didn't love him like *that*. She just loved the color of his skin, his beautiful eyes, his muscles and his cock still pressed firm and hot in her mouth. She felt some vibration under her fingers. Perhaps some groan or exhalation. He wished she could hear herself laugh.

She wished she could hear him come. Just once.

She felt almost mournful as he slipped away from her. Unthinking, again she slid her hand down between her legs. She was wet, her clit perky and swollen under her fingertips. When Constance looked up at him, Kai was buttoning his shirt and giving her an assessing look. She hoped he wasn't wondering about the absence of blood. She didn't want to have to explain the concept of a menstrual cup to him in sign language. Much less draw a diagram, for God's sake.

But no. He was probably smart enough to have already figured that out. He was giving her a different kind of assessing look. He ran his tongue over his bottom lip.

"You like that?" he asked. "It turns you on, serving me this way?"

How could he doubt it? She curled her fingers away from her tingling clit to make one very simple and heartfelt sign. "Yes."

"Masturbate for me then." The predatory look on his face excited her. "Is that permissible? Can I make you do that at this time of the month?" His lips pursed in a half-smile. "Is that giving or receiving?"

She made a naughty looking sign. "Both."

He chuckled, but she was still, feeling pinned by his direct gaze.

"Lie down on your back. Spread your legs so I can watch."

Constance lay back right where she was, her shoulders on the soft deep pile carpet. Her legs tensed as she spread them slowly and braced her heels on the floor. He watched her from his full height, imperious now. Her Master.

"Masturbate and make yourself come."

It was hard to be one hundred percent sure of his words from this angle, but she knew without a doubt what he wanted her to do. Her gaze never left his face. His lips moved slightly, but she didn't think he was talking.

His eyes were her whole world.

She parted her slick pussy lips with eager fingers, stroking over her clit. Her hips rose of their own volition as the swarm of heat and desire in her center seemed to spread out to her whole pelvis. Her nipples tightened with a delicious ache. She imagined Kai pinching them, biting them. She stared up and remembered him hurting her and fucking her. Taking her. Her fingers moved faster, rubbing and pressing, seeking release for the hot lust that had overtaken her as she'd sucked her Master's cock.

She wanted to draw this out, this glorious torment under his scrutiny. He was breathing even faster than before. She could see his chest rising and falling, and felt blood pumping in her ears like a drumbeat. *Yes, yes, yes, yes, yes.* She closed her eyes, ready to fall over the edge.

But then she felt him moving, felt his presence beside her. She opened her eyes and stared up into amber pools edged with blue-gray. Dark brows, and full lips parted over straight teeth. He was crouching beside her, and their gazes locked just as a shattering orgasm contracted within her. Her hands flew off her clit. The sensation was too much. She clutched at his arm and he swallowed hard, his Adam's apple bobbing in the column of his neck. His five-o'clock-shadow stubble rubbed against her hand. He was pressing her fingers to his face. For a moment he wore a look of pure animal violence.

Constance curled up on her side, needing to look away. He released her. If he said anything before he left the room, she didn't see. She only remembered, like imprinting, the feel of his rough cheek scratching against her palm.

Chapter Nine:
Perfect

Kai took an hour, a full hour, to calm down. Odalisque. Fucking hell. She had some kind of superpower to turn him into a mindless maniac. So brazenly sexual. So unashamed. So submissive to his will. She'd touched herself like nothing fucking mattered but making herself come. If he hadn't left—if he hadn't stood up and marched his ass out of the fucking room—he would have fallen on her until the saffron-colored shag carpet was running with red. Human sacrifice.

Goddamn period.

Well, there would only be eleven more of them to endure. Unless he renewed her contract for another year. And another year. Six fucking years. He'd sign on for all of them, the way he was feeling tonight.

But he had to find some kind of restraint and self-discipline for the rest of the evening. For tonight, they would just hang out and talk. He was determined on that account. No blowjobs, no hand jobs, no masturbating, no giving or receiving of any kind except him cooking her dinner and pouring her a glass of wine.

He made some stir-fry and then went to the odella to get her. Constance was curled up on the bed, writing in a notebook. She'd showered, and her hair was still a little wet, dark-shiny against her pale skin.

"Come have dinner with me," he signed. He had to start signing to her at least some of the time if he ever hoped to get fluent. She nodded and smiled. She also raked her eyes over his body. Head to toe. She did it a lot. It made all those hours on the treadmill seem worthwhile, but she was going to turn him into a narcissist if she wasn't careful. Even though he only had on some sweats and a faded UCLA tee shirt, she seemed pretty pleased with what she saw.

Hopeless narcissist. Yep.

"You might want to bring that notebook." He was talking again now, too brain fried from her eye-raping to make coherent signs.

She shoved the one she had under the pillow and got a different one from the desk, then preceded him down the hall. His eyes were riveted to her ass as she sauntered down the steps ahead of him. It fascinated him, how comfortable she was in her nudity. He wanted to get nude too, just to see if he could be as nonchalant about it, but then he liked the power imbalance of being dressed while she was naked.

At the bottom of the stairs he took her hand and kissed it, and led her to the café table in the kitchen, beside the picture window with the view. The veggie stir fry was still steaming. He sprinkled some sesame seeds on top and served it with basmati rice. She took a few bites and then picked up the notebook.

This tastes awesome. How long have you been a vegetarian?

He read her loopy, scrawled hand and smiled over at her. "I don't do it for any philosophical reasons. I just don't like the taste of meat. My mother never made it for me when I was a child. She was from India. A lot of vegetarians there."

Is Kai an Indian name?

He finished chewing a snow pea and picked up the pen. *My real name is Kaivalyan.* He wrote the name out. He would never have attempted to fingerspell it. He put the pen down and propped his head on his hand. "It means isolation, or aloneness. My mother picked the name out and told my father it meant 'victorious.' He was angry later. They were always doing passive-aggressive shit like that to each other. My mother was a very lonely and bitter woman."

Constance picked up the pen. *So was mine. Is your mother still alive?*

"No. Cancer. My father remarried. He's...somewhere."

Do you have any brothers or sisters?

"One sister. Satya. See, she got a great name. Satya means truth. And my sister is very truthful. If you ever meet her, you'll see what I mean. She's very...in your face sometimes."

"Is she older or younger?" Constance asked, signing now.

"Younger. What about you? Any brothers? Sisters?"

She signed, "Too many to count."

"What do you mean?"

She grabbed the pen again, and heaved a sigh. *My mother married nine times. I have eight half-siblings and God knows how many step-siblings. I've long since lost count. She died*—Constance paused in her writing, such a short pause he almost didn't catch it—*in an accident. She overdosed on prescription medicine. And alcohol.*

Kai rubbed his fist in a circle on his chest. "I'm sorry."

Constance shrugged and signed, "She was a mess." She grabbed the pen again and wrote furiously for a minute.

My mom was a piece of work. She only ever married soldiers. I've lived on fifteen military bases. She told me it was the smart thing to do. That if you were a soldier's wife, you would always have something to eat, medical care and a roof over your head. But even soldiers don't like to be used. One would dump her, divorce her, and a couple months later she'd have a new one. She'd either get to them with sex, or get knocked up somehow. Anything to secure another military husband. Another roof over her head.

She stopped a moment and rubbed her chin.

She was like an odalisque, only a lot more lowbrow and sordid.

Constance hadn't had an easy childhood. That was clear from her words and her beleaguered expression. Kai winked at her to lighten the mood. "So it's a family legacy, this odalisque thing."

She laughed softly and went back to broccoli and carrots, dragging the slivers through sauce. She didn't seem to have much appetite.

He waited until she looked up at him. "You'll have to tell me what you like to eat. I'll buy it for you. Whatever. It doesn't matter that I'm a vegetarian. Like I said, it's not an idealism thing. You can eat meat if you want." She shrugged, and he worked hard to sublimate the suggestive joke in his head about "eating" and "meat."

He leaned back, nearly finished, and took a sip of wine. "My voice sounds so loud in here. It feels weird sometimes, like I'm talking to myself."

Kai knew at once from her expression that his comment didn't sit well with her. She wrinkled her nose and made a blunt sentence with her hands. "Sign, then." She turned away with a frown. He nudged her head back, forcing her to look at him.

"Don't get angry. You don't understand how silent it is here. All I hear is my own voice. I'm not used to it echoing off the walls."

She pursed her lips and signed, "Put something on the walls then. Or put on some music." She looked away, her version of ignoring him. She ate a few more bites and put her fork down. Her signs were still curt. "I'm sorry I can't hear you. I'm sorry I can't talk to you. I sound stupid when I try to talk."

He shook his head. "Stop. You need to understand, I don't know all the right things to say. Okay? I didn't mean anything by what I said. And Jesus fuck, don't apologize for something you have no control over." He flushed with misplaced frustration and anger. He was angry at himself for making her feel shitty, making her feel like she had to apologize. And he was angry at her for apologizing when he knew she was pissed.

"Look," he said, waving a hand in her face so he knew she was listening. "I like you just as you are. Deaf or hearing, I'm pretty damn sure I'd like you the same. I think the way you deal with it is amazing and...inspiring. But I'm the jackass here. I can't sign worth a fuck. I can't help you hear all the things I wish you could hear. It makes me feel fucking helpless sometimes, and fucking irate."

Constance rolled her eyes and made a sign it took him a moment to decipher. *Potty mouth.*

She started to fingerspell, but he stopped her. "I got it. Potty mouth."

"You curse too much."

The sign for *curse* was new, but he figured it out pretty easily in context. He shrugged and raked his eyes over her full, pretty breasts and her trim waist. He reached out, running a thumb over one pink nipple and watching them both draw up tight. "Did we just have an argument, Constance?"

She signed *maybe* with so much petulant attitude he started to laugh. She cracked a smile too. He squeezed her breasts and enjoyed watching her squirm in her chair. "You're a very bad girl, aren't you? To argue with Master?"

She raised one eyebrow, and gave what could only be construed as a smartass look. He had her over his lap in an instant. She peered back at him as he landed a glancing blow over the lingering light bruises. "Are there any rules about spanking an odalisque at this time of the month?"

She signed awkwardly, her arms raised in front of her. "Didn't you read the contract?"

He went off on an unheard rant about disrespectful odalisques, the slap of his hand clearly audible over the music of her laughter. It was a play spanking, but it was a real spanking. Her legs started to kick after the tenth or twelfth blow, and her ass cheeks gained a new rosy red glow.

She was beautiful to spank, her wiggles and moans as arousing as her hourglass figure, and his cock hardened against her hip. She gazed up at him, begging with her eyes for respite. He pushed her down on the floor and freed himself, thrusting inside her welcoming mouth.

You'll wear her out. You're asking too much of her. But she was a cockslave. She was his slave to use as he wished. It was just getting a little confusing, who was enslaved to whom.

Afterward, she rested her head in his lap, sitting back on her ankles. She was very still. He thought she must be tired, and was going to send her to bed for the night. But then she looked up at him and asked if he played the piano. The sign was unmistakable, the nimble running of fingers along a keyboard.

He nodded. "Yes, I play. Music is one of my passions." *You are quickly becoming another one of my passions.*

"Will you play for me?"

Kai hesitated a moment. Was it a trick question? She gave a half smile.

"I mean, I would like to watch you play. I think you would look really sexy doing it."

She accompanied the sign for *sexy* with a little wink. Well, he couldn't argue her wishes, especially after she'd given him the second mind-blowing hummer of the night.

He nodded toward the living room and they crossed together to the piano on the other side. She leaned against it like some kind of sultry songstress. He asked, "What do you want me to play?"

She shrugged. "Anything you like."

"I like classical music. Booming concertos and lilting sonatas." He thought he lost her on the word *lilting*. He slid a hand up the keyboard. "Do you have a favorite composer?"

Stupid, stupid, *stupid*. How long was he going to make these stupid, annoying comments to her? He grimaced. "I'm sorry. Of course you don't."

"I like Mozart," she said. She spelled out *Mozart* with a kind of reverence. "I've read about what his music sounds like. And he seemed like a really interesting guy."

"He was sort of crazy," Kai muttered. He smiled up at her. "Okay, Mozart it is." He played a few notes of a familiar sonata, then lifted his fingers from the keys.

"Do you know Debussy?" Kai had to spell it for her twice. He sucked at fingerspelling. When she finally got it, she shook her head.

Kai lifted up the piano bench and went rooting through the music. "Debussy didn't so much write songs as stories—"

He stopped as her face appeared before him. "I can't hear you," she signed.

He looked up at her so she could read his lips. "He didn't write songs so much as feelings, moods, scenes. Stories. Watch this."

Kai closed the bench and sat down to pluck out a fast-moving tune. "He called this *Golliwog's Cakewalk*." He hunched his shoulders and hammed up the rollicking opening stanzas of the piece. "It looks like what it is, huh?"

Constance nodded, her eyes meeting his. He jumped up, suddenly animated. He started riffling in the piano bench again, remembering to look up at her to talk. "There's this other song by him. One of my favorite songs to play." He found the songbook he sought and leafed through, holding up the page when he found it. "*La Cathédrale Engloutie*. The Sunken Cathedral. The way he wrote the piece—"

Kai sat down, opening the sheet music in front of him.

"It's written to be visual. It's based on the legend of this grand cathedral sunken in the deep. It rises up out of the water on mornings when the sky and sea are clear. The composition starts out slow..." Kai began to play, touching the keys lightly. "It paints a picture of quiet, peace. Imagine the dawn, the morning sun just starting to shine over the water. Then, a chime begins to sound." He played the chimes with careful, deliberate fingering. "I guess the chimes are bells tolling in the distance. Morning bells. Then it starts to pick up."

He looked at Constance. She was watching him, spellbound.

Encouraged, he started into the rolling, wave-like chords of the cathedral's majestic ascension. He made sure to face her so she could see what he was saying. "At this point, it grows louder. The chords are more complex." He shifted his shoulders to give emphasis to a peaking phrase. "And then—"

He played the crashing chorus of chords that made the piece one of his favorites. "So, it's really loud here. Majestic. Climactic. You can really picture this huge, dripping wet, ornate cathedral standing out against the sky." Kai fell silent and just played, doing the runs and raising his left hand in a dramatic flourish to bang against the lower register keys. "And then..."

He drew back and played the dissonantly soft, rhythmic chimes. "Then, suddenly, the crashing music calms to near silence, and the bells toll again. It's time for the cathedral to sink down into the depths. This part sounds quiet and melancholy. It's the same music as earlier, only calmer, more wistful. It's meant to sound as if the music is muted by water, and then finally sinks into only the silence of the distant chimes." Kai caressed the final plinking notes with a light touch, and lifted his fingers from the keyboard.

He looked over at Constance, still standing motionless beside his piano. She stared at him, her gaze moving to his hands resting now in his lap, and back to his eyes again. Some jolt of connection or emotion passed between them, powerful but fleeting, before she blinked and looked away.

* * * * *

Constance tried to act casual. Tried to act like he didn't affect her the way he affected her.

But fucking *come on.*

Why did he have to be so gorgeous and kind and talented and...amazing? He wasn't playing fair.

Constance was resigned to the fact that she was deaf. She really was. Like many deaf people, she didn't consider herself disabled or less than anyone else. But there were times, like now, when she would have given anything on earth to be able to hear. Just for one minute. Ten seconds. Five seconds. If she got to hear his voice, even for five seconds, then she would know. She would know that mystery. She would never forget it once she heard it, she was certain.

Constance had wanted to see him play out of curiosity, but had never imagined how it would move her. She'd pictured some handsome, polished showmanship, her lover at the piano. Some entertaining motion to watch while she drooled over his arms and his abs. What she had gotten was a musician who played so well, who felt the music so deeply, she really could almost hear it. She could "hear" the loud parts and soft parts just from how he played them. She could imagine the majesty of Debussy's cathedral just from the expression on Kai's face.

No, Constance. No emotional attachment.

"Are you okay?" Kai asked, closing the keyboard lid. "I didn't mean to upset you."

Constance realized she was frowning. She circled her fist over her heart. "I'm sorry. No...it's just... It was beautiful. So special, how you explained it to me." *But could you please stop making me fall so hard for you?* "Thanks for trying to help me hear the music. You came really close. How long have you played?"

He waved a hand. "Since I was a kid. But I don't want to change the subject. I wish there was something I could do to help."

"Help? You mean, help me hear?"

He nodded. "I'm sure you've been to doctors, tried hearing aids and everything. But isn't there some kind of surgical thing? A Coch—"

She finished the spelling for him. "Cochlear implant?" Kai nodded. "I wasn't a candidate."

"What does that mean?"

She blew out her breath in frustration. "If there was a way to help me, it would have been done by now."

"But you went to military doctors. Moved around a lot, right? How do you know you got the best care? Let me take you to a specialist—"

"No."

"Maybe there's some new, cutting edge research—"

"No."

"I have more money than I know what to do with, Constance. Money can sometimes buy things you don't expect. Let me try to help you at least—"

"No." This time when she made the sign, she snapped her fingers hard. He still didn't shut up. Constance left the dais and went to the kitchen for the notebook. She returned, writing as she walked. God, she had to make him understand that there wasn't any hope of her hearing. Ever.

Kai, I appreciate your offer but please accept the fact that there's no way to change me. There's not enough money in the world to make me hear the way you hear. There just isn't. It's okay.

He stared at the notebook and frowned. "This is really hard for me, you know. I like to fix things."

She shook her head. "You can't fix me. I'm sorry if that upsets you."

Kai looked on the verge of giving in, but then he turned those eyes on her, those deep pools. "Please, please, please, just see one specialist. For me. Just one visit. Please."

He took her three days later. It was marvelous what money could buy. A morning appointment with a well-known leader in the field who was certainly booked solid for months. She would have done anything to spare Kai the disappointment of the doctor's frank evaluation. Well, she'd tried to explain to him.

Kai was subdued on the way home. Constance sat beside him in the backseat, unaccustomed to being clothed. She was also unaccustomed to Los Angeles, the soaring skyline and crowd of humanity, the snarled roads and belching traffic as far as the eye could see. Kai stared out the window, lost in his own thoughts. He seemed so sad. She reached over and put a hand on his thigh. He gave her a half-smile, grasped her hand for a moment, and then threaded his fingers through hers.

She loved his fingers. She didn't know why. They were so long and yet so well shaped. Each knuckle had a little sprinkling of dark hair. She stared at his hands and felt an ache in her chest. She was falling in love with him, no matter her convictions. No matter that it was against the code.

It was only the newness of it all. The devotion of a slave for her Master. She reminded herself in her weak moments that theirs was a temporary arrangement by agreement. Kai had paid a million dollars more or less for the convenience of having her go away at some point. He could get tired of her next week and send her away. He was rich enough to buy another girl. He was rich enough to do whatever he wanted. She turned his hand over and spelled his name against his palm.

Kai?

He leaned down and touched his lips to hers, a chaste, sweet kiss that inevitably turned darker. He tilted his head and kissed her more deeply, then slid his tongue across her lips. He smelled like aftershave and sunshine, and tasted like honey. *You're in love. Idiot.*

93

She pulled away and started signing, just to get her mind off that train of thought. "Thank you for trying to help me. It's kind of you to care so much."

He pursed his lips, looking partly annoyed and partly amorous. "Of course I care. But you're perfect as you are. I shouldn't have pushed the issue."

She unbuckled her seat belt and moved closer to him, resting her head against his shoulder. She got another noseful of sunshine and the scratch of light stubble against her forehead. "You know, my other senses are more powerful because I'm deaf," she signed to him. "I taste and smell and feel things more strongly."

He seemed amused by that. "Really? How do you know you taste and smell and feel things any more strongly than anyone else?"

She made a face at him. "I do. I know I do. I notice more anyway. Like the way your skin feels a couple hours after you've shaved. The way leather seats smell different from fabric seats in hot cars. I notice the way each variety of orange tastes a little different."

He put a hand on her fingers, stilling her. "There are different varieties of oranges?"

Constance giggled. Kai smiled back and nudged her over in the seat. "Buckle up for safety."

"We're almost to your house anyway. And guess what?" Constance paused for maximum effect. "My period is officially over. I'm yours to..." She made the famous finger-in-a-hole sign.

He got a suggestive gleam in his eye. "I might have to stay home then, rather than go into work."

"I'll put you to work, big boy," she signed with her own suggestive leer.

He threw his head back and laughed. They were only a mile or so away from his property. He took her arm and pulled her against him, and this time his kiss wasn't chaste at all. It wasn't even passionate. It was just plain dirty. Constance felt it in her breasts and her pussy, a heavy, horny ache. She twisted her fingers in his hair and felt his hand working its way up her fitted skirt. He plunged his palm down the front of her silk panties while he bit on her lip. God, she wanted to pull the skirt up to her waist and straddle him, and rub her clit right against the rigid rod she could feel through his pants.

Kai pulled away with a gasp as they drove through the gate of his house. "Stop for a minute." He took her face in his hands, forced her to focus in the haze of her arousal. "Wait. We're almost there."

They both turned to look at the front drive at the same time. A silver sedan was parked to one side. A woman in a black suit with short dark hair stood with a portfolio in her hands, waiting for the car to pull around.

Chapter Ten:
Please, Please...

Ms. Dresden closed the door to the odella and had Constance undress. Constance knew why. She was grateful she had nothing to fear in her owner, no abuse to hide. She hung up her blouse and shimmied out of her skirt, then took off her panties. Ms. Dresden smiled softly and ran her hands over the light marks remaining from her spanking a few nights ago.

"Come sit beside me, and we'll have a candid talk."

Constance sat across from the older woman and curled her knees under her. She hadn't known Ms. Dresden very long. She'd met her the first time on the flight across the Atlantic. But they'd had plenty of time to become friends on the plane, and Constance loved that she knew ASL. It would be fun to have a conversation without all the starts and stops and missing words she'd become accustomed to with Kai. And it was nice to see someone from Maison Odalisque. Constance sometimes missed Bastien and the other girls. Although her current situation was certainly fulfilling...

"How are things, Constance? Has Mr. Chandler adhered to the contract between you? Have you been kept in comfort? You haven't been made to work or keep house for him?"

Constance shook her head. "I haven't done a thing. And I couldn't be more comfortable."

"There is adequate chemistry between you and your owner?"

Constance couldn't help the broad, wicked smile that spread across her face.

Ms. Dresden chuckled. "That wonderful, is he? I'm glad to hear it. And has he used you anally thus far?"

Constance nodded, biting her lip. *Oh yes, he did.*

"He was cautious? He lubricated you adequately?"

She thought about the itching, warming lube tormenting her asshole and shifted slightly on the bed. "Yes, he used plenty of lube."

Ms. Dresden seemed very pleased to hear that. "And I perceive you have already engaged in some sado-masochistic play. How did it go?"

Constance flushed, remembering the intensity of that scene. "We've only played once. Oh, and I got one spanking."

"Did he play within your limits? Was he attentive to your needs?"

Both Constance's hands fluttered in the affirmative. "Oh, yes."

"What about a safe word? How are you handling that? Did you discuss it?"

"I didn't want a safe word, but eventually we agreed that it would be me saying no."

Ms. Dresden nodded in approval. "That sounds workable. And how is the rest of the communication between you? You've found a way to make it work?"

Constance looked down at her hands, and then signed to Ms. Dresden with a rueful grin. "His ASL is terrible. Really pathetic." Both of them laughed. "It's actually a relief to sign with someone who's fluent. But he tries so hard, it's really endearing. So it's okay. The lip reading fills in the rest."

"That's good. So he hasn't been impatient with you at all?"

Constance shook her head. "Never. Not once."

"He is even-tempered? Has he showed any anger to you, any intense emotion?"

"No. Actually..." Constance stopped signing a moment. She was ashamed to confess the depth of her own emotions to Ms. Dresden.

"Constance?" Ms. Dresden tapped Constance's knee. "Did something happen?"

"No..." If Ms. Dresden knew the true extent of her feelings, would she make her leave? It was such a desecration of the code, to fall in love with your owner. "A few days ago...Mr. Chandler was playing the piano,

97

and it was just... He looked so beautiful. He was explaining to me how the music sounded and I—I—"

"You what?"

"I don't know. I suddenly felt a little…kind of…emotional toward him." Constance couldn't meet Ms. Dresden's eyes. "It was only emotion about how lovely he looked while he was playing. And the kindness of trying to explain it to me. Do you think— Is that kind of emotion an acceptable thing?"

Ms. Dresden's hands were silent for a long while. Then she gazed at Constance and signed, "He is very kind to you in everything, isn't he?"

Suddenly it seemed to Constance that Ms. Dresden knew everything. That she knew Constance was falling in love with Kai, and that the overmistress was disappointed in her. Constance was supposed to be for Kai's sexual use. She was supposed to be his vessel, his relief. And she was doing this to gain independence, not an emotional connection.

"Well..." Constance shrugged. "Mr. Chandler is just a really kind person. He said he wished he could help me hear. That's where we were today. Some big, famous hearing specialist he found down in the city."

"He took you to a hearing specialist?" Ms. Dresden looked slightly scandalized.

"I told him he didn't have to, but it was what he wanted. Isn't that part of my duty? To do as he wants?"

There was a long, horrible pause as the overmistress's pen flew over her notepad. Constance twisted her hands together.

Finally, Ms. Dresden raised her eyes. She put her pen down and leaned close. "I know that you learned about the danger of emotional attachment in this lifestyle. I also know that the first few weeks are the time a new odalisque is most likely to conceive an unnatural affection for her Master. Sometimes it can't be helped. Just remember, the code requires that an odalisque not tax her owner emotionally. It cannot be done."

Constance nodded. "I know. The night he played the piano…it was...one weak moment. It wasn't really about any emotional attachment to him." She signed that lie without the slightest tremble in her fingers. She almost convinced herself. But she doubted she convinced Ms. Dresden at all.

"If you are falling in love with him, Constance—at all—you must stop it. Remember why you are here. Focus on serving his sexual needs.

Avoid him when you're feeling emotionally needy. When we next meet, I'm sure you'll be in a very different place. The glow wears off, and you settle into the dutiful aspects of the job. It is really much simpler then." She tweaked Constance's nose. "Mind the code. Promise me."

Constance promised, flushing red under her guardian's gentle rebuke.

Ms. Dresden made a few more notes in her leather portfolio, then put down her pen and looked up. "Has Mr. Chandler shared you with anyone yet?"

Constance shook her head.

"I suppose he hasn't had much time to plan anything like that. Well, if he does before I see you again next week, remember that he agreed to certain protections for you. Hold him to them."

"I will."

Constance waited until Ms. Dresden was finished packing up her portfolio before she signed again. "It was nice to see you."

The overmistress took her hands and squeezed them. She let go and signed, "Have you been lonely? Sometimes the occlusion is an adjustment. Has he taken you out and about at all?"

"Only today. To the doctor. We've been staying in at night. But I'm not lonely. He's wonderful company."

"Do you miss the Maison?"

Constance thought a moment. "Yes," she finally signed. "But not enough to want to go back any time soon. I feel like this adventure is just beginning."

Ms. Dresden smiled at her. "I hope this adventure turns out to be everything you dreamed."

* * * * *

Moments after Ms. Dresden took her leave, Kai appeared in the door of Constance's odella wearing nothing but a smile. He led her into the saray, to the iron bed in the center. Constance was sure she was about to be thoroughly fucked.

But Kai proved to have other plans, and Constance wasn't happy about them. He regarded her now over the top of his tablet computer.

"I remember quite clearly Bastien telling me that bondage was essential to an odalisque's fulfillment. Deepening your feelings of slavery and all that. I am one hundred percent certain he talked to me about it."

Constance whined in misery, arching her hips toward him. She was leaning back, her shoulders propped against a cushion on the wide white mattress. Her wrists were cuffed to straps around her upper thighs so she couldn't touch herself. Her ankles were tethered with rope to each corner of the footboard, spread wide. He'd given her just enough slack to fidget and try to draw her legs together to soothe the ache.

But the ache could not be soothed.

Kai lounged across from her, the picture of masculine perfection, his cock cycling between hard and half hard, resting against the fur of his lower belly. He was long, lean male, tormenting her like some demon with the nearness of his physicality. Every so often he leaned forward to play with her pussy lips and run the lightest teasing fingertip over her clit. He'd make some flippant comment like, "Yep, still wet," or "Wow, you look pretty horny," before returning his attention to his computer screen. As he read, he'd run his fingers lazily over his abs, then down to rearrange his cock.

Oh God, he was killing her. This was abuse, plain and simple. Where was Ms. Dresden now that Constance needed her? Helplessly, she shifted her hips forward even more and begged with her eyes. Begged for a touch, a fuck. An orgasm. *Please...*

He looked up at her and got a thoughtful gleam in his eye. "You know, this won't do at all. I've given you absolutely no means to communicate with me. That's not safe, is it? Maybe I should release your hands."

She nodded frantically. *Yes, yes. Pleeeease!*

"Oh, but...wait. That would kind of defeat the purpose of the whole bondage and enslavement thing. Hmm."

Kai rolled off the bed and went in the other room. He was gone a few minutes while she furiously tried to free her hands and pull her legs together. Oh God, her throbbing clit. Damn him. She gave up and lay back against the pillows. He was right. This was submission. Enslavement. She was his sex toy to use, if and when he decided to use her. She was his slave to frustrate, to deny, to whip into a frenzy of desperate need.

Kai was back again, raking his eyes over her quivering form in approval. "Oh, yeah. That's a nice view. Bastien really knew what he was talking about with the bondage. Now, here." He held up two sheets of paper, each with a message. One said, *Oh, please, please, I'm dying!* The other said, *I hate you so much right now!*

He put one down by her left foot and one down by her right foot. She immediately started grinding her ankle into the *I hate you* one.

"Ah, you're sweet," he said, laughing.

She laughed too, she couldn't help it. This was all hilariously funny, or would have been if she wasn't about to jump out of her skin with the need to be fucked. He leaned down to kiss her as she kicked helplessly at the other sign. *Please, please!*

Kai stood and crossed to his cabinet full of BDSM gear. She watched with dread as he took a shiny stainless steel anal toy out of its fuchsia-lined box. He dripped some lube on it. *Please don't let it be the jacked up stuff*, she prayed to herself in silence. *Please.*

She felt a whimper rise in her throat as he crossed back to her. "This should make things a little more interesting for you."

He knelt on the bed and for a moment she scooted her butt back, clenching her cheeks. *No, no, no!* She could say the words and he wouldn't do it. But she was here to serve and obey him, not her own needs. She rested her head back against the cushion and tried to relax as he worked the silver bulb into her asshole.

Oh, shit. The jacked up lube. *Damn it.*

She squirmed as the burning, itching sensation grew inside her. Clenching her ass only made the sting worse. The plug wasn't huge, but it was heavy and solid within her, stretching her anal channel. She gave him a desperate look that she hoped communicated the depth of her suffering. For good measure, she kicked the *I hate you* sign again. That was probably a mistake, since he went back to the cabinet and came back with a pair of clover clamps on a chain. Kicking the sign a few more times did not dissuade him.

He pinched and tugged at one nipple, closing the wicked pincers over the thrusting tip. As the sharp pain bloomed across her nipples and chest, she came off the bed, arching her hips as far as she was able. She loved the agony of the clamps, but she hated it too. As he applied the second one, she cried out with all the frustrated lust she was feeling. God knew what she sounded like, but Kai must have liked it, because he grabbed his cock in response.

He was fully hard now, his reddening rod thrusting up toward his belly. She wanted him so badly. The stinging ache and stretch in her ass had her pussy soaked and her clit swollen with the need for release. The clamps added that extra layer of inescapable pain that made her crave his touch, his rough possession.

He gazed back at her. "I know you want my cock inside you. I know you want to feel me splitting you open, rubbing against that little toy in your ass." Her pussy flared even hotter, pulsing instinctively at his coarse words. "But for a moment I just want to watch you like this. I want to watch you wanting me. Needing my cock." He paused, then leaned closer, running soft fingertips down the side of her face. "You have no idea what this feels like. Watching you crave me so hard."

She held his gaze. *Crave* wasn't even a strong enough word for what she felt. Her heel crinkled the *please, please* sign, but it was all pointless now. He was in complete control of her, a lesson he'd surely intended to impart with this little torture session. She felt her body unwind as she came to terms with her powerlessness. She subdued the insistent needs of her body to his will.

His gaze softened as they communicated without words, without signs. The bed shifted as he leaned closer. She clenched on the ass plug in anticipation, only to be rewarded with another wave of torment. *Relax, relax...*

He licked up her belly, dropping warm kisses around her navel and beneath her breasts. He ran his tongue along the sturdy metal chain that connected the clamps, and then drew it between his teeth. She cringed at the pain of the clamps tightening, and pulled at the cuffs that held her wrists. She wanted so badly to touch him, to pull him against her. He leaned to kiss her mouth, and in doing so, pressed the cool metal chain between her teeth.

She did as she knew he wished, and held it tight in her mouth when he moved away. Her chest strained at the tugging discomfort, and the worst part was that she had to give that pain to herself. He watched her struggle for a while, calmly stroking her breasts and the curves of her hips. She stared into his light-dark eyes and felt lost for a moment. *I'll die if you don't take me. I really will.*

The silly signs he'd written had been pushed aside by now. There was no hate or pleading, just desire and need. He reached down and slipped a finger into her pussy. "Look at me," he said. "I'll tell you when you're allowed to come."

Her eyes went wide. When she was *allowed* to come? Jesus Christ, as soon as the head of his cock breached her, she was going to go off like a fucking rocket. She shook her head at him. He shook his head back at her.

"Concentrate. Pull on this if you're coming too close too quickly."

He pulled the chain from between her teeth, causing the clamps to tighten suddenly. "Focus on this pain, not what you feel between your legs." He replaced the chain and traced a finger about her trembling mouth. "Be a good girl."

She bit down on the smooth metal links. She felt like crying as he positioned his cock at the entrance of her cleft. She would never survive this. She felt him begin to enter her and yanked hard on the clamps, sending a sharp ache down her body. It didn't completely erase the pleasure of him filling her, but it dulled it enough to keep her from immediately orgasming. Oh, why, *why?*

But she knew why. This was all about control. The first day she'd arrived they'd been like newlyweds, fucking mindlessly, however they liked. She got the feeling those days were over. It was probably for the best. He was supposed to be the one in control, the one being pleasured. It would be within his rights not to let her come at all if that heightened his sexual satisfaction. She wanted to be a good odalisque. She wanted to fulfill her owner.

She chanted those words in her mind as she pulled the chain even tighter, chanted those words each time she hovered on the brink, driven there by his thick cock filling her and yes, rubbing against the plug in her ass. He was fucking her in a languid, slow rhythm, his own body tense and shuddering. She watched his abs bunch and relax as he moved over her and withdrew again, and again, the depth and power of his thrusts never wavering. She looked up at his lips every few seconds. She didn't want to miss it when he finally gave her permission.

Then, his thrusts came faster. His knees spread hers on the bed so her ankles pulled at the rope bindings. Oh God. She jerked her head back, yanking on the clamps, but even then the pain was too much intertwined with pleasure. She felt his hand in her hair. Her eyes came open even though she didn't remember closing them. Somehow, through the haze of lust and desperation, she read the wonderful words on his lips.

"Come with me."

His thrusts were practically lifting her from the bed. The ache in her ass was replaced by something headier, a knowledge that she was filled to the hilt with the plug and Kai's pounding cock. With each stroke, he pressed down against her clit, and she shivered from the powerful tingling suffusing her entire pelvis and breasts. She was a sexual creature, tied down, held down, and bursting with the feeling of being thoroughly used by her Master.

His hand slid from her hair and caught the chain in her mouth. He pulled it down against her belly as he arched over her, twisting his hips. Constance cried out and felt her whole body transported to a place where all that existed was screaming pleasure turning her inside out. Her pussy contracted around the thick length of his cock as he bucked against her.

She looked up to find his mouth thrown open in ecstasy, his entire face transformed and softened by pleasure. *Oh, please, please, I'm dying*, she thought.

What she really needed was a sign that said, *I love you so much right now.*

Chapter Eleven:
Sharing

By the end of the second week Kai had everything set up. Flashing fire alarms, vibrating and flashing smart phones. Two, in case she misplaced one somewhere. His odalisque watched all this with a serene detachment, lounging nude on her bed, or following him around like a sex-starved puppy.

Okay, maybe the sex-starved-puppy thing went both ways.

After subsisting on the world's best blowjobs for the duration of her period, they were back to fucking like zealots. Kai would fuck her all evening, sleep the sleep of the dead, and go to work and think about fucking her all day.

It was like a new world, and only he and Constance lived there. Kai watched everyone else schlep around, whine and complain bitterly about the single life, or irritating husbands and wives. It was all he could do to hide his self-satisfied smile. He had an odalisque. His life was sex-drenched and sweet.

Kai loved the delicious mystery and privilege of it so much that he waited almost three months before he let Mason in on the secret. He knew his friend would be pissed that he hadn't told him sooner. He also knew Mason would want to come over and play.

They'd shared women before, when they were younger men, and Kai had an open invitation to hook up with Jessamine any time. He hadn't, only because at first he'd been married to Veronica, and afterward, he'd felt too emasculated to even look at a siren like her. Now, compared to Constance, Jess wasn't such a turn on.

Jessamine was a sexy piece of female, but she was no odalisque.

Kai invited Mason to lunch in his company's dining room. His female employees always appreciated when he did that. Kai knew Jessamine wouldn't come with her husband, since she was currently filming a movie in Toronto. Mason showed up looking rough, with the start of a beard and bloodshot eyes.

"Taken to drinking in the afternoons, my friend?" Kai eyed him suspiciously. Mason usually lived pretty straight.

"Aw, no," Mason said, rubbing his face and leaning on the table between them. "Just a bad night. Sleepless night. Way too much shit going on."

"What kind of shit?"

Mason waved a hand. "The usual. Scripts to read, meetings to go to. Jessamine carrying on."

"I thought she was out of town?"

"She is. She still carries on. I worry about that woman sometimes. But what's up with you? You look a little smug, you bastard."

Kai shrugged, pretended nonchalance. "Yeah, I've been sleeping better than I've slept in a year."

Mason grinned. "You met a girl? You seeing someone? You look damn happy about it. Who is she?"

"I found her in France."

It only took Mason a few seconds to connect the dots. "Holy fucking hell!" His friend's eyes practically popped out of his head. "Holy fucking hell!" he repeated. "You did not seriously go over there and buy one!"

"Well, it's more of a rental situation, but yeah. Her name is Constance."

Mason sat and gaped. His eyes darkened then, and narrowed in reproach.

"Why the hell did you not tell me? Why didn't you ask me to go over there with you?"

"I thought you didn't want one."

"Yeah, I don't. I still would have loved to check the place out."

"I don't think they allow tag-alongs. Serious buyers only." Kai twirled the ice in his drink. "Jesus, Mace, it was really something though.

106

Girls everywhere, all horny, submissive females. The agent, this guy Bastien, he leads you around like you're in a furniture showroom, pointing out the various models. And they definitely have a try-and-buy policy."

Mason let out his breath in a long gasp. "You lucky fuck. You lucky bastard. How long ago did you go? How long have you had her?"

"I went in January, and I've had her about three months."

"You fucking bastard. Well, what's she like? And more importantly, when can I meet her?"

Kai laughed at his friend's salacious stare. "You can definitely meet her. But listen, I don't want any of this getting out. I don't want to share her with any strangers or anything, or throw any orgies. I'll probably only share her with you. At least for now."

"Possessive, are we? Yeah, that's fine."

"If I decide to throw any sheik-style sex parties I'll let you know, but she's kind of the quiet type."

"They're all quiet. They're sex slaves."

"No, she's...especially quiet. She's deaf. So if you're going to share her with me and everything..."

"She's deaf, really? How do you talk to her? How do you tell her what you want?"

"She reads lips, and I've learned to sign a little."

"You know sign language?"

"I do now. A little. I'm getting better. And she doesn't like to talk, so she either writes things down or uses ASL."

"ASL?"

"American Sign Language."

Mason stared at him a moment. "So not only do you have a sex slave you can drill in any hole whenever you like, you don't have to deal with any chit-chat either. You're living the dream."

Kai chuckled softly, but something unnerved him about Mason's crass, objectifying language. He was past the point of thinking about Constance as some slave with holes to fill. It annoyed him to hear Mason talk about her that way.

"Anyway," Kai said, "she's really cool. She's pretty and laid back and just...always in the mood."

"Does she like your kinky stuff?"

Kai snorted. "What do you think? Would I have chosen her otherwise?"

"Ah," Mason sighed.

Kai studied his friend. "I don't get it. If you're so into BDSM, why don't you do scenes with Jess? I can get you guys into LoveSlave. Jeremy can too. All you'd have to do is drop your name at the front desk—"

"Jess isn't into it. She's into everything but that. And even if she was into it—"

"She'd be a domme."

Mason's shoulders slumped. "Exactly."

"Sucks to be you. I'll let you dom my odalisque. How about that?"

"More than I'm getting from Jess. Can I spank her? Mark her?"

"Within reason." Kai got the distinct, uneasy feeling all was not well between his friend and his wife. He'd always considered them the strongest, most solid couple in town. "So, if Jess won't do the kink stuff with you, why don't you get it on your own? You have an open marriage, don't you?"

"It's not that simple. Jess can be very, very jealous. Insanely jealous."

"And controlling," Kai added quietly.

Mason met his gaze, then looked away. He clearly preferred not to talk about it. Kai would give him space, for now.

"Hey, Kai. If it comes up in conversation, don't tell Jessamine you have an odalisque."

Kai laughed. "Don't want her to start nagging for her own again?"

But Mason didn't laugh.

"Jesus, man," said Kai. "You look awful. When do you want to come over? When are you free?"

Mason propped his head on his hand and blinked a couple times. "Meh. How about tonight?"

* * * * *

"Lucy, I'm home!"

He always said it in his best Ricky Ricardo voice, even though he knew she couldn't appreciate his cleverness. He left his briefcase in the foyer, dropped the takeout in the kitchen, and then loosened his tie, taking the stairs to her odella two at a time. She was lying on the bed with her usual notebook in her hands.

"What are you doing?"

"Writing," she signed, sliding the notebook under her pillow. As usual. He wondered what was in there, why she was so secretive. Poetry, she'd said. Maybe she was planning some terrorist attack, or plotting to take over the world. Drawing diagrams of a build-at-home nuclear weapon. She was giving him that lustful, wide-eyed look, and he burst out laughing at the idea of her hatching world-domination plans from her odella.

"What?" she signed in the face of his mirth.

"Nothing," he answered, waving his hands. "How was your day?"

She stretched and signed that she'd gone swimming. "It felt so warm, like swimming in a Jacuzzi."

"It will get hotter before the end of summer. It's almost July."

Constance tilted her head at that, and he knew she was thinking the same thing he was. The months were going by too fast. "Time flies when you're having fun," she signed with a smile.

"Don't I know it," said Kai, already unzipping. After his daily "welcome home" blowjob, he lay down beside his nude odalisque, still fully dressed, his fly done up again. He knew it excited her when he was in his work clothes and she was naked. Sick little perv. He tugged lightly on one of her curls.

"Constance, do you know who Mason Cooke is?"

She gave him an exasperated look. "Of course I do," she signed. "Who doesn't?"

"I know Mason pretty well. He's a good friend of mine. He wants to meet you."

Constance did a decent job of disguising her shock. She laughed and signed, "Wow. I thought you were going to ask me to the movies."

"No. It's more like asking you to have sex with Mason Cooke. Is it okay?"

She made a quick sign. "Of course."

"He's coming tonight. I'm sorry I didn't give you more notice."

"I don't need notice. I'm always ready to please you in whatever way I can."

In the last couple weeks, she'd been using an awful lot of what Kai thought of as "odalisque talk." Pat phrases and rehearsed-sounding replies that he knew were meant to distance them, and remind him of her place in his life. It annoyed him, although he knew that was what she'd been trained to do.

"Speaking of advance notice," he added, "we're taking a two-week trip to New York in September. I'll tell you more about it when it's all ironed out, but you might need to buy some formal clothes, gowns and accessories. We'll have parties to attend. Banquets and charity events, that kind of thing. I'll have my driver take you downtown, and I'll give you my credit card. You can buy whatever you like."

Constance lounged across from him, looking skeptical.

"What? What's wrong?" he asked. "You'll do anything I like sexually, but you balk when I ask you to buy clothes?"

"I don't know how to buy clothes," she signed. "And when they ask what I need, they won't be able to understand me. And I won't know what to buy anyway." She dropped her hands, looking frustrated. Kai rubbed the back of his neck.

"Okay. I can send someone out to shop for you. They'll have to take your measurements. Does that work?"

She nodded and signed, "Thank you."

It was really no big deal. He should have just done that in the first place. Somehow he'd imagined she might like going out with his credit card and buying whatever her heart desired. He'd pictured her sashaying down Rodeo Drive with fistfuls of boxes and bags with a big grin on her face, like in the movies, but instead she'd acted like he was asking her to do something distasteful.

But when he actually asked her to do something distasteful, like perform sexually for his friend, she was one hundred percent fine with the idea.

Duh. Because she's an odalisque.

"When is he coming?" she signed.

Kai looked at his watch and rolled off the bed. "In an hour. There's takeout for dinner. I'm going to go change."

* * * * *

Constance breathed in and out, slow deep breaths, drawing on her training. *He's just a mega-movie star, girl. No biggie. Even if he has a massive dick.*

Constance lounged against some pillows in the saray while Kai gave his friend Mason Cooke a tour of the facilities. Kai didn't bother to sign any of what he was saying for her benefit, and she couldn't read their lips since they kept turning their heads. She could easily read their expressions though, and their relaxed body language.

And their erect cocks—they were hard to misunderstand.

It was clear to her from their manner—and the fact that they were unfazed by one another's huge erections—that they were good friends. Constance would be happy to serve any friend of her Master's. There was actually something exciting about handling more than one man at once. It was more strength, more brawn, more cock to deal with. More passion and more lust. She wasn't nervous. Kai used all her holes regularly, to the point where she wasn't uptight at all about penetration.

Kai was showing Mason his cabinet of toys now, and Mason's cock stood up even stiffer. So it was to be one of *those* types of nights. Constance let her legs fall open and fingered her pussy as she watched the men. It was about to get painful—and erotic. Her favorite combination. She was ready to go.

Kai turned to her and smiled while Mason pulled out an armful of implements from the cabinet. Strap, crop, paddle, tawse, whip, another strap, another paddle. Balancing them in one arm, he also grabbed a pair of nipple clamps and some lubricant. Thankfully, it appeared to be the non-stinging kind.

She raised her eyebrows at Kai as Mason jogged across the room to dump all the stuff on the bed. Kai laughed and signed, "Mason is a BDSM noob." He fingerspelled *noob* with a hilarious look of forbearance on his face. "He wants to try just about everything. He's maybe a little overeager right now."

Constance made one lone sign. "Ouch."

Kai shook his head and threw some condoms on the bed beside the toys. "It'll be okay. On your feet, beautiful."

Constance stood and presented herself to the two gentlemen. She waited with one hip cocked slightly, her breasts thrust out and displayed to full effect. She wanted to touch herself again, just from the hungry way they looked at her. Kai had brought Mason straight to the saray, rather than having them all meet somewhere else in the house and have a drink first. She hadn't even really been introduced yet to Mason. She preferred it that way. She liked that she was here to be their toy, their pleasure vessel. She didn't want to be their friend, not at moments like these.

Kai looked at Mason, who, having just pulled every toy out of the cabinet, seemed unsure of his next move. "You want to make some marks on her?"

Mason nodded. Kai led Constance over to the lattice side of the iron bed. He turned back to his friend. "Do you want her restrained or unrestrained?"

Mason only took a second to answer. "Restrained. Yes!"

"Go get some cuffs."

Kai turned her then and pressed her forward against the cool metal structure. Without hearing, she habitually wanted to turn her head to see, to watch. To know what was coming. She was trying to train herself out of it, to just trust in Kai to manage things. It was harder now, though, with another man in the room. She leaned her forehead against the lattice and took more deep breaths.

She jumped a little when she felt warm, rough hands stroking and parting her ass cheeks. With great effort, she didn't spin around to see who was touching her. She just let the feelings of subservience and submission sink into her mind. The hands left her and her arms were pulled behind her. Cuffs were attached to each wrist. Her wrists were then pushed forward and fixed to either side of the lattice. She was caught now. Powerless. Well, she could still kick...

No, maybe not. She felt a tug at her ankles and looked down to see Kai with a spreader bar. Her pussy gave a little throb as he nudged her legs apart. It was harder to dodge blows in the leg spreader, and damn impossible to kick, although she would never really do any of those things during a scene. But knowing she had the power to do them if she chose was somehow soothing. Kai liked to take her power—and choices—away.

She moaned weakly at that provocative thought. Kai placed a hand under her hips, forcing her ass out. She scooted her tethered feet back and arched her spine, and watched Mason come around the bed and pick up the crop. The noobs always loved the riding crops. She braced for impact as Mason disappeared behind her, but all she felt was the soft, dull thud of the handle across her ass. She looked back over her shoulder. Kai shrugged as if to say, "What can you do?"

He took the crop from Mason, demonstrating in the air how to flick the whippy end of it. He gave it back and Constance turned away, wrapping her fingers around the metal bars. Mason landed a blow correctly this time, right on the sweet spot of her left ass cheek. Before she even had time to react, he whapped the other cheek—way too hard. Constance pulled at the cuffs, wanting to cover herself. She looked pleadingly back at Kai. He came toward her and took her chin in his hand.

"I know it's scary playing with someone new. Some of it's going to hurt, and he wants to leave marks, but this is nothing I haven't done to you before. I won't let him really hurt you, okay?"

Constance let out a breath and turned away. She wanted this. *She wanted it.* She was just a little scared. She was used to Kai hurting her, but Mason was something new, an unknown quantity. She closed her eyes and steeled herself to take the pain. She thought Kai must have taken over the crop for a moment. She was given a series of stinging, rapid slaps that had her dancing on her toes. Each time she tensed and drew her ass forward, she'd feel that patient tap on her hip. He liked for her to keep her ass thrust out at all times, as if she craved the punishment of the various implements. It was sexy, yeah. But it was hard to do.

After Kai got her ass and inner and outer thighs all warm and tingling, Mason took over for a while. His shots were more random— some light, and some a fierce, stinging shock. His rhythm was slower than Kai's. Constance imagined them consulting between blows. Finally, Mason put down the crop and picked up one of the paddles. He seemed to have no great difficulty using that. The first one Mason used was a long, principal's-office-style slab of wood that gave more thud than sting. He soon abandoned that—probably at Kai's urging—for a smaller, sleeker red paddle with what Kai liked to refer to as "pain holes." The little holes drilled in the wood increased the sting and heat fifty-fold from the large, thuddy instrument.

Oh, God! It was so hard to stand still, helpless, with her legs spread and her ass arched out, and take each blow. The paddle would connect, which was painful enough in itself, but then that pain would bloom into a torturous, flaming heat she couldn't soothe or rub away. She didn't know if it was Kai paddling her, or Mason, or both. She hoped to God Mason would lose interest in it soon. She lost count of the blows, but she was sure her ass was angry red by now. She was making begging sounds, instinctive, uncontrollable noises that she knew probably sounded awful. She couldn't help herself.

Finally, the paddling stopped. Constance sagged, drawing her aching ass in as far as she could without stumbling from the damn spreader bar. *Please, let me go. Fuck me now. Fucking is awesome!*

Constance was overjoyed when Kai released her feet. He kissed her on the neck, on the shoulder. She breathed in his familiar scent and let her body relax back against him. She rubbed her ass against his erection with needful, blind intent. He turned her head until she was looking at his lips, and then he said, "Not yet."

Not yet? Damn, Mason was on the bed in front of her, nipple clamps in his hand. Kai soon joined him. Her owner reached through the iron latticework to pinch her nipples. She blinked, watching them talk through the metal barrier.

"So, these are called clover clamps," Kai explained to Mason. "Pulling on them tightens them. They're a really nice torture device. You can't leave them on too long, but they're really fun for getting a reaction. So...put one on this tit first."

Constance bit her lip as Kai released her nipple with a painful pinch, only to have Mason take over and pinch it again. The concept wasn't difficult. Mason closed the biting clamp over the soft, vulnerable flesh, his face breaking into a wide smile as she writhed in reaction to the pain. *Another fine sadist in the making*, she thought with a groan.

"Now," Kai said, angling his head toward her so Constance could read his lips. "We're going to thread this chain through the bars and over to here." He took her other nipple in a ruthless grip. "And then every time she jerks or pulls away from the bedframe, she's going to get a nice dose of ouch."

Sadist! Both of them were grinning like maniacs as Mason applied the other clamp. Constance wrapped her fingers around the metal, as far as the cuffs on her wrist would allow, and thought about her predicament. Sure, it was easy to stand still at the moment and bear the rollicking ache at the tip of each breast. But once they started hurting her again—Mason was already palming Kai's leather tawse—it was going to be really hard not to move.

Mason had definitely gotten his groove down with corporal punishment. The first blow was confident, not tentative. It had to be him—Kai was still standing beside her, doubtless enjoying the *oh-shit* look on her face.

From BDSM noob to skilled sadist—Mason took only four blows to make her shift enough for a painful reminder tug. On the sixth blow, Constance rose on her toes, and then a quickly-delivered seventh achieved full pulling-away pain. Her ass burned from the bite of the leather, and she shuddered from the awful ache in her nipples. Her pussy was on fire. She felt empty and frustrated and angry that she couldn't get away from the torment of the tawse at her back and the clamps at her front.

She closed her eyes, blocking out Kai. Blocking out everything. *Take it, take it.* A moment later, the blows stopped and her ass cheeks were parted. She looked up but Kai was gone. A cold dollop of lube and something hard pressed against her ass. A glass plug—the large one. Again, she struggled to be still, to accept the invasion lest her nipples pay the price. Her breath was coming in stutter spurts as the dull, unpleasant pain of the plug's insertion peaked. It was driven home, a dubious relief. She could still feel it in there, both making her horny and tormenting her. There was more tawse, or was it strap? Paddle? *Owww....*

Then Mason's strong arms came around her, and she felt his cock poking against her burning cheeks. The glass plug slid out, leaving her empty only a moment before something larger and longer filled her up. Mason was taking her ass, skillfully, thank God. No wild jabbing or thrusting. With a tool his size, Constance supposed he knew better.

As he fucked her, she became aware of his scent, like Kai's but not like Kai's. She got used to the contours of his muscular body, the unfamiliar girth and feel of his cock. She smelled latex and lubricant. The scent of sex. She felt weak, like her legs wouldn't hold her, but Mason held her up. The pain in her nipples flared and desisted as he manipulated her body, but the sensation of fullness in her ass nearly overpowered the ache in her breasts.

Then, without warning, the clamps were removed and rioting pain suffused her breasts. She struggled against it even as her eyes popped open to find Kai gazing at her. Did he understand how much this aroused her? How exciting it was to serve him, to be used and hurt this way just for his pleasure? Just for that glazed, infatuated look in his eyes?

Mason was fumbling with the cuffs on her wrists, his cock still buried in her ass. He took them off as Kai sat on the edge of the bed, his cock standing up swollen and rigid from his fist. Mason moved her like some kind of rag doll, nudged her over the few steps. He bent her over with a firm hand between her shoulders.

Constance knew what was expected. She opened her mouth and took Kai's cock deep between her lips, down into her throat. She tasted salty pre-cum and wanted more. She sucked her Master while her Master's friend drilled in and out of her ass, and she felt her own arousal reach an almost crippling peak. She didn't just feel it in her pussy, or her reamed ass, or her tortured nipples as they scraped against the wiry hair on his legs. She felt it *everywhere*. She felt it in her soul.

Constance braced her hands on Kai's thighs, ran them up the muscles defining his hips. His chest rose and fell as she sucked him. If he said anything, she didn't know and didn't care. Then she was halted, pushed forward again. Mason lifted her knees on either side of Kai's waist and she fell forward against her Master's chest. Kai slid a hand between them and started to ease the head of his cock into her slit.

This was something she'd been trained for, this kind of licentious excess. Trained with dildos and plugs and all kinds of depraved exercises, but she'd never experienced the immediacy of two real men— breathless, panting men—thrusting into her, until now. She hadn't felt the hard flesh of male bodies trapping her between them, or the pressure of their fingers as they guided and cradled her.

Kai's cock stretched her pussy while Mason still fucked her ass. She couldn't move at all, except as they let her. Her whole body tensed with the knowledge of her powerlessness. The men were careful, skillful, working smoothly in tandem so she could concentrate on sensation rather than mechanics. And the sensation was incredible, like nothing she'd ever known. Such warmth, such fullness. Such complete possession and submission to powerful male lusts. Each stroke resulted in a surge of delicious pressure in her pelvis and heaviness in her breasts. Mason squeezed and pinched her sensitive nipples until she almost screamed from the pleasure, until her pussy and ass spasmed subconsciously around the men's lengths inside her.

Then Kai was reaching, fingering her again. She braced against his chest as he parted her pussy lips, wet with the waterfall of her excitement. He tapped her clit with one of his questing fingers, and that last, shimmering note of sensation was all it took. Constance plunged into a racking, mind-exploding orgasm. Firm masculine hands held her down, held her still, even as her orifices clamped down on the massive cocks filling her. Again and again the pleasure rolled, and rolled, and rolled until she lost the ability to comprehend it.

She didn't know what happened after that. She fell, panting, against Kai's chest, her hands curled in the hollows of his neck. She wasn't in control, didn't want to be. She was just Constance, lost in the aftershocks of her orgasm, nestled between two shuddering, thrusting men.

Chapter Twelve:
Questions

Kai and Mason stayed up drinking vodka and Red Bull downstairs, long after Constance passed out in her pillow-strewn bed.

They'd fucked her three times in a row, various couplings and intensities, broken up with sessions of teasing-to-hardcore BDSM play. Kai watched his friend over the rim of his glass. Mason had been like a kid in a candy store while it was happening. Now, sprawled back against an ottoman, he was significantly more subdued.

"So, she sleeps away from you every night?"

Kai nodded from the couch. "That's the way it works."

"But I mean, could you sleep in there if you wanted to? If you wanted to...I don't know..."

"Snuggle?" provided Kai with a grin. "Are you a snuggler, Mace?"

"You know what I mean. Is it by her choice, or yours? If you decided you wanted to sleep in there with her..."

"She's supposed to serve me sexually. Once the sex is done, I'm obligated to leave her alone. Could I go in there now and snuggle with her? Yeah, if I wanted to have more sex. But just to sleep with her all night? No. There's supposed to be this kind of...space between us."

Mason considered that, glancing up toward the open door of Constance's odella. "Twisted. I mean, really? That's in the contract?"

Kai rolled his eyes. "Poor little cuddlebear. Put on some pants and I'll give you a snuggle."

"Fuck you, Chandler. I'm just saying."

Kai put his glass down with a bang on the coffee table and slung his legs up over the couch. "No, seriously. Put on some pants. I'm tired of staring at your flaccid dong and your saggy balls."

"Tough. I like being naked."

"You'd make a good odalisque."

"Ha. I'm an odalisque already. I live for Jessamine's pleasure. That's how she sees it anyway."

Mason's voice had an unmistakable edge of bitterness. "I sense all is not well at the Casa de Cooke."

Mason shrugged. "Eh. It'll work itself out." He took another drink, then leaned closer and whispered, "Do you ever get the urge to cheat on her? Sneak a nut with someone else for a change? Do you ever get bored with her? You've got her for what? A year?"

"First of all," Kai whispered back, "she couldn't hear you even if you yelled. So there's no need for the whispering. And it's kind of impossible to cheat on someone you're not in a relationship with," Kai added in a normal voice. "So no, and no. Not yet anyway."

The men drank a while in companionable silence. Kai reviewed the finer moments of the evening in his mind, and flicked a look at Mason, who seemed to be doing the same. "So, how did you like getting your kink on? Was it everything you hoped for?"

Mason let out a low whistle. "Jesus Christ, that shit is hot. I mean, I imagined it would be fun and all, but it was...more than that. It was more than fun, more than messing around. It really gets intense."

Kai nodded. "Yep."

"I mean, I always imagined doing that kind of shit to women, but I never thought about how exciting their reactions would be. The reactions were better than the—"

"Actions? Yeah. That's why you do it. The thrill of watching your partner fall apart from the pain while simultaneously trying to hump your leg. It's great if you're with someone who's really into it." Too late, he remembered that Mason's partner wasn't. "Anyway, I'm glad you had a good time."

"You know, she wasn't like the sheik's odalisque at all."

"No?"

118

"Constance was a lot more...slutty. No, I don't know if that's the right word. The sheik's girl was all about seeing to everyone else's needs. Constance seemed to be enjoying everything a lot herself."

"Yeah, well. I think that makes her better."

"Me too. I mean, Constance seemed a lot more into it. It was really exciting."

Mason sounded a few shades shy of worshipful. Kai fixed him with a look. "You're not falling for my odalisque, are you? I still think you should get your own."

"Yeah, maybe." Mason drained the last of his drink. "Hey, can I crash on your couch?"

"I wouldn't think of waking my driver at this hour," Kai said. "I'll even give you a room and a bed of your own. As soon as you put some damn pants on. At least a pair of boxer shorts."

"Can I borrow some boxer sh—"

"Yes."

"Jesus, Kai," Mason murmured. "You're a hell of a friend."

* * * * *

All three of them slept late the next day, which was probably why Kai didn't hear the doorbell, or notice a key turn in the lock. He opened his eyes to find Satya in his face, frowning ferociously.

"You haven't called me in forever, Kaivalyan. I hate when you ignore me."

He shot up out of bed. This was the reason he couldn't sleep naked. His sister had no sense of boundaries.

"Jesus, ever hear of knocking?"

Her eyes went wide and indignant. "I knocked and rang the bell. And then I let myself in. I just came to get something I left here last year before I went on that trip to Nepal. I won't keep you, since you seem hung over or high or something."

"I'm not high," Kai muttered, pulling some sweatpants over his boxers as Satya trotted out of his room. His sister was sort of like a volcano and sort of like an earthquake. And sort of like a hurricane mixed with a cyclone, all rolled into one.

"What do you need, Sats?" he asked, stumbling after her.

"I think I left it in the guest suite upstairs. That leather bag with all the pamphlets about the child brides. You remember? The pamphlets are kind of outdated now, but they were well designed. They'll work in a pinch."

"Let me look for it." He was practically chasing her now. Satya was so fast. She was petite and perky and way too fast for ten in the morning. She was already halfway up the stairs. "Satya! Stop! Let me get it."

"I'll get it." She waved a hand over her shoulder. "I know exactly where I left it."

Me too, thought Kai. *Because I moved it when I was fixing up that room for my odalisque.*

The door was standing wide open, as it always was. *Shit. Shit. Shit.* Satya barreled in, her usual frenetic self. *Please let Constance be in the bathroom. Please let her be under the covers.* Damn, she never slept under the covers. And she never wore clothes.

Please, God, don't let her back be to the door when my sister sees her. If Satya saw the evidence of their play last night, she'd go ballistic.

"Satya, stop!" he yelled one last time, pointlessly, since she was already backing out of the room. Satya turned to him with narrowed eyes.

Kai lifted his chin and met her gaze. "Your bag's not in there. I did some redecorating. I'll show you where I put it, and then you can run along on your way."

Yeah. Did he really believe it would be that easy? Satya came down the stairs and dogged his heels all the way to the office where he'd stowed her bag and the other various things she left at his place whenever she blew through. He located it and handed it to her.

"I don't suppose you'll mind your own business and leave now."

His sister crossed her arms in front of her. "I don't suppose I will. Why is there a naked woman lounging on the bed in your guest room? And why did you decide to decorate it like a bordello on crack?"

"A bordello on crack? I think it looks great, and I decorated it that way because she likes it that way. And she's naked because she's...she's a nudist."

"Don't lie to your sister. Does she live here? Is she your girlfriend?"

It spoke a lot to the closeness of their relationship that they could talk about nudism and bordellos. Kai still sensed disaster. He grabbed his head and groaned. "Just leave it. Can't you just leave it? For once?"

"No, I can't. Is she really your girlfriend? Because it seems kind of skanky, her hanging around naked in your guest room which now looks an awful lot like a whorehouse on acid."

"Whorehouses can't be on acid! What is it with you talking about buildings being on drugs?"

"Hey, Satya," came a cheerful voice from the room across the hall. Kai turned and did a facepalm. Mason was in nothing but tight-fitting boxers, lazily scratching his chest. "What were you saying about acid?"

Satya looked from Mason to Kai and back again, silently arching her brows.

"Okay," said Kai. "She's not exactly my girlfriend."

"Then what exactly is she? A prostitute? Did you and your degenerate friend spend last night with a prostitute?"

"Degenerate?" Mason protested, but Satya was barreling on, in full scold mode. She poked a finger into Kai's chest.

"You know, Mother would be spinning in her grave if she knew how you lived. You rich men and your vices—"

Kai held up a hand. "Excuse me. My vices are none of your business. And these rich men"—he indicated himself and Mason, who was now yawning and scratching his balls—"these 'rich men' finance your numerous pet humanitarian projects. So I would pipe down with the accusations and judgments if I were you."

"Judgments? No judgments, just facts. Prostitution is not only a crime in this state, it also exploits women. And I know—" Satya stopped to take a breath, her bronze skin flushing dark. "I know my big brother would not involve himself in the exploitation of women." She threw Mason a dirty look, as if she might believe it of him.

Kai grasped for calm as Mason shrugged and loped off toward the kitchen. Satya looked so much like his mother sometimes, and yet she was nothing like their mother, that silent, submissive woman. Satya was just getting started with him.

"Listen, Sats," he said as they walked back to the living room. "I'm not exploiting her. That's all I'm going to tell you. The rest is none of your business."

"Just answer this question. Does she live here?"

Kai gritted his teeth. "Yes. So if you don't mind, please don't come barging in here anymore without a phone call first."

Kai looked up then to see Constance standing at the top of the stairs. She was wrapped in a thick terry robe that just skimmed her knees. Thank God he'd bought it for her, to use poolside in the spring and summer. *Please don't let my sister see the marks on you.*

At his expression, Satya turned too. Kai watched his sister—women's rights crusader—and his contractually purchased odalisque size one another up.

"I'm sorry I walked in on you while you were undressed," Sats said to Constance, her back poker-straight and nearly as stiff as her voice.

Constance looked back at him. He almost broke down laughing at her exasperated expression. She signed, "Tell her it's okay. That I'm always undressed."

Kai shook his head and signed back. "No, I'm not telling her that."

Satya spun to face him. "What did she say? Can't she hear me?"

"No. She's deaf. She said it's okay, about you walking in on her."

Constance started signing again, almost too fast for him to catch all the words. "Tell her I'm not exploited. That I chose this."

Kai paused a moment, then shook his head. "She won't understand. I won't tell her that. No." He turned to Satya, who looked about ready to murder him.

"That's not fair, Kai. If she wants to tell me something, let her tell me."

Instead, Kai gestured toward her and turned to Constance. "Let me introduce my sister, Satya." He fingerspelled her name for Constance, who nodded. "And Satya, this is Constance. Constance stays here with me. She is very, very happy and content."

"I want to talk to her. Privately."

Kai shook his head. "Absolutely not."

But Constance was waving her hands to get his attention. "It's okay. I would prefer not to be your shameful secret for the next eight and a half months. I can explain it to her so it's not creepy."

Kai didn't really have an answer to that. He gazed up at Constance and silently signed, with emphasis, "Whatever you do, don't let her see the marks from last night."

* * * * *

Constance told Satya the truth about why she lived in Kai's house, the whole truth in blunt terms. She left out the hardcore sex and kink stuff, but Satya wasn't stupid. Constance wasn't sure at first how she'd react, but Kai's sister surprised her by being inquisitive rather than condemning.

They were sitting at the desk in Constance's room, the notebook open between them. Satya asked many questions, spoke them slowly and clearly so Constance could read her lips. It wasn't that hard. Her lips and speech patterns were very much like Kai's. In fact, she looked very much like Kai, only shorter and prettier with longer hair.

It was clear that Satya was trying hard to understand Constance, her thoughts and motives in choosing to be an odalisque. She was also frank about her misgivings.

"You understand why this unsettles me, don't you? In India, where my mom was born, there are child brides, arranged marriages. Women have so few choices. They're forced to live under the dominion of men. So I don't understand how you can choose to live in such subordination when you don't...when you don't have to."

Submission, not subordination, Constance corrected her in writing. *I chose this. No one made me do this, and I didn't choose it as a last resort. I chose it freely over many options I had. This seemed like the best one.*

"But why?"

Constance thought back on her life. On struggles and heartbreak and her search for security and independence. It was too personal to put it all in words. *I can't answer that in any way you'd understand.*

"Try," Satya urged. "Confide in me."

Constance thought a moment. She knew it would give Satya some peace of mind if Constance could make it make sense. *Satya, my childhood was crazy. My mom dragged us from town to town, from man to man. We always had to depend on his good graces, whoever he was. It was true slavery. No choices. My mother was helpless. I think, in hindsight, she made herself that way on purpose.*

Constance paused and thought a moment, chewing the pen. *I was so angry with her. I blamed her for making me live that way, with so much upheaval and fear. I never felt safe. As I got older...more mature...she used me as a lure too.*

Satya put a hand on Constance's pen, her eyes wide in alarm. "She didn't! Tell me she didn't..."

Constance shook her head and started writing again. *She didn't offer me to them or anything, but she flaunted me. Her looks were fading and it worried her. She thought if I could just catch their interest, she could do the rest. But it didn't work out. Not quite that way. And when the men came onto me, my mother blamed me and said I invited their attentions. I left home when I was fifteen. My mom's newest soldier had been stationed on an Air Force base in Germany, so I ran to France. I survived through a lot of nasty, awful situations. I scraped and schemed to survive. All I ever wanted was some security for myself. The chance to make my own destiny, and not let life control me the way my mom did.*

Satya nodded. "That's understandable."

I met Sebastien, the owner of Maison Odalisque, when I applied for a job as a maid. I thought it was a bed and breakfast. Constance laughed, remembering that meeting, when he'd misunderstood the position she'd been applying for. Constance had decided pretty quickly she preferred the other one.

Constance pulled her robe closer around her and turned the page to write more. *Just picture it. I went from having nothing, and no prospects, to the possibility of earning half a million dollars a year. There's something about security and a calm, predictable life, especially to a person who's never had either. The work isn't degrading. It probably seems so to you, but it doesn't to me. I'm proud of my sensual skills. I developed them like any other person who works with their body—a dancer, a model, a gymnast. I've worked very hard to become the best at what I do.*

Satya thought that over. "I guess in a way it is sexist, that women can be celebrated for doing all kinds of physical things, as long as they're not sexual. You know, throughout history, men have always feared female sexuality and tried to control it. It's still going on in a thousand harmful ways. I see it all over the world. It's disgusting. Disheartening."

Every odalisque contributes a quarter of her salary to combat sex trafficking, Constance wrote. *Believe me, I feel as strongly about these issues as you.*

"Do you love my brother?"

The abrupt question was the last thing Constance expected. She toyed with the edge of the notebook, thinking before she wrote.

I love this life he affords me. I love to serve him. He's very kind to me. Very generous. And an excellent lover. Really over the top as far as lovemaking skills.

Satya slammed her hand down on the page, and made some gawping protest like la-la-la-la-la-la. She shook her head at Constance. "I don't want to know what kind of lover my brother is. The point is, you don't love him. At the end of this year, you'll walk away from him?"

Maybe, Constance wrote. *I might stay another year. We are limited to six years of service to one owner.*

"Why?" asked Satya.

Constance realized how ludicrous the words were before she even wrote them. *To prevent us falling in love.*

Satya looked at her hard, and for the first time, Constance couldn't meet her eyes with total steadiness. Fortunately, Satya seemed satisfied that the overall situation was not harmful or illegal. She stood up and nodded.

"Thank you, Constance, for being honest with me. You might not love my brother, but I do. He's the only family I have. Mom's gone, and our dad's been out of the picture for a while. I might seem overprotective, but he is my big brother and we're very close."

Constance nodded. Satya asked, "How do you sign 'thank you?'"

Constance put her fingers to her lips and drew them forward in the familiar sign. Satya smiled.

"I remember that from preschool ages ago." She repeated the sign to Constance. "Thank you. Now I promise to leave you alone. Unless you'd like a visitor now and again? Do you ever get lonely here by yourself?"

Constance thought a moment. She liked Kai's sister. Satya was slightly scary, but Constance could tell she had a huge heart. A lot like her brother. Constance picked up the notebook. *I don't exactly get lonely, but company is always fun.*

Satya read it and shot her a grin. "I'll be sure to call first. Or text, I guess."

Constance nodded and wrote her cell number for Satya, then led her back down the stairs to the living room, where Kai sat on the couch. Constance chuckled inwardly at his woebegone expression.

"Your sister and I had a very nice talk," she signed.

Kai stood and put his hands on his hips. "A nice talk. Right." But his relief was palpable. His sister reached up and popped him on the head, which was kind of funny since he was at least a foot and a half taller than her.

"I'll never understand why you won't let me fix you up with someone, brother. But Constance is pretty cool."

"Just don't go starting some fund to save the odalisques. Some odalisque awareness campaign. I won't be contributing to it, and I'll deny everything."

The siblings faced off, and then they both smiled. Constance felt some pang of jealousy, or admiration. During her childhood, she and her myriad step-siblings had competed for every scrap of love or attention. Both were always in short supply. What would it feel like to have a brother or sister love you unconditionally? Protect you so fiercely? Laugh with you so easily?

Constance stared at Kai as he hugged his sister, and fell in love a little more still. They broke apart and Kai tugged on Satya's wispy, swingy black locks.

"Now that you've made each other's acquaintance, perhaps you and I can agree on some other time and place to get together and catch up."

Satya scowled at him. "Yeah, right. You'll put me off, like you've been doing for the last three months."

"You've been out of town!"

"Still, I'm your sister. Your flesh and blood. Do you know how it breaks my heart—"

"Hey, Sats." Mason came out from the kitchen, juggling a couple of pans. "Stay for breakfast. I'm making omelets." He dropped one of the pans, barely missing a toe. Constance wondered if he was planning to cook in Kai's boxers. They didn't appear to provide much coverage. "You got any eggs, Kai?"

"I have to be on my way," Satya said quickly.

"I swear to God, I will call you," Kai promised. "We'll go out to lunch or something."

"I want to talk to you about New York. You're going, right? In September?"

"I'm planning to."

"I'll be there too. Human Rights conference?"

"Among other things."

Satya rolled her eyes. "But you'll be at the glitzy events, swilling champagne. I'll be outside waving the placards."

"You wouldn't have it any other way."

Kai handed Satya a leather bag, and she slung it over her shoulder. He walked her to the door, their faces turned away from Constance, so anything else they said was lost. Constance wandered into the kitchen, where Mason was indeed cooking eggs in tight blue boxer shorts and nothing else. She watched him for a while before he even realized she was there.

Odalisque

When he finally turned to her, he waved a spatula to get her attention. "Hey you. I had fun last night. Thanks."

Any irritation Constance felt at being called "Hey you" was softened by the fondness in his gaze. There really was something irrepressible and boyishly appealing about Mason Cooke. Constance saw it in Kai too sometimes. Constance smiled back at the blue-eyed megastar. She flipped open a notebook on the counter.

I had fun too. Do you want to see the bruises?

Mason blinked at her. "Bruises? Are they bad?"

Not too bad. And I like them. They're like souvenirs. With Satya gone, Constance shed her robe and showed Mason her backside. He looked partly horrified and partly excited. He reached out to trace over one of the welts, which had faded overnight from bright red to dull lavender.

"Jesus Christ, that's hot. You're going to make me burn the fucking toast."

He turned away from her, yanking charred bread out of the toaster. There was a definite bulge growing against the front of the boxers. Being small on him already, they were quickly approaching critical mass. Constance imagined him busting out of them completely like some comic book hero, the sagging seams torn and ragged. He waved the spatula at her again.

"Go. Stop tempting me. Go see where Kai is."

Constance expected to find him in the living room. She looked down the main hallway and didn't find him there either. The only place he could be, unless he'd gone outside, was—

She ran up the stairs to the odella and pushed the door open. Kai looked up with her notebook in his hands.

"How dare you?" she signed through a red haze of anger.

"What?" Kai protested as she crossed the room and ripped the notebook from his fingers. She threw it on the desk beside the others, filled with her most private writing and thoughts.

"You're eavesdropping!" She spelled the word out in furious staccato. *E-a-v-e-s-d-r-o-p-p-*

"Yes, I got it," said Kai. "I was eavesdropping. I'm sorry. I was curious—"

"I don't care how curious you were. How dare you read my private notebooks!"

"Private notebooks? We write in these all the time to talk together."

127

"We write in one notebook, with a purple cover, which is downstairs. You knew that notebook wasn't the same one. You were eavesdropping. Spying on me."

She couldn't tell if he was catching all her angry signing, but he got the general message. "I'm sorry," he said. "I was just curious what you and Sats talked about."

"I don't want your excuses, I want your apology."

Kai was staring at her. Okay, so she was acting like a raving bitch. But it was the first time since she'd arrived that Kai had disappointed her, the first time he'd done something that made her uneasy. Insecure.

He held up his hands. "I said I was sorry. I have a trust problem, okay? You would understand if—if you knew."

"Knew what?" Constance signed impatiently.

One side of his mouth turned down in a frown. His eyes were dark, growing blacker. "I don't want to talk about it."

"Oh, why? Is it private? So you're entitled to privacy, but not me?"

She could see him draw in a deep breath. She moved closer, looked up in his eyes. "I didn't say anything to your sister that I wouldn't have said to your face."

"I know. I don't know why I even looked." His lips twisted in a bitter smile that hurt Constance's heart. "I was betrayed by my ex, Constance. Maliciously. Thoroughly. When I found out..." He stopped, looking down at the floor. "Well." He kicked at the rug. "I have issues with trust."

"Because she betrayed your trust, that means you get to betray mine?" Constance swallowed hard. Kai looked so bereft. She ran her fingers over the notebooks on the table, then signed, "You want to see what I've written about you? Then ask me. I have no reason to hide the way I feel about you, positive or negative. I just have to submit to you sexually. Right?"

He recoiled as if she'd slapped him. "Jesus! I just wanted to know what you said to my sister."

"Then ask me what I said to your sister. Don't go poking around in my notebooks!"

"Why? What are you writing in there that's so top secret?"

"My thoughts. My *private* thoughts. You bought my body. You own my sex. My ass, my pussy. Not this! Not my mind."

They stood, facing off like pugilists. Constance felt blindsided by his betrayal, but also cowed by his pain. She wanted to comfort him but she was too upset. So he had a shitty ex-wife. Who didn't? That didn't give him the right to read through her notebooks while she wasn't around.

While she was trying to think of something to say to diffuse the rancor between them, Kai turned to the door. Mason was standing there, looking from one of them to the other.

"Hey guys, what's up? Everything okay? Breakfast is ready."

Kai looked back at Constance. "We'll be down in a second." Mason left and Kai came closer to her. "I'm sorry, Constance. I won't do it again."

Constance reached out for his hand and squeezed it in truce. She let go and signed, "I'm sorry I flipped out."

Kai leaned to kiss her forehead, then brushed back a lock of her hair. "I don't want to fight with you. I prefer you horny, not angry."

She gave him a flirtatious smile. "Well, you know how to get me that way."

"I think maybe a nice long session tied to the bed with a rope knot against your clit and a plug in your ass." Constance could feel herself flush, feel the arousal dampen the cleft between her legs. "And then...after..." He leaned closer as she watched his lips. "Hours and hours of lurid, debauched sex."

Constance was caught in his gaze and the wicked pleasure it promised, but Kai glanced away, sniffing the air.

"But first, how about some burnt toast and overcooked eggs for breakfast?"

Constance burst into laughter at Kai's long-suffering expression. "You've eaten Mason's breakfasts before?" she signed.

"Many times," Kai admitted. "You just have to power through it. It's the only way to get him to go away."

Chapter Thirteen:
Secrets

Summer went by in a blur. Constance spent many hours in Kai's designer pool, floating on her back and reminding herself that she wasn't here to get lost in the sex, or to fall in love with her owner. She spent the rest of the hours in his arms, or tied to the bed in the saray, or writhing beneath his bronzed Indian-god body, being urged to greater and greater orgasmic heights.

They had no more arguments after the eavesdropping incident. Ms. Dresden's visits continued out of routine more than any real purpose. And Kai continued to respond to Constance with avid arousal and enduring kindness, which made it that much harder to think about the inevitable end.

Constance also gained a new and unexpected friend in Kai's sister. Satya visited every couple weeks, and Constance would dress in clothes and sit across from the animated woman at Kai's kitchen table, eating *nankhatai* cookies and drinking tea. Satya would talk about her humanitarian work and the many causes she supported. She also talked about her boyfriend, who worked with her at Amnesty International. Constance admired Satya's sense of purpose and her strong ideals.

Kai only tolerated these visits. It didn't help that Satya wouldn't let him hang around while they talked. His sister said Kai dampened their ability to "girl talk." Kai believed, rightly, that Satya was using the visits as an excuse to check on her. Constance gained another overmistress, in a sense.

However, there were very few attempts on Satya's part at trying to talk her out of being an odalisque, and no attempts to make Constance feel she was doing something wrong. It didn't take long for Constance to realize that Satya believed, above all, in choices for women. As long as those choices were not forced or made out of desperation, Satya kept her peace even if she disagreed with them. Or couldn't quite understand, as in Constance's case.

Soon the pool grew a little chilly, the breezes a little cooler. September arrived and they set off on Kai's New York trip. He worked on his laptop during the flight, sipping occasionally at sparkling water and lime. Constance shifted, sighed, and stared out the window. She had to stop obsessing about him. She had met just that morning with Ms. Dresden, and spent the whole interview carefully choosing her words and avoiding the overmistress's gaze. Kai confessed to Constance that to him, Ms. Dresden's visits felt like job evaluations. For Constance, the visits were an unwelcome reminder that her sojourn with Kai Chandler was another month gone.

More than *six months* gone.

Mason had been a frequent guest at Kai's house since he'd first joined them a few months ago. Constance didn't mind. Mason could be coarse and immature, but she knew inside he had a good heart. She often caught him watching her in a kind of fascination. It was flattering and sweet, and then they'd go to the saray and it was like the two friends competed for who could fuck her and turn her on the most. She *really* didn't mind that. She'd gotten a little graphic trying to describe it all to Ms. Dresden, and had actually seen the iron-tempered, worldly woman blush.

But she hadn't met Mason's wife, Jessamine, or any other of Kai's friends besides Mason and his sister. Satya. *Truth.* Constance was still, for all intents and purposes, a dirty little secret. Kai's dirty little secret who'd be paraded around in thousand-dollar gowns and jewelry and be introduced to all his politically and financially powerful friends over the course of this New York trip.

She snuck a look at Kai, shifting in the wide, comfortable seat. She wanted to talk with him, interact with him, but flying in side-by-side seating wasn't conducive to conversation when you were deaf. She could read signs sideways from long-time experience, but Kai wasn't to that point yet, and reading lips sideways was out of the question. He was also engrossed in some document he was typing at in fits and spurts. She reached beside her and dug in her bag for a notebook.

She wrote, *What are you working on?*

He shrugged and took the pen. *Party speeches. I have to be on my game.*

Are these high stakes types of parties?

Some of them, he wrote back. *I want to say the right words to move people and make them want to get involved.*

But none of this is business, is it? All charity stuff?

He shot her a crooked smile, twirling the pen once around his fingers. *It's still important. My business is booming, making money. It practically runs itself. Charity work is like swimming against a current. There's always more that's needed.*

How many charities are you involved in?

He started writing a long list. *American Cancer Society. Livestock for Life. Kids Making Music. Battered Women's Network. ASPCA. Wounded Warrior Project. Make a Wish. Pediatric AIDS. Project Playground. Amnesty International, which Satya works for. The Foundation for Auditory Research. There are more I can't think of right now.*

She circled the last one. *I never heard of this.*

Kai looked over at her and then down at the page. *I just started it. Don't be mad at me.*

Why would I be mad?

He still wouldn't look at her. He wrote, *Because I know you don't want to be able to hear.*

Wow. He missed the mark on that one. Not wanting to be pitied and fussed over wasn't the same thing as not wanting to be able to hear. She scratched her cheek and turned away to watch the blinding sun reflecting off the clouds. So he was throwing his money at auditory research now, thanks to her. She hoped it came to some good for someone. Maybe someday they would find a way to make every deaf person hear. It might not help her, but it would help those who came after her. She picked up the pen again.

I think you're a really amazing person. I really admire you.

Kai looked at her words and gave her that devastating smile. He made the sign for her name right against his cheek, an endearment, and turned back to his laptop. Her heart flip flopped in her chest. *Sigh.*

After a moment or two he stretched back in his chair, rubbing his neck in frustration.

She turned toward him and signed, "Can I help?"

He shrugged. "It's mostly written already. But it sounds kind of stilted. I don't know what's wrong with it."

"Do you want me to look at it? I study words."

Kai laughed. "That's right. Your etymology. Sure, take a crack at it." He pushed the laptop her way, and Constance looked over the short speech he'd typed. *I study words.* Yeah, sure. She actually studied the great orators, speeches, and the craft of speechwriting. She wrote speeches of all kinds in her notebooks, a secret hobby that seriously embarrassed her. She didn't even remember now how she got so interested in it. She'd watched speeches on TV perhaps, subtitled of course. Something about the act of public speaking had fascinated her from her earliest years. *Because you'll never be able to do it...*

But here, now, a chance to finally use the skills she'd furtively honed. She added a few juicy words and sentences to Kai's existing work and even added some parenthetical sections where he should pause for maximum effect. But then she took them out. A little too over the top.

She pushed it back over to Kai when she was done. He scanned it, one corner of his mouth hitching up. "Wow, thanks. That's actually a lot better now. You really do know your words. Or your insects. Or something."

She tried to act casual, laughing and waving off his praise.

"So...all those speeches I saw in your notebooks the day I"—he paused to look guilty—"eavesdropped on you. You wrote them, didn't you?"

Scarlet humiliation flooded her face. Even if she wanted to deny it, her blush would have given her away. "Go ahead," she signed. "Make fun of me. A non-verbal deaf person with oratorical dreams."

Kai shook his head. "Don't mock yourself. I could tell from the few I scanned that you're good at it. Have you ever considered trying to work as a speechwriter?"

Constance wished this painfully embarrassing conversation was over. "Odalisque money is better," she said with a shrug.

"I'm not joking, Constance. In a few minutes you made my lame speech a hundred times better. This should be your life's work."

"I can't talk! Who do you think would hire me to write speeches?" She set her gaze somewhere in the middle of Kai's chest. "I used to try to talk. People look at you with pity. Or they smile and nod even though you can tell from their eyes they're not understanding a word you say. It didn't take long for me to give up. So let me have my dinky little speechwriting hobby. But don't tell me I should do it for my job. That's ridiculous."

Kai dipped his head to catch her gaze. "You don't have to deliver them, you know, only write them. Presidents have speechwriters. CEOs like me. Public relations firms. They all need people who can write good speeches."

"I already have a job," Constance signed, then turned away. She prayed he would let the topic drop. Well, he didn't really have a choice when she purposely looked away from him.

He put a hand on her knee and squeezed it. She turned warily but his gaze was less incisive now, more thoughtful.

"Why did you decide to become an odalisque? Because of the reasons you told my sister?"

Constance raised a brow. "Did you think I lied to her?"

"You lied to me," he pointed out. "You told me you wrote poetry in your notebooks."

She searched his face for anger, but he was teasing. "Please don't tell anyone I write speeches. Don't go hounding your rich, famous friends to give me a job."

Kai stroked a hand up her forearm. "I'll keep your secrets. But...I mean...are you really happy? Being an odalisque?"

Constance knew he didn't mean to be insulting, or reproachful of her choices. He really wanted to know. She thought for a moment before she started to sign. "When I was still at the Maison, I worried I might end up with someone who was only interested in using me in the most basic sense of the word. An owner who just fell on me and pumped away and came in me, like I was only some kind of receptacle. Day in and day out. I thought that would be the worst thing that could happen."

"Yeah, I'd say so," said Kai with a grimace.

"The thing is," Constance continued, "I would have been content with that. I would have put up with it and been happy enough. Because I really was just seeking a safe situation. A way to make good money and find the security my mother never had. But this...you..." She paused, feeling a blush rise in her cheeks.

"What?" Kai prompted.

"When I came over here to be with you... I hoped for the best but braced for disappointment. I thought, 'He must be too good to be true.' But I was wrong. You're better. Better than I thought the best lover could be. And I'm really grateful." She had to wrap it up before she started bawling. "I guess all I'm trying to say is, I don't regret becoming an odalisque for a minute, because it brought me to you."

It was almost too much to say. It probably crossed a line, but it felt good to let it out for once. And Kai was practically glowing at her praise. He looked pleased, and affectionate. "I'm glad it brought you to me," he signed. "And I feel very much the same."

When he looked at her like that, with that half-crooked smile, those white teeth and those amber eyes you could drown in... *Good God, help me please.*

* * * * *

Normally Kai found travel tedious, but he'd enjoyed flying across the country with Constance. There was something delicious about taking her out into the world, where no one knew what they were to each other, or the charms Constance possessed beneath her reserved outer shell. And for him, she was like a curtain being pulled back, revealing new aspects of herself every day.

Like her bizarre speechwriting talents. The day Kai had snooped in her room, looking for her conversation with his sister, he'd found notebooks full of speeches written in Constance's hand. He'd assumed she'd copied them from somewhere for some reason, perhaps the "word study" she did. But on the plane he'd realized she'd written them herself.

He loved that she wrote speeches. He would have asked her about it sooner but it would have brought that awful day back, when he'd breached her privacy and she'd called him on it in the most condemning terms. And he'd spilled out the crap about his ex-wife, like Constance cared whether he'd had one or one hundred failed relationships. Like that exonerated him.

He'd deserved every ounce of her scorn, but he'd still been shocked by the way she went for his throat. As much as Kai enjoyed her calm, submissive nature, it had kind of thrilled him to realize she had a hell of a spine when she wanted to.

He had been proud to lead his odalisque through the luxuriously appointed hotel lobby on his arm, and happy to fuck her twice in a row on their new hotel bed. They'd picked over a room service dinner and then Constance had fallen asleep like a kitten in his arms.

But Kai dreaded the night ahead, and fought sleep. Kai always dreamed in hotel rooms, and the dreams were always the same. He tried to change things to make the dreams stop. Turn the air on louder or softer, pile the pillows higher. Drink less coffee, or more wine at dinner. It never worked.

The dreams always started on a beach, a wide expanse of silty sand dotted with broken seashells. The horizon was always blindingly bright, the sun a ball of wonder in the sky. But the water always looked murky. There was always wind, and the oppressive feel of an approaching storm. Then the voices would start, excited, high pitched voices. The children would run toward him, all of them three years old, or maybe four. Two boys and a little girl. He would open his arms to gather them close, to embrace them, but they were too excited. They would run away from him, toward the shoreline, toward the ever-heightening waves.

"Be careful," he would yell. "Come back." But they never listened. He would chase them, trying to corral them, but in trying to catch all of them, he'd manage to catch none. While he watched in helpless horror, all three of them would be overtaken by the surf. They would be pulled under the waves, gasping for air, their black locks turning drab and dark, their eyes wide in surprise.

They would stare at him, calling "Help, help" in those sweet, childlike voices that made him want to cry. They would bob in the water, struggling, and then they'd be gone while he stood with his feet rooted to the spot. Their little dark heads would disappear, leaving only the water dragging sand and shell pieces out into the deep. He would be left feeling, somehow, like he forgot to save them. *Oh God, I have to save them!* The realization would hit him like a kick to the chest—

Kai bolted up in bed, reaching out, running for them now, but the dream was over as always. Too late. There was only Constance beside him, looking alarmed and sleep-dazed. Kai took a deep breath and reached out to stroke her face.

"Are you okay?" she signed. "You were shaking the whole bed."

If she wasn't deaf, she probably would have heard him howling too, yelling unheeded words at his children. *Be careful. Come back!* He felt the grief still on him and in him, like the oppressive air and the salty smell of the ocean. He swallowed past the lump in his throat, terrified he might break down and cry in front of her.

"It's okay," he said. "Go back to sleep."

But his jaw was so tight he could hardly say the words. Constance slipped out of bed and came back a moment later holding a glass of water. He took it from her and held it, and made the mistake of looking in her eyes. They reflected his own pain and the concern she was feeling, and then a few tears did shake loose. He put the water down on the bedside table and wiped at them angrily. They weren't tears of sadness. They were tears of rage, of anguish. Of helplessness.

He kicked the sheets away and fell on her, kissing her hard, tasting his tears in her mouth. He knew he was acting abrupt and crazy. She was afraid. He could tell it, but he couldn't stop. He searched her warm, firm curves and whispered reassurances against her neck that she couldn't hear. He spread her legs and thrust inside her roughly, but it was okay. She was wet, so wet. She was wet from the last time he'd fucked her and she would be wet, he knew, until the very last time they fucked. That's what he loved about her. She was there, ready for him, always. He could depend on her.

Constance held onto his shoulders, pressing close against him, seeking solace from his storm. His grief and rage were subsumed into mindless wild need for her. He was fucking her, but he could just as well have been hugging her, or swimming beside her in the grotto, their hands groping one another under the glittering ripples of water. *Ah, Constance.* He would hurt her if he wasn't careful. Hurt her now with his pounding strokes...or hurt her later when they had to part.

He fucked her until the last bitter tear streaked down his face, until the lump of desolation in his throat allowed him to draw breath again. When he came inside her, it was like a great unwinding, a great exhalation of air. She didn't come. She hadn't even tried to, only held him through the torrent of his meltdown. *I'm sorry, Constance. None of this is your fault.*

Afterward he pressed her down against the fine hotel linens until his cock softened and slid away from her. He heaved himself off and rolled onto his back, his arm slung over his eyes. She lay still beside him a long time, and then shifted as if to leave. He shot out a hand to grab her.

"Where you are going?"

She made the sign for "t" and shook it. Bathroom. Her eyes were wide. He was still scaring her. God, he hated hotels and the dreams they brought him. Tomorrow he'd put her in a separate room. Except he was pretty sure the hotels in this area were all booked. Why the hell hadn't he bought a place in New York ages ago? Or booked a goddamn suite so she could have her own room?

Because, for once, you had an excuse to sleep with her in your arms.

Constance stayed in the bathroom a long time, probably hoping he'd fall back to sleep before she came out, but Kai knew he wouldn't do any more sleeping tonight. When she finally crept back to the bed, he held out his hand to her. He used the other hand to sign "I'm sorry." He really was.

She shrugged and sat across from him on the bed, so serene and accepting. He suddenly wanted to tell her everything, unburden the painful secret he kept in his heart.

"I had children." He had to sign it, because he knew she couldn't read his lips in the dim room. "Three of them. They died."

Constance looked shocked. "Oh, God. How?"

"Well, they were never born. My ex-wife aborted them." He didn't know the sign for *aborted*. He used a word like throw out or throw away, coming from his middle, and she seemed to understand. Her eyes went wide and sad.

"I'm sorry," she signed.

Kai rubbed his forehead. "I never knew until...after. Now I carry them around with me like ghosts. I feel them here," he said, pressing his hand against his chest. "I see them everywhere. I see some kid walking around... God, little Indian kids are the worst. Like a punch in the gut. I wonder what they would have been like. What they might have done in life. I think of grandchildren I might have had." He stopped, his throat clenching up tight again. "I know it's stupid. I don't know why I can't just let it go. They were never even born."

Constance shook her head. "It's not stupid," she signed with emphasis. "It's normal to grieve for children you lost. Even ones that weren't born." She thought a moment, biting her lip. "If you want a family, you could still have one. They wouldn't be the same as the children you lost, but—"

"No. No, no, no." Kai snapped his fingers together in the negative sign.

"Why not?" Her gaze was intent in the darkness. "I'm sure some woman would be happy to marry you and have your children."

Kai snorted. "You think? Once she realizes how rich I am, maybe. I don't trust women. I can't. Three non-children tell me I can't trust women."

"That's a pretty broad statement, to not trust women just because one did this to you."

"One?" Kai was waving his hands around, signing a little loudly. "Constance, when you have money, you can't trust women. Ever."

Constance's hands fell still a moment. She looked away, past his shoulder and then back again. "I don't believe that. I think you're a smart enough man to know if a woman is using you."

"Ha. No. I'm not." He didn't know why he was being so rude to Constance when she was only trying to help, when he'd felt so close to her just moments before. But she had no idea what the world looked like from his vantage point. Constance, for whom everything was cleanly and contractually spelled out. Constance, who had an overmistress looking out for her best interests.

"You seem upset," she signed finally. "May I serve you again?"

Serve him again? His mouth twisted and the signs came out garbled and frustrated. "'May I serve you again?'" he repeated. "That's your answer to everything. You want to serve me? How about you give me a baby? Three of them, in fact. Oh wait, that's not in the contract. These things need to be in contracts I guess, or someone ends up getting fucked over." His face started to flame from regret before he even slapped the last words out.

Constance watched him in awful stillness, a statue in the darkened room. Then she dropped her eyes and her hands came to rest, like a period, in her lap.

He reached out and took one of her hands. "I'm sorry. Go to bed, Constance," he said in the darkness. "I don't need anything. I just had a bad dream."

Kai lay back on the pillow, and after another moment of watching him in silent question, Constance did the same. He still held her hand, reluctant to release it. Over time, he felt it relax, then fall open as her breaths lengthened. He listened to the in-and-out of her breathing until dawn lit the slivers at the edges of the heavy hotel curtains.

Next thing he knew, he was awakening to the sound of rain beating against the window. He shifted and felt Constance beside him. Half-asleep, he thought he'd forgotten to leave her room. Then the haze of confusion cleared and he remembered they were in a hotel. Then he remembered his breakdown the night before. Jesus, he'd *cried* in front of her. He must have been more stressed out about this trip than he thought.

He rolled over to look at the clock. It was nearly eleven. He still needed to unpack and go over his speech for that night. Not to mention get Constance to look at his other speeches. In a few minutes time on the plane she'd turned his so-so speech into a standing ovation type thing. Talented girl.

But Constance was out, fast asleep. She slept until noon most days, no matter how much noise he made. She'd even slept through an earthquake once, which had amused her but startled him. He'd fretted about fires and her inability to hear the house alarm, but she'd just shrugged and pulled him into bed with her.

"I can take care of myself," she'd said. Maybe she was right. Last night, anyway, when he'd been beside himself and freaked out, she'd reacted with equivocal calm. Probably one more thing she'd learned at Odalisque School. How to deal with freaked-out lovers. Constance's solution, as always, had been sex.

Her lashes moved and then she was staring up at him with sleepy green eyes. He kissed her right cheek and licked her face from chin to temple. She laughed softly and pushed at him. She tasted like flowers. His cock was stone hard, just as it was every morning. Was she angry with him over his outburst yesterday? Still freaked out? He shouldn't have mocked her for offering to serve him. Her service was precious to him.

Kai wanted to show her how much he loved her. And he did love her desperately. That was suddenly clear to him in the dim hotel room with the rain beating on the windows and her warm, lithe body pressed against him. Her legs opened without prompting, welcoming him to come inside.

He pulled away instead. He wanted to see her better. He went to pull back the curtains and paused to look out at the city through the blur of raindrops. They were high up, high enough to look down on buildings and roads, people hurrying along with their tiny dots of umbrellas. He turned back to her.

She signed, "It's raining?"

He nodded. "It sounds nice. Relaxing."

She gave him an impish smile. "I know something else relaxing." Her hands paused as her eyes dropped to his upstanding cock. "I think you could use some relaxing."

He chuckled and crossed the room, basking in her admiring gaze. He shouldn't love her. He usually tried not to love her, but this morning he'd allow himself to fail in that endeavor. He crawled into the bed and ran his hands up her calves and over her thighs. He parted her, staring at her most private place. She let him look his fill, unlike other women who usually squirmed away or clamped their legs shut. He loved the smell of Constance, the taste of her, the sleekness of her pussy with its swollen glistening folds.

He looked up at her. She was watching him, placid, expectant.

"You're so beautiful."

Kai said that to her every time he went down on her, and she smiled every time. He slid his thumbs into the valleys of her labia and lapped up the sheen of nectar he found there. Until Constance, he'd never been much into going down on women. He did it for their pleasure, because he believed in giving as good as he got, but he'd never really enjoyed it until he'd tasted Constance. She had a flavor other women didn't have. A responsiveness that was natural and not contrived.

He took his time, and she never rushed him. He explored all the parts of her he'd come to know with lips, teeth, and tongue. He nudged her clit with the tip of his nose and then laved it with a flat stroke. Her hips undulated and bucked under him. When she really got close to orgasm, she became very vocal. He didn't think she even realized it. She was normally very self-conscious about her vocalizations. But when he teased her and drew things out, and tickled that spot on the tip of her clit, she made the most wonderful noises. Noises like any hearing girl might make.

She was making them now, sighs and whines and moans low in her throat. She wrapped her fingers in his hair. She was a hair puller. Kai reached up and caught her hands in his own, pinning them beside her. She shuddered, strung tight like a bow, as he nipped and sucked and kissed her pussy. He let go of one of her hands to press a finger inside her, then two. She ground her mound against his hand and went right back to pulling his hair at the same time. With a pitched groan, she tensed, and then he felt her sheath contract around his fingers with almost enough power to force them out. The orgasm seemed to go on and on, and he gently licked her clit until she nudged his head away.

"No," she signed weakly. "I'm too sensitive now."

She said that every time too. Kai smiled and eased up the length of her sated body, cupping her pussy in his hand, giving her time to

141

recuperate. He was near to bursting. He kissed her, and she licked her scent from his lips with an avidity that almost banished his control. A moment of rest, and she was practically climbing him. He rolled under her and pulled her astride him, driving in to the hilt. He shivered, overwhelmed by the sensation of her tight pussy enveloping him so suddenly and completely. He grabbed a handful of her ass cheeks and squeezed.

She arched her back and ran her hands over his chest. From the noises she was making, she'd never really lost the arousal of her first orgasm. She swiveled her hips, riding him with abandon. He pushed one of her hands behind her and she fondled his balls the way he'd taught her, building pleasure and pressure at the base of his cock. He started groping her breasts, pinching the nipples. They'd gone from his leisurely oral enjoyment of her charms to a frenzy of fucking.

And then he heard her say his name. *Kai.* She whispered it, her eyes closed, her head thrown back in passion, but he heard it even over the pelting of the rain. She said it perfectly, a breathy, throaty rendition.

Again, please. He wanted her to say it again, but she was lost to him, in her own erotic world. She twitched her hips and her hands clenched on his shoulders, then she collapsed, her pussy milking his cock with waves of orgasm. He was helpless to hold off any longer. He came along with her, his hips coming off the bed, his cock driving as deep as he could go. The pulses of his climax were divine, gratifying relief. His orgasm was like the rain—drenching. He let it settle over him, holding onto it until the last possible moment.

Then his whole body relaxed, as did hers. She slid to the side and buried her face against his chest. After the delight of his orgasm, he got this too, her sex-drunk affection. She toyed with the trail of dark hair on his lower abdomen, her fingertips nearly bringing him to arousal again. He finally pushed her hand away.

"Stop," he signed in front of her eyes. "I'm too sensitive now."

She looked up at him and laughed, and he thought *I love you.* He almost signed it. His hands made fists to prevent the words. He couldn't love her. It wasn't how this was supposed to work. Love had caused all the problems he'd wanted to escape, and he was pretty sure she felt more or less the same way. That was why she'd become an odalisque, and why he'd gone in search of one.

Still...

He pulled her up until her head rested on his shoulder, and ran a finger down her cheek. "You okay?"

She sat up beside him and stretched her arms over her head. "Sure, I'm fine. I'm glad you're feeling better this morning."

"I'm sorry about the way I acted last night. I shouldn't have taken my frustrations out on you."

She thought a moment before she signed again. "I understand. You were just feeling really emotional. I guess that's why Bastien always warned us not to get emotionally involved."

He didn't know what was worse—her dismissive words or the fleeting censure on her face. Kai hadn't told anyone about his lost children, not even his sister. This morning, he'd felt so close to Constance. Now she was back to pushing him away. His whole body went tight and he felt unreasonable anger. "I'm sorry I burdened you with my emotional problems. I won't do it again."

He turned away before she could answer. He got out of bed and went to the bathroom, scowling at himself in the mirror. *I guess that's why Bastien always warned us not to get emotionally involved.* Fuck Bastien. That fucker. Even if it was true—even if he'd been thinking the same thing a few minutes before—he hated hearing it from her.

Kai listened to the rumble of thunder. The storm was getting worse, not better. The storm outside, and the storm in his soul. He walked back into the room. Constance was writing in her notebook, her face expressionless, blithe. She barely spared him a glance. She was so cool, so untouchable. He felt like an outsider beating on the window of a wonderland, peering through the glass at the marvels inside. Unable to get in.

Chapter Fourteen: New York

They had been in New York a week. Constance was getting used to spending each evening dolled up in glittering gowns. Diamond necklaces and earrings were delivered to the hotel each afternoon, and returned by courier the following day. Rentals, Kai said. She was afraid to ask what they were worth.

Constance wasn't sure how she felt about all this charity business. Tonight they were at a fundraising concert at Lincoln Center. There was a reception and dinner first, followed by a performance. Kai told her the tickets cost between ten thousand and twenty-five thousand dollars each.

Kai wasn't making a speech tonight, but he was still "working," pulling off a combination of posturing, socializing, and schmoozing which he did very well. Constance's job was easier. She just had to look pretty on his arm, and smile at all the very rich people filing by. She both admired and disliked these people. She couldn't help but be impressed by their jewels and ornate gowns, and the air of *richesse* they communicated. It was so natural and effortless, it had to be inborn.

At the same time, there was something disingenuous about these events. The champagne, the caviar, the thousands of flowers decorating the ballrooms and tables. How much of the money they were donating went to pay for these things? Constance thought you could send a hundred inner-city children to private school for the cost of one party.

Feed a hundred homeless teens for six months or even a year. When she questioned Kai about it, he only shrugged and said that was how things worked.

He'd been somewhat short with her since the night he cried. He still fucked her regularly, and even tied her up now and again, gazing at her with a thoughtful look in his eyes. But he kept an emotional distance. Of course, that was for the best. That was what she'd been trying so hard to accomplish herself.

She had never in her life seen a man cry, except on TV and movies. She thought hard, trying to remember, but she hadn't, not in real life. It had frightened her to her very core, to see Kai lose it, even though she understood more than anyone how real nightmares could feel. And when he'd asked her for children, a little part of her heart had died.

Maybe he hadn't even been serious. Still, like his ex-wife, she would never give him children. She didn't want children, not her own. She wanted to help other people's kids, the runaways and throwaways of the world, not fritter her life away changing diapers and arranging society playdates. One more reason to hold Kai at arm's length. It was for his own good.

She watched Kai now—confident, smiling, rubbing shoulders with the glitterati—and she couldn't place that falling apart man from the week before. Kai had a way of standing with his chest out, his chin up, his body moving easily and gracefully. He had that manner of *richesse* like all the others, but she knew he hadn't been born rich. So perhaps it could be learned. Constance became highly aware of how she moved, how she held her head. She tried to trick the golden society around her into believing she fit in.

The rental diamonds probably helped.

Kai introduced her to everyone as Miss Constance Flynn. It sounded very retro and romantic. He didn't specify if she was his friend, girlfriend, or work acquaintance. She supposed he was content to let everyone draw their own conclusions from the way he treated her, from his manner of remote affection. He returned to her now from a conversation a few feet away. He tilted his head, slid a hand down her bare arm.

"You have goosebumps. Are you cold?"

She nodded. Yes, she was cold. She missed her nakedness, her warm odella and saray back at Kai's home. Kai slept restlessly, and she wasn't used to having a bedmate. The diamond necklaces scratched her neck and the earrings were heavy at her ears. Her head ached because the stylist Kai had hired to do her hair used a thousand sharp pins for every up-do. But she couldn't wear her hair down. No one here did. All the feminine hair in sight was twisted, pinned, and bejeweled into submission. All the eyes were fastidiously made up, all the lips pink or red, many grotesquely altered by plastic surgery.

Kai pulled her next to him, squeezing her a little. He was trying to warm her up, but his tux was silk and slippery and not warm at all. Then, with an abrupt movement, he turned her and tapped her chin. A shorthand he'd developed for *Listen to me*.

"Mason is headed this way with his wife. You have to pretend you never met him before."

Constance was puzzled. "Why?" she signed. "I thought he had an open marriage."

"He does. But she doesn't know about you. It's a long story. Just play dumb."

Just play dumb. That was a really insulting phrase to someone who chose not to speak. Long ago, Constance would have been described as deaf and dumb. No one used dumb anymore, except as a synonym for stupid. Constance knew Kai didn't know any of that, but she still seethed inwardly as Mason approached with his sexy, glamorous wife. Constance knew who she was, of course. Jessamine Jackson had a big film that had just come out, about some mistress of international intrigue.

Up close, the starlet looked smaller than she did on screen, more brittle. She had tiny lines beside her eyes. Constance thought she was probably already conferring with the plastic surgeons. Mason looked suave and haughty beside her. It annoyed her, the playacting. His eyes swept over her, feigning polite curiosity. Constance frowned back.

Kai greeted them and introduced her the same way he'd introduced her to everyone else. *This is Miss Constance Flynn.* They both shook her hand. Mason was a consummate actor. He acted exactly like someone who'd never met her before. Who'd never fucked her or spanked her or fixed her with nipple clamps to a huge iron bed. Jessamine sized her up openly and then gave Kai an assessing look. Kai deflected it with a question.

"How long are you two in New York? I didn't expect to see you here."

Jessamine rolled her eyes. "We were bored." She said more, but it was hard for Constance to read her lips. She had a pinched way of talking, and a lot of flirty business going on with her mouth that obscured the syllables Constance needed. Instead, Constance looked at Mason. He might have been blushing a little. Constance sidled closer to Kai, wishing she was anywhere but here. It bothered her that Mason was sneaking around with her behind his wife's back. Constance had assumed it was all in the open. It bothered her more that she was forced to play along now, right in front of his wife's face.

Kai nudged her. Jessamine had asked a question. He asked it again, signing at the same time. "Jessamine asked if you come often to New York."

Constance shook her head. "Just tell her the truth," she signed to Kai. "You dragged me here."

Kai chuckled and told Jessamine that Constance had come along on the trip to support him. Jessamine made some more flirty remarks about Kai having a new love and keeping secrets from her. *No*, thought Constance. *It's your husband keeping secrets.* Through all this, Mason stood in silence. Before long, Jessamine turned her attention to him, and in that moment Constance knew that, despite Mason's acting, his wife suspected something.

Jessamine looked back at Constance, who tried her best to appear rich and blasé. Constance turned to Kai. "Tell them whatever you want. I'm going to the ladies' room." She escaped the little pow-wow with a sense of relief. She stayed in the bathroom until it started to empty and then found Kai as everyone sat down for dinner. To her relief, Mason and Jessamine were a couple of tables away. Constance gave Kai an arch look.

"Did Mason keep himself out of trouble?" she signed.

Kai gave her a harried smile and flicked his napkin into his lap. "I had no idea they'd be here. I'm sorry if that was awkward. They have a...complicated marriage."

"It would seem so."

Constance let Kai do all the introductions at the table, and all the talking. Sometimes being deaf came in handy. None of the other eight people at the table were brave enough to draw her into conversation. She got painfully awkward smiles whenever she looked around, so she kept her eyes on her plate. Of course, then she started wondering, *how much did this gourmet lamb cost? How much for this china and silverware? How much for this gold-dusted dessert?*

After dinner they filed into the adjoining Metropolitan Opera House, a confection of a theater with tiers of balconies like some wedding cake. The whole auditorium glittered when everyone was in their seat. Mouths moved everywhere. Constance thought it must have created a din, all that talking, but then the lights went down and all the heads turned to the stage. Constance tried to read the playbill by the dim glow of the runner lights. *Faust*, an opera about a successful man making a deal with the devil in order to gain unlimited knowledge and worldly pleasures. Ironic. She searched the theater for Mason and Jessamine, but it was impossible to pick them out from all the other people in the dark.

Constance turned her attention to the stage instead, following the action with the help of the opera summary. It wasn't easy, since a lot of the time people were just standing around singing. There was some bit with jewels. Faust trying to seduce a lover, Marguerite, with gifts and diamonds. Hmm.

By the fourth act the opera descended into melodramatic craziness. Marguerite got pregnant and killed her child, and some other nonsense went on, with Faust going to hell in the end and Marguerite to heaven. The two main characters sang a long, histrionic duet to close the opera, and Kai gave her a sideways look from beneath his lashes.

"You're so lucky you can't hear this," he mouthed.

Constance had to smother her laughter behind her hands.

* * * * *

Ugh, *Faust*. Kai had spent his irritation with the bloated opera in Constance's arms afterward. He'd left her sleeping, curled up in a nest of pillows, and was headed down to the hotel bar for a much needed drink. Kai thought he was a lot like Faust, only he hadn't made a deal with the devil for worldly pleasures. He'd made a deal with Sebastien Gaudet, and Constance Flynn, of course. She was Marguerite. She would go to heaven at the end, with his money, and he'd be left in hell.

Such thoughts. He was turning into an ass, wallowing in self-pity. He had to pull himself out of this slump. Kai headed across the bar to find Mason already seated at a table.

"What are you doing here?" Kai slid into a seat across from his friend.

"Same thing you're doing. Trying to get that opera shit out of my head."

Kai laughed and leaned back in his chair. "Where's Jess?"

"With some female she knows in Tribeca."

"Ouch."

"It's better than her being here, asking a lot of questions."

"You should have gone too. Must be fun to watch your wife with another woman."

Mason shrugged. "We've been married six years now. I've seen it a million times. What are you drinking?"

Kai flagged down the waitress for a vodka tonic, then listened as Mason launched into a scathing deconstruction of the night. By the end Kai was laughing so hard he could barely breathe, as Mason re-enacted both the male and female roles from the opera they'd watched.

"The food was good anyway, wasn't it?" Kai asked.

"Oh hell, the food was delicious. Speaking of delicious, your odalisque seemed uncharacteristically cranky tonight."

Kai wagged a finger at him. "I don't think she approves of you keeping secrets from your wife."

Mason snorted. "Oh yeah, that would have been a scene, if Jess had found out she was an odalisque I'd been seeing behind her back."

Kai stirred the ice in his drink. "You know, she's going to find out eventually, Mace."

"Yeah, yeah, she'll find out. I'll cross that bridge when I come to it. So really, Constance disapproves? She told you that?"

"She didn't have to. I know her well enough by now to tell. You said yourself she looked cranky. I don't think she liked having to pretend for your sake."

"Hm." The idea seemed to puzzle Mason. "I love pretending. Anyway, she's a sex slave. She doesn't exactly have a moral high ground to stand on."

"Oh, but she does, my friend. Constance is all about honesty and frankness. She follows that damn odalisque code obsessively. With *religious* zeal."

"And I'm sure you're fucking her with equally religious zeal, so why don't you just shut the fuck up and stop whining? Oh, that reminds me. Jess wants to organize a scatter party for New Years Eve, and she wants to hold it at your house."

"Oh, yeah? Nice of you to let me in on the plan."

Scatter parties, one of Jess's favorite perverse pastimes. A group of couples showed up, scattered, and had sex with whomever they ran across. Kai had been to a few in the past. He always hoped they'd be exciting and erotic, but they were usually more awkward than anything. Kai shrugged. "I guess it's okay. I don't have any plans yet for New Years. Who's she going to ask?"

Mason shrugged. "Let her handle that. She knows all the beautiful people. She won't invite any gremlins."

"I wasn't worried about gremlins. I'm more worried about how many people are actually going to be fornicating in my house."

"Well, what do you want to cap it at?"

"I don't know. Some reasonable number."

Mason chuckled. "Jess is never reasonable. How about we tell her eight? Eight couples. Too many? Me and Jess, you and Constance, and six beyond that. I know Jeremy and Nell are itching to get out and swing a little now that they're back in L.A. And maybe the sheik and his odalisque..."

Kai gave Mason a suspicious look. "Who's planning this? You or Jess?"

Mason held up his hands. "I swear, it was her idea. But I might have encouraged her. Some of us have to get by in life without odalisques. It's not fair, you know."

"You get plenty of use out of mine." Kai punched at the lime in his drink with his fingertip. "And not everything about odalisques strokes the ego. Constance is very insistent about the fact that she only cares for me as her owner, for instance. She never lets me forget it." Kai clamped his mouth shut. He had apparently had quite enough to drink. He was getting sloppy. And bitter.

"Huh? Hold up." Mason looked befuddled. "Are you saying you want her to care about you as *more* than her owner?"

"Well, no. I mean... Look, the whole thing has just been—" Again, Kai shut his mouth.

"What?" Mason prodded. "Better or worse than you expected?"

"It's not better or worse. It's just not what I expected, and I'm not sure..."

Mason's eyes went wide. "She's not doing it for you? Really? When you shelled out a million bucks?"

"No, it has nothing to do with her. It's—it's probably my problem."

Mason blew out a breath. "I'm sorry, man. That really sucks. Can't you, I don't know, exchange her or something? Try another girl?"

Kai sighed. "Let's just drop it, Mace."

"But—"

"Why don't we start talking about you and Jess's problems then?"

"Fine, I'll drop it." Mason hunched over his drink. "Hey, if you're just going to hang out here boozing and bitching, mind if I go up?"

Kai looked sideways at his friend. "Without me?"

"I don't need you there to get hard, bro. No offense."

"No, that's not what I meant. I'm not supposed to give her to other men if I'm not there to supervise." It wasn't really a hard and fast rule. In fact, Kai was pretty sure he'd just made it up. He was jealous that Mason could still look at Constance like some commodity to be shared. Mason was the one who should have gotten an odalisque. He would have been great at it. He wouldn't have been fighting himself, like Kai, to stay in the right mindset.

Kai rubbed his forehead and gave Mason an exasperated look. "It astounds me that someone with such a hot wife is always sniffing after my girl."

"Ah, but my wife is not here, and your girl is."

"Constance is probably sleeping."

Mason rolled his eyes. "If you don't want to share, Kaivalyan, man up and say so."

Kai wanted to say so, but another part of him wanted to prove to himself that he could be as matter-of-fact about Constance's status as Mason was. As Constance was herself.

"Okay," Kai said, draining the last of his drink. "But only a quick fuck. No big play scenes. I've had enough theater for one night."

"Spanking?"

"No, you pervert. What's wrong with you?"

They stumbled into the hotel room in the dark, and before Kai could stop him, Mason shook Constance and startled her. Kai knew Mason didn't realize how deeply she slept without the intrusion of sounds. Kai watched Constance, hoping for some kind of overt reaction. Distaste, resentment, indignation. If she had reacted with any kind of negativity he could have sent Mason away with a clear conscience, but she turned and opened her body to them before she was even fully awake. Mason was naked in a heartbeat, rolling on a condom and sliding into bed behind her.

"You fucking her too, man?" he asked, running a hand over Constance's hip.

"No. Help yourself."

Mason frowned slightly and gave him a look, which Kai ignored. His friend slipped his fingers between Constance's thighs. She arched back against Mason in a sleepy feline stretch. She had grown close to him. It was beautiful to watch, and yet disgusting. No, he was disgusted with himself. Mason was an excellent lover. Let him have her. Let her have the pleasure. That was what she was made for.

Kai undressed, hanging up his tuxedo pants and Mason's too. Fastidious details to distract him from the soft moans on the bed. Kai hesitated a moment, and then joined them, lying against Constance's front. Why not? She belonged to him. She stroked his shoulders, smiling her graceful smile.

Kai kissed her softly, drawing her close even as Mason drilled her from behind. Finally Kai pulled back and fingered a twisting lock of her hair. It was still wet from the shower, cool and silken in his fingers, in contrast to her body heat.

Mason was fucking her harder now. Constance reached between her legs, her eyes glazing over. Kai knew she could orgasm from penetration without clitoral stimulation, but she told him it felt better when she had both. He added a third sensation for her, pinching the taut peaks of her nipples with ruthless ferocity. Her mouth fell open in a gasp of pleasure. When she came, her whole body shuddered. Mason came soon after with a jerk and a shout. Kai watched, fully aroused but too conflicted to follow Mason into her pussy. Not tonight.

A few moments later, Mason gave Constance a squeeze and extricated himself from the tangled bed sheets. "Thanks, man," he said to Kai. "That always hits the spot. She's so fucking respo—"

"Responsive. I know. You say that every time."

"I'll have to think of a new word. Refreshing. Enthusiastic. Marvelous. Superb."

"Mason, just go. I'm tired."

Mason gave him another look, then dressed and took himself off without another word. Kai rolled onto his back with a sigh of frustration. Constance sat up beside him.

"Is everything okay?" she signed. "May I serve you too?"

Yes, you can serve me. By refusing to sleep with Mason or any of my other friends again. By falling in love with me, the way I've fallen in love with you.

He didn't say that, of course. He didn't say anything. He really was way, way too tired.

Chapter Fifteen:
Party

Constance returned home from New York with a renewed determination to adhere to the *Code d'Odalisque*. Being out and about on Kai's arm had felt way too girlfriend-y. She even started to entertain some far out secret fantasies about becoming his wife, and that's when she knew she was crossing a line.

She really needed to be with someone she didn't love so much, like Mason Cooke. Mason was as sexy and rich as Kai, but he didn't affect her the way Kai did.

But then, Mason wasn't doing so well. He still showed up at Kai's house a couple times a week, but he spent the rest of his time working too hard and drinking himself to sleep. Mason never talked about his wife, the statuesque, glacial-eyed woman Constance had met at the Lincoln Center fundraiser. He didn't have to. Things clearly weren't going well. Mason and Jessamine were featured on the covers of the tabloids, smiling and clinging to one another at red carpet events, but Constance knew those smiles for a lie.

November turned to December and Kai had to turn the heater up again in Constance's odella. Somehow she hadn't felt quite as cold at the end of last winter, when she'd first arrived. Now the next winter was starting. *Winter. That's it, girl. One more season. Then you leave.*

The holidays came, and Constance steeled herself against sentimentality. It was harder than ever when Kai was playing Santa at the Kids Making Music Christmas Eve concert. She couldn't hear the underprivileged children's orchestra play, but she could see the shining faces of their proud parents, and Kai's own blissed-out smile under his white Santa beard. Why did he have to be so perfectly wonderful? Satya was there too, applauding and jumping up to help her brother distribute gifts.

The three of them had gone home afterward and talked long into the night, and opened gifts in the wee hours of Christmas morning. Satya stayed the next few days, hanging out with Constance and showing off all the sign language she was learning. By this point, Kai signed practically as well as Constance. Satya, quick as she was, wasn't far behind.

It had all been too perfect and heartwarming. Constance managed, barely, to keep her emotions reined in. And then the scatter party happened.

Constance had always loved New Years Eve. The celebrations, the revelry, the way people naturally sought each other out. So she'd been totally on board with the party Kai described to her. It was part swinging, part running around naked, and part getting drunk. None of them bad ways to ring in the New Year.

Jessamine and Mason arrived first, just after dinner. Jessamine leaped on Kai and wrapped her legs around his waist while Constance looked on, somewhat taken aback. "I'm searching for you first, big boy," the actress said. At least Constance thought that's what she said. It was hard to tell when she was crawling all over Kai like a nympho. *Jealous, are we?*

Constance looked over at Mason, who raised his shoulders and gave her a vaguely disgruntled look. Kai finally peeled Jessamine off him. "I think the guys get to search first."

"It's definitely the guys' turn to search first," Mason agreed. "Ladies second. Third round is anything goes."

"Only three rounds?" asked Kai, with a wink at Constance.

"Three rounds," said Jessamine. "Then the general fuckery begins. Hey, Kai, you remember the sheik I told you about? He has a new odalisque, and he's bringing her tonight."

Constance took in that information with interest. She wondered if it would be anyone she knew. She didn't have much time to think about it as the other guests started to arrive. The Grays showed up next, laughing and greeting everyone. Another power couple. Jeremy Gray's wife, Nell, wasn't an actress, but he cast enough light for them both. He was muscular, blond, with eyes even bluer than Mason's. Mason did the introductions while Kai admitted another pair of couples. Constance scrutinized each man, wondering who she would end up with.

The concept of a scatter party was simple. Everyone got naked. Then either the men or women got ten minutes to "scatter," that is, hide somewhere in the house. The lights were turned low, and then the players searched until they found someone. And they fucked whoever they found. It was kind of like an x-rated version of hide-and-seek.

So far, there wasn't anyone Constance wouldn't mind being found by. She knew Kai and Mason well already, and Jeremy Gray was the epitome of cosmopolitan, manly cool. The next two couples were older attractive men with smiling, sexy wives. Second wives probably. Trophy wives. A little disgusting, but she had a thing for older men. Another couple arrived and Mason nudged her.

"That's the sheik," he mouthed for her benefit, but she already knew. She recognized the odalisque on his arm. Constance gave Jenna a furtive wave, and was rewarded with a dimpled smile.

"Hey," said Mason, touching her arm. "No odalisque bonding tonight. Jess doesn't know...still..."

Constance rolled her eyes and dug in her pocket for the small notebook she'd be using for the night. *Why don't you just tell your wife what I am? I don't think she would care.*

Mason shook his head, grimacing. "She would care. She would be mad I haven't shared you with her."

I'm not yours to share, Constance wrote.

"That wouldn't matter to her."

Jeremy beckoned Mason over to help open bottles of bubbly, and the champagne started flowing. Constance stayed on the outskirts of the chattering couples and wondered when the clothes would start coming off. She was dressed, like everyone else, although she'd argued with Kai that she didn't see the point.

"Be civilized," he'd signed to her with a smirk. "You'll freak everyone out if you open the door naked. But you'll be able to take your clothes off soon enough." They were still waiting for two more couples. The next couple was not long in arriving. A tall, handsome black man and his strangely demure wife. Interesting, how conservative she looked.

Just as Constance was picturing the shy woman ripping off her clothes and pouncing on one of the men—Kai perhaps—the doorbell rang again and the last couple came in.

They were both drop dead gorgeous. He was broad, compact, with a great smile and a laid back air. He had a stunning woman on his arm. She was petite and curvy, with large doe eyes and a full head of cascading blonde hair. It seemed that every head turned in unison to stare at her. Then they all turned to stare at Kai.

* * * * *

Jessamine turned to Kai, her hands outstretched already to calm him.

"Now, honey—"

"Jess! You invited my wife? Seriously?"

"Your *ex*-wife. It's been a year already, and she happens to be one of my best friends. And her new guy is just—" Jessamine licked her lips and rolled her eyes back in her head. "Too yummy to leave out!"

Kai took her arm and scowled at her. "You are truly an epic bitch. You know that?"

Jess was nonplussed, pulling away and laughing off his anger. "I love when you get rough, Kaivalyan. Look, just be a grown up. Veronica has moved on. Why can't you? You have your pretty little girlfriend to keep you happy." Jess flicked a hand over at Constance, who was watching every word between them. He felt bolstered by her expression of outrage, and the narrowed eyes she turned on his ex.

Kai hated that Veronica looked better than ever. Jess moved off to welcome her and the guy she was with. Kai refused to look at either one of them, heading over to Constance instead. She touched his forearm.

"That's her? Your ex-wife?"

Kai gritted his teeth. "Unfortunately, yes."

"Can't you make her leave? Get rid of her? If you want me to be the bad guy, I'll happily boot her out on her ass."

Kai grabbed her hands, feeling unlikely laughter bubbling in his throat. How she could have him going from furious rage to mirth in the space of a few seconds, he'd never know. But he thought about his sweet-tempered odalisque marching over and strong-arming Veronica out the door, and laughed again. He pulled Constance close, shooting a look over at his ex. Veronica was watching him, and he could see the curiosity in her eyes. Did she think she could just show up and ruin his New Years?

He looked down at Constance. "As much as I would enjoy watching you drag Veronica out to the street by her fake-blonde hair, I have a better idea. Let's have a fun time in spite of her, and show her how little I really care."

Constance smiled back at him conspiratorially. "I think that's a fantastic plan. But what if you're the one who finds her after we scatter?" she signed, raising her eyebrows.

"Fuck that," answered Kai. "I'll walk on by."

Jessamine clapped her hands, calling for everyone's attention. If Jess had wanted a big scene when Veronica arrived, she was certainly disappointed. Kai detected an edge of pique in her voice.

"Everyone! Listen!" Jessamine started taking off her top. That brought the room to a standstill. She flung it across the room to land on top of Kai's piano, and picked up her champagne glass with a grin.

"I want to begin by thanking everyone for coming together tonight to ring in the New Year the best way I know how—with lots of horny sex!"

A chorus of cheers and ribald comments went up from the assembled company. God, they were all a bunch of pervs, thought Kai. And he was included in that group. He looked over at Constance. She smiled back at him, then returned her gaze to Jessamine's lips.

"So, you all know how this works. You have ten minutes to hide in some secret corner—preferably a corner conducive to fucking. Whoever finds you gets to have you." Kai reached over to squeeze Constance's ass, eliciting a giggle from her.

"Tonight is going to be a three rounder," Jess continued. "As our gracious host Kai reminded me, it's the men's turn to hunt first. The ladies hunt second, and then for the third round, it's whoever stumbles across whoever first." Another round of cheers went up as Jessamine batted her eyes suggestively. She really was good at this stuff.

"Around midnight, we'll reconvene and ring in the New Year all together"—she raised her eyebrows—"if you know what I mean. Just so everyone knows, the rooms up those stairs are private and off-limits. There are plenty of rooms down here and in the back wing, which you can get to behind the kitchen. Men must wear condoms. No exceptions. You have one hour to play with your prey, and then we reassemble here.

And no searching out the same partner in subsequent rounds!" She gave all of them a vixenish look. "Variety is the spice of life, no?"

Kai scanned the room, lightly rubbing Constance's back. Who would he end up with first? Who would his odalisque end up with? He knew all the men, except for Veronica's other half. He hoped to God she didn't get found by him. He knew for sure Constance wouldn't seek Veronica's guy out in the second round, unless it was to kick him in the nuts. Kai tapped her shoulder while Jessamine fielded some last minute questions.

"You're okay with this?" he asked. "Now that you've seen the candidates?"

Constance swept a look around. "Pretty impressive company," she signed with a grin. "I like you best, but I guess they'll do for one night."

"Oh!" Jessamine's voice rose again over the chatter. "I almost forgot. Kai's partner Constance is deaf. She can read lips, but if she wants to talk to you she'll use her notebook." All the eyes in the room fixed on the woman beside him. Constance held up her notebook with a half smile. Kai wanted to say more, the overprotective owner. *Don't cover up her eyes. Make sure you look at her when you talk. Don't startle her.* But he held his peace, because he knew Constance preferred to take care of herself.

With the preliminary announcements done, everyone downed the last of their champagne. Jessamine started distributing boxes of condoms she'd grabbed from the counter, like some perverse dessert course. "I think it's time for the first round to get underway. We don't want to miss the ball dropping at midnight. So ladies..." She started working at the waistband of her skirt. "If you would all so kindly disrobe and prepare to scatter. Men, time for you to get naked too."

Amid cracks about balls dropping, sixteen revelers started to undress, some coyly, some with bawdy glee. Again, it struck Kai how jaded they all were about sex. He was no exception, of course. Constance was evidence of that.

Kai piled his clothes on the sofa with everyone else's, and didn't even glance at Veronica, who seemed to intentionally flaunt herself to him. Was she insane? When all the women headed off in their various directions, Kai went the opposite way from where she went. He heard Jessamine's hiss and let her pull him into the coat closet. So much for guys finding girls. It was okay though, they had a score to settle. He closed the door behind him and regarded her across the cramped space. "Down on your knees," he said in a gruff tone.

Jess stiffened for a beat, and then her eyes went liquid and hot. She knelt in front of him, feigning some very realistic fear. "Are you angry with me?" she whispered. "Are you going to...force me to do reprehensible things?"

"Jessamine," Kai replied, grabbing a fistful of her hair. "By the time you leave this closet, you won't be able to face yourself in the mirror. Now open." He jerked her hair again, using the other hand to roll on a condom. "You can start by sucking my cock."

* * * * *

Constance's first partner was one of the older men. He was tall, taller even than Kai, and slim. In fact, he was quite attractive, one of those old guys who was too rich to ever look aged and worn. He reminded her a lot of Bastien, so when he found her in the laundry room and ran a hand down her arm, she acquiesced right away. They fucked on a pile of towels. He was very slow and leisurely, and very skilled. She came twice, which seemed to delight him. He spent a long time afterward just looking at her, running his fingers over her body until the hour was up. She learned later that his name was Michael, and that he was the second most powerful studio exec in Hollywood.

After that, they returned to the living room with everyone else. Kai and Jessamine stumbled out of the coat closet, both of them a bit worse for wear. When Constance grinned and eyed the scratches on Kai's chest, he shook his head at her. Then he asked, "Did your first partner work out for you?"

Constance nodded and signed, "I won't ask about yours."

Jess announced the second round. Now the men had to scatter, and the girls got to do the finding. It seemed like most of the ladies already had a man in mind. Constance saw two or three go off like a shot in Kai's direction, including his ex-wife. But Kai was a big boy, he could handle it.

Constance wandered down the hall and stopped in front of the only door that was still open. She poked her head in and almost left, seeing no one. But then a hand closed around her wrist. She almost dropped her notebook.

Mason Cooke was crouched behind the door. Hiding.

159

He pulled her down beside him and kicked the door shut. He took her head in his hands and gazed into her eyes. He looked miserable. Constance reached for her notebook and wrote *What's wrong? Aren't you having fun?*

Mason read it and gave her a rueful smile. He wrote *NO* in capital letters, underlined twice.

Constance grimaced and wrote, *Who was your first partner?*

Veronica. Mason tapped the pen and thought a moment. *She spent the whole time talking about Kai. Which is fine, because I couldn't get it up for her anyway. She wants to get back together with him. Apparently Jessamine agreed to help.*

Constance's mouth fell open. She wrote *Traitor!* and turned the page. *Kai is going to be furious.*

Mason took the notebook back. He took a long time to write, but it was only a few words. *I'm not in love with my wife anymore. I don't even think I like her at this point.* He looked over at Constance, as if to see what she thought. Constance wanted to pull him close and cradle him in her arms. He looked so devastated. She ran a hand down his cheek, over the sexy stubble that set so many hearts aflutter, while his own heart secretly ached.

Oh, Mason, she wrote. *Does she know?*

I don't think she cares. She barely acknowledges my existence anymore.

But you look so happy when you're together.

When have you ever seen us together? Out in public? At events? That's all an act. Public relations. She doesn't even look at me at home. Spends all her time out dredging up new sex partners.

Constance gave him a reproving look. *You have secret sex partners too.*

You're right, he wrote. *At least she's in my face about who she sleeps with. But you're the only one, the only secret I've kept. To protect you. Otherwise she'd want you for herself. She loves pretty girls.*

He put the pen down, and they both sat in stillness for a moment, shoulder to shoulder. Then Constance wrote, *What are you going to do?*

Mason smiled a self-deprecating smile and took the pen. *Well, when I grow some balls, I'll leave her. The tabs will have a field day. Hollywood's premier marriage on the rocks. It'll be a fucking mess.*

Constance put her hand on the back of his and took the pen. *But you'll have to do it at some point. You shouldn't be so unhappy. No matter the blowback, or the expectations, you have to be true to your heart.*

Mason looked up at her from the page, and she couldn't quite interpret his expression. Some fleeting accusation was there, perhaps, and then gone. He shrugged. *It's my problem, Constance. Don't worry about it. But thanks for listening.*

In the awkward pause that followed, Constance picked up the pen. *So, do you want to have sex? This is a scatter party, after all.*

But Mason still had a faraway look. He wrote, *Constance, do you think I'm a good person? A worthwhile person?*

Of course I do. Tons of people do. You have millions of fans.

He wrestled the pen from her. *No. They don't count. That's not really me, that person they worship. You know what? My real name is Darwin. Darwin Kulik.* He looked over at her. "It's okay, you can laugh."

Constance shook her head. *I like Darwin as a first name. It's original. Why did you change it?*

He nudged her with his shoulder and wrote, *If you ever tell anyone I'll kill you.*

Then, in a lovely release of tension, they both started to laugh. Constance watched Mason's chest expand and contract with what must have been roaring laughter. But then he wiped his eyes. Constance sobered and scooted around to the front of him.

He shook his head at her, and let her read his lips. "No, no, I'm not crying. I'm just tired. Tired of feeling like a piece of shit ornament on my wife's arm."

Constance reached down for the notebook. *You're not an ornament. You're not a piece of shit. You're a warm, loving man and a faithful friend. You're funny and talented. And very generous in bed.*

Mason took her hand. "You know, it's been so long since anyone's said anything like that to me. When they weren't, you know, obviously trying to suck up."

Constance shrugged. *I call it like I see it*, she wrote.

Mason looked back at what she'd written, running his fingers over the paper.

"Can I tear out these pages and keep them? For when I need to read those words?"

She nodded and wrote, *Maybe you should show them to Jessamine.*

Mason chuckled as he ripped out the pages of their conversation and gave the notebook back. "I don't know if I'm brave enough to do that." He folded them over and held the paper in his palm. He rested his head back against the wall and toyed with his half-hard cock. "Ugh, one more round of this." He looked at Constance. "How was your first guy?"

She lay down on her side, resting her head on her arm. She wrote, *He was a very good lover. But a lot less enthusiastic than you generally are.*

Mason leaned down to read her writing. "I'm not at my best tonight. Although things are looking up." He gave her wry smile and gestured to his cock, which was definitely perking up. He came down over her, nudging her legs apart with his knees. Constance stroked his cock and caressed his balls. Within moments Mason was fully erect. He grabbed a condom and rolled it on.

Right before he entered her, Mason pulled back and touched her cheek. "Thank you, Constance. You're so good at what you do."

They fucked on the floor, there beside the door, and ended up returning to the living room a few minutes late. But Constance was heartened to see that by the time they did, Mason was nearly back to his normal cheerful self.

Chapter Sixteen: Scattered

After the second round, Constance expected everyone to be winding down, but they all appeared to be going strong. The guests had more drinks and grabbed some of the finger foods and sushi Kai laid out.

Kai came to meet Constance by the piano. "So you snagged Mason, huh? What took you guys so long in there?"

Constance frowned. "I'll tell you later. And it's not what you think. Who found you?"

"I ended up with your odalisque sister. She was lovely." He leaned down to drop a kiss on Constance's forehead. She shivered as his fingertips grazed her nipples in a teasing touch. "Lovely, but not nearly as lovely as you."

"Such flattery," Constance signed.

"You're the loveliest girl here." Kai tapped her chin, making sure he had her attention. "Jeremy noticed the bruises on your ass, and he happens to be a serious kink player. He's already snuck up to the saray, waiting for you to 'find' him during the next round."

Constance glanced around the room. No sign of Mr. Gray. "That was very forward of him."

Kai smiled. "I told him to do it. He can be trusted. He's a good guy—and from what I understand, very fun to scene with."

"You share your toys so nicely."

"Which toys?" Kai asked. "The ones in the cabinet or the one currently snarking at me? Anyway, he told me where his wife would be hiding, and I hear she's pretty fun too." Kai pulled Constance close and gave her a squeeze. "Just save some energy for after the ball drops, because you're all mine then."

Constance gave a little shiver at the promise in his eyes, and then lurked around the shadows of the room until all the other guests had headed off into Kai's hallways for round three. Then she scurried up the stairs and snuck into her suite. It was dark in the odella, but a faint light issued from the adjoining saray. *Jeremy Gray, the movie star, is waiting in there for me...* Jeremy Gray, who must have been staring at her ass pretty intently at some point to notice those bruises, as they were nearly faded to nothing.

She walked in, searching for him, and found him standing beside Kai's cabinet. Wow. She'd been surrounded by naked bodies for the last two hours, but something about Jeremy's nakedness was impressive indeed. Maybe it was the authoritative nature of his stance, or the fact that his body didn't have an ounce of fat—only lean, gorgeous muscle. Or maybe it was the size of his—*oh my!* She blushed when her gaze finally meandered up to his eyes. She found him watching her with a knowing smile.

Well, really. The man had nothing to be ashamed of.

He beckoned her over, and when she was close enough, he put his hands on her shoulders and looked in her eyes. "Is it true? Can you tell what I'm saying from reading my lips?"

Jeremy was quite easy to read. Something about the shape of his face and his mouth. She nodded, and then remembered her notebook. She wrote, *I can hear you pretty well, as long as I'm looking at you when you talk.*

Jeremy nodded and smiled. "Fair enough. I was glad to get your owner's permission to play with you. This seems like a pretty vanilla crowd." He turned and picked up one of the straps, a particular favorite of Kai's. He ran his hand over the leather a moment, then looked back at her. "But then, I'm awfully kinky. Much like your owner, I'd say."

Kai was right. Jeremy Gray was shaping up to be pretty interesting. She eyed the strap in his hands, wondering how it would feel. Would he play with Kai's intensity? Or with Mason's playfulness? She wrote in the notebook, *It's a secret that Kai is my owner. That I'm an odalisque.*

Jeremy nodded. "I know. Fortunately, I'm good at keeping secrets."

He seemed so casual about the whole thing. A little too casual. She wrote, *Is your wife really an odalisque too?*

Jeremy threw back his head and laughed at that. "No, my wife is really my wife, and I love her desperately. Although, to be honest, I originally hired her on for a term of service too." He raised his eyebrows at Constance. "Of course, that's also a secret."

Constance made a lip-zipping motion that even a non-signer could understand. Jeremy smiled lightly, but Constance could sense the time for small talk was over. Jeremy ran his steely, blue-eyed gaze up the length of her body and back down again. "If I'd known I would have this opportunity, I could have planned something in advance. Something very elaborate and devious."

Constance bit her lip. Intense like Kai. Definitely.

"Well," Jeremy said, his chest rising and falling in a sigh. "I've never been afraid to improvise." He took the notebook from her fingers with a smooth authority that turned her on. "Shall we put this down? Kai told me about your safe word procedures, and I plan to keep you a little too busy for any more writing." He placed the notebook on one of the cabinet shelves and took her arm to lead her over to the bed. His grip was warm and firm. Within moments, she was draped face down over the padded footboard.

She looked back, nerves thrumming. Honestly, she was a little scared of him. Jeremy frowned slightly and pointed forward. "Eyes front. Keep them there."

Constance swallowed and looked ahead at the lattice of the headboard. Things could have been worse. She could have been tethered there with the nipple clamps, one of Kai and Mason's favorite games— *Ouch!*

Jeremy's first blow wasn't vicious, but it was crisp enough to have her clawing at the sheets. A couple more came on the heels of the first, burning both her ass cheeks. Jeremy paused, and it took every ounce of her control not to look back and anticipate the next stroke. It came seconds later, a real stinging one.

This wasn't safe word play, not really. Constance could take this kind of pain for hours, but it was uncomfortable in the moment. She tensed her ass, which only made the next stroke feel harder. Jeremy was laying them on faster now, warming all her sweet spots to a burning hum. Her clit was coming alive, her pussy throbbing along with her heartbeat. Sex was fine, it was great, but pain added a shimmering sheen of excitement. Pain made her wild.

By the time Jeremy finished with the strap, she was grasping the sheets in earnest, stuffing them into her mouth to keep from screaming. Jeremy stroked and squeezed her cheeks, making the burn sizzle even hotter. He nudged her legs open and parted her with his fingers, driving them deep into her pussy. She grasped at the slick protrusions, ground on them, pleasure and pain combining to near the breaking point. He withdrew them before she could come, and hauled her over to the spanking bench.

Jeremy made her straddle the narrow top platform, her pussy slipping along the vinyl. He folded down the lower platforms so her legs hung down, trembling, on either side. He worked below her to fix her ankles to a spreader bar beneath the bench, then cuffed her hands behind her back. When he was finished, Constance was powerless to do anything but squirm and fidget against the padded wooden bar between her thighs. She was so close to coming, her legs clenching with the effort to tip her hips forward. If she could only rub her clit against something...

Firm hands stilled her hips, impeding her efforts. Constance looked over into Jeremy Gray's implacable gaze. "No. I'll tell you when you're allowed to come."

Constance swallowed a groan. It wasn't fair. She'd been trained to be orgasmic. It was ten times harder for her to hold off orgasm than anyone else. She threw a pleading look at Jeremy, but he was rooting around in Kai's cabinet again. Perhaps while his back was turned, she might twist her hips a little...just to take the edge off the nearly unbearable ache—

A searing line of fire erupted against her flank. She yelped and spun to find Jeremy beside her, brandishing a crop.

"I'll let you know when you can ride the horse, little filly. Now, eyes front."

Constance threw her head back in frustration, suddenly not at all excited about playing with Jeremy Gray. He was a sadist. A *teasing* sadist. The worst kind. Jeremy took his time landing biting flicks of the crop all over her ass and outer thighs. The orgasm was building inside her, teeming and expanding, with no way to break free. She arched forward and back in an effort to evade the stinging licks, but that only got her more worked up. She glanced back at Jeremy, her eyes begging for mercy.

He put his hands on his hips, unmoved. "If you can't stop looking behind you, perhaps I'll just stand in front."

He came around her and, to her horror, started giving the same stinging series of licks to her front side. He flicked the underside of one breast and the nipple of the other, causing a sharp, agonizing pulse in her clit. *Oh, God, if he didn't let her come soon...* She threw her shoulders forward protectively, but he would have none of that. He pushed them back and made it quite clear without words that she was to keep her breasts outthrust. She closed her eyes, racked by pain, tormented by pleasure. At last the cropping ended and Constance was left gasping for breath. *Please, please, let me come now!*

Jeremy undid her bonds, helped her off the bench, and stood her before him. A quick assessment had him shaking his head. "I still plan to give you a thorough fucking, Constance, and you're already way too close. I'll have to find something to get your mind off that lovely ache between your legs." *Please, not the clamps, not the clamps!* "Like maybe a nice wicked pair of nipple clamps." *Damn!*

She was quite certain Jeremy was enjoying her anguish. If his huge, upstanding cock was any indication, he was enjoying it very much. He returned from the cabinet with a pair of alligator clamps on a chain. Oh, God, she hated them, but if that's what she had to wear to get fucked by him, so be it.

"Hold your breasts out to me," he said. "Show me how much you want me to make them hurt." Constance gritted her teeth and offered her breasts with trembling hands. Each clamp delivered searing torture. It was so hard not to just grab them back off, but that wouldn't have been a very submissive thing to do. The clamps did achieve one aim. They got her thinking about something besides the overwhelming desire to come.

Jeremy was rolling on a flavored condom. One look from him was all it took to have her falling to her knees. He grasped her face between his hands, guiding his cock to her mouth and invading her throat without quarter. Any other woman would have probably gagged and threw up all over him, but Constance stayed calm and drew on her lessons from the Maison. *Breathe through your nose. Swallow if you start to gag. Open. Open. Stay open to the cock of your Master.*

Within minutes, Jeremy's stern and staunchly controlled veneer began to crack. He reached down, legs trembling, to tug at the chain between her nipples. She moaned against his cock, then pulled away to lap at his balls. After a moment, he stopped her with a jerky motion and pushed her back on the floor. He lowered himself to thrust between her thighs and fucked her hard, with the chain and the clamps trapped between them. Part of her wished to pull away, to escape the pain and intensity of his possession, while another part of her reveled in it. *More pain, more pleasure.* The pain in her nipples interwove with the pounding, grinding invasion of his cock. She lifted her hips, meeting each thrust. Her swollen clit ached in rhythm to his strokes.

He slid one hand under her hips and fucked her from up on his knees. Her eyes nearly rolled back in her head as he contacted her g-spot over and over again. She was shuddering, imploding, and then she felt him nudge her against the cheek. She could barely make out his words.

"Now, little filly. Finish the ride."

Or something like that. It was all she needed to hear. She cried out from the force of her orgasm, racked with rollicking spasms of completion...and blessed relief. Jeremy pressed her down into the floor and went rigid over her, his head buried against her hair.

Their passion spent, they both relaxed by slow degrees. As always, reason seemed to flood back to Constance at the most inopportune times. *Who is this stranger on top of me? What am I doing here? And when is he going to take off the clamps?*

Jeremy moved away from her, stood to remove his condom and throw it away. He was back in a moment with her notebook and an apologetic smile, the dominant sadist replaced by a smiling gentleman. "I guess I should have taken those off first, shouldn't I? What a good submissive you are, not to take them off yourself."

Constance moaned softly, then sucked in her breath as he removed the biting clips, bringing feeling back to her tender nipples. Jeremy licked each peak gently, a soothing touch of warm tongue. He leaned back then, regarding her with curiosity. He was probably having the same thoughts. *Who is this stranger I just took to heaven and back?*

He asked, "How much longer will you be with Kai?"

She raised an eyebrow and took up her pen. *Why are you asking? Are you in the market for an odalisque?*

Jeremy chuckled. "I have to admit I find the *Code d'Odalisque* fascinating, but my wife is enough for me. No, I was thinking that Nell would probably like you. Perhaps, if you're going to be with Kai for a while, the four of us can arrange our own little party."

Constance felt a curious ache in her chest. She forced a smile for Jeremy, and wrote, *My year is up in February. So I don't know. Maybe.*

Jeremy scrutinized her for a long moment. "Don't you think he'll want to keep you beyond that?"

Constance thought, and then wrote as honest an answer as she could muster. *I'm not sure I could survive another year.*

Jeremy nodded. "I thought so. You're in love with him."

It was pointless to disagree. Constance wrote, *That doesn't matter. Love isn't part of the code. Anyway, we don't belong together. I'm deaf.*

"I'm quite sure he doesn't care about that."

And I have plans. Dreams. Things I want to do. Kai wants children, and I don't. There are a lot of reasons it wouldn't work out. She put a heavy period at the end of that line and tucked the pen into the edge of the book.

Jeremy waited a moment for her to look up at him. He pushed the pen back toward her. "But are there any reasons it *would* work out? Say, for instance, if he was in love with you too?"

God, she was in trouble. He had that implacable look again.

* * * * *

Kai and Nell were relaxing down in the living room after a very rousing session. If Constance had the most spankable ass in the world, Nell certainly ran a close second. Kai went to get her a drink, and on the way back was waylaid by Veronica.

"Oh. You." He looked down his nose at her, all the satisfaction of the past hour's scene ebbing away. "Can I help you with something?"

Veronica batted her eyes at him in that passive-aggressive way she had. "Why are you avoiding me, Kai?"

"I don't know. Maybe because I hate you?"

Veronica pouted, folding her arms over her pert breasts. "Are you still angry about that old stuff?"

"That old stuff?" Kai gave Nell's drink to Mason to deliver, and took his ex-wife's arm and steered her toward the back hallway. "That 'old stuff'? Is that how you refer to the fact that you secretly deprived me of three children?"

"Oh, you never wanted children," Veronica spat at him. "You just wanted a reason to be mad at me."

"You grifting me out of 35 million dollars wasn't a good enough reason? Why are you here?"

Veronica stuck out her chin. "Jessamine invited me. You and I have a lot of the same friends. I don't know why we can't get along together. I had kind of hoped we might stay friends."

Kai stared at her, his jaw open in disbelief. "Really?"

"I miss you, Kai."

It was unspeakably rude, but he laughed out loud. "It's New Years Eve, Veronica, not April Fools Day. Sorry. I was stupid enough to fall for your games once—"

"Games? What games?"

"The games where you pretend to care about me in order to take my money and abort my kids. Those games."

"Kai—"

"What about your date there, your handsome Mr. Universe?"

"I don't care about him. Being with him has made me realize how much I need you. How much I miss you."

"Is the money gone already? How do you buzz through 35 mil in one year?"

"The money's not gone. This has nothing to do with that. Can't I have a change of heart?"

Veronica blinked up at him, lower lip trembling, in full blown delicate-flower act. How he'd loved her once. For a moment he was that impressionable young man again, who couldn't believe such a beauty would be interested in him. But he was wise enough now to look past the delicate flower to the thorny stalk beneath. "Not a fucking chance, woman. Give it up."

"Kai—"

She grabbed his arm and he pulled away. "Either leave my house, Veronica, or leave me alone. Just stay out of my face—"

Jessamine's shriek interrupted their argument. With a muttered curse, Kai pushed past Veronica and into the living room. All the conversation had stopped, the various couples clustered on the outskirts of the room. In front of the New Years telecast, Jessamine was waving a fistful of papers in front of Mason's face.

"You fucking bastard. Explain this. Explain it to me!"

"What's there to explain?" Mason yelled back. "You're an intelligent woman. I'm sure you can fucking figure it out."

"Oh, I figured it out all right." She slapped Mason upside the head so hard Kai flinched. "You're fucking Kai's little deaf girl right under my nose. How many times have you had her? I knew it! I knew it at that Lincoln Center bash in New York. Where is that little whore?"

"Jessamine." Kai crossed the room. "Look, calm down. It's twenty minutes to New Years. Sit down, have some champagne—"

"You knew about this?" Jessamine turned her fury on him. "I should have known. The two stooges. He's always loved you more than me. What are you, a couple of closet homosexuals?"

"Jess," Mason warned.

"What are you even talking about?" asked Kai, prying the pages from her hand. He scanned them, recognizing Constance's handwriting, and Mason's. "Where did you get this?"

"They were sitting on top of the piano," Jess fumed. "Apparently Mason spent one of his hours plotting the end of my marriage with your sanctimonious, whoring little bitch."

"Enough," Kai snapped. "Don't talk about Constance that way."

Jess spun on Mason again. "How dare you? We promised never to keep secrets. Where *is* she?"

With impeccable timing, Jeremy appeared at the door to the odella with Constance at his side. Jessamine went tearing up the stairs. Jeremy positioned himself in front of Constance, but Jess went pushing past, into the odella. Mason and Kai ran behind, along with the other guests.

Jessamine took in the bright bed, the harem-like curtains and decor, and spun toward the saray. She looked inside, and when she turned around to Mason, her face was white and drawn. Her voice shook with the force of her rage. She pointed at Constance and barely spoke above a whisper. "Is that woman an odalisque? Answer me. Is she your odalisque?"

Mason shook his head. Kai held Constance close and said, "She's mine. I went and got her on my own. Mason had no part in it."

Jess fixed her gaze on her husband. "And you slithered over here behind my back to be with her. For how long?"

"I invited him, Jess," Kai interjected. "Don't just blame him—"

"You stay out of this. Just fucking shut up." She gave Constance an eviscerating glare before she turned back to Mason. "I'll ask again. How long?"

Mason looked as enraged as his wife. "Since summer. Six months ago—"

"You fucking ass!"

171

"Since you started spending all that time with your fucking *Out of Bounds* co-star!" Mason's voice rose, hoarse and tortured. "Since you started hooking up every other night with those slutty waitresses from Eau de Vie. Since you started swinging with your fucking personal trainer and your bodyguard. Since you left me!"

"I never left you! You knew about every one of my lovers. You agreed! We agreed to an open marriage."

"What choice did I have, Jessamine?" Mason's voice cracked and broke. "Yes, I agreed. But I don't agree any more. I've had enough."

In the frozen silence that followed, Kai heard, with a sick sinking feeling, his sister's bright voice from the stairs.

"Constance! Hey, are you up there?"

Satya's face appeared in the door. She took in the sixteen naked bodies and Mason's stricken expression, Jessamine's rage and Kai's flustered scowl.

"Brother," she asked softly. "What's going on?"

Kai swallowed past the tightness in his throat. "We're having a little party." His voice sounded strangely normal, considering the circumstances. He belatedly remembered to put a hand over his genitals, after seeing the other men covering up. "What are you doing here?"

Satya was looking anywhere but him, anywhere but at the naked party guests. "It's New Years Eve. I was lonely and I wanted to come spend it with you and Constance."

"I thought you were spending it with your boyfriend."

Satya's eyes were shining, like she was about to start crying. "We actually just broke up." From downstairs, the sound of the countdown blared up from the TV. *5...4...3...2...1...*

HAPPY NEW YEAR!

Satya put a hand to her throat, turned, and fled.

Chapter Seventeen:
Enough

What a fucking disaster. Kai had been to boring scatter parties and weird scatter parties and awkward scatter parties, but he'd never been to an Oh-my-God-what-the-fuck-just-happened scatter party. That was a first.

He felt terrible for everyone involved, including Satya, who wasn't answering her phone. Kai went over to see if Mason and Jessamine were all right only to find Mason had already moved out and left no forwarding address. No contact number. Jessamine had flown back to Toronto after filing divorce papers. It hit the tabloids the next day.

While Kai processed all these events, his odalisque moped around, obviously feeling unsettled and guilty. It had been Constance's notebook pages, after all, that brought down the Jackson-Cooke Hollywood dynasty. To Kai's chagrin, Constance held up the whole debacle as proof that intimate emotional relationships really were something to be avoided. Whenever she started harping on this assertion—which she did frequently—Kai went a little more insane.

Less than two months left.

Kai didn't know if he could make it. The tension between them was almost as unhealthy as Mason and Jessamine's fucked up shit. Of course, Constance didn't perceive things the way Kai did. All she saw was the damn *Code d'Odalisque*, with its rituals and duties. Oh, she was a hell of

Odalisque

an odalisque. He still fucked her and played with her, sometimes two or three times a day, and she still excited him. His body anyway. He still loved her—yes, *loved her*—but the distance she insisted on was starting to drive him mad. His nightmares came fast and furious, perhaps spurred on by the scatter party encounter with his ex-wife. Overall, Kai was pretty damn miserable, and the only person who had the power to soothe him was the same person who agitated him the most. Constance Flynn.

It was late January when Bastien finally contacted him. Kai had gone into work early, meaning to knock out some overdue tasks. Just before lunch, his secretary patched through an overseas call from a Mr. Gaudet. Kai was tempted to put him off. Bastien would want to know about Kai's future with Constance, about what he intended to do. And Kai had no idea what he intended to do.

"Hello, Bastien," he answered warily.

"Mr. Chandler. How are you?"

I've been better. "I'm fine, and yourself?" Kai stood to shut the door. "How are things at the Maison?"

"Ah, it's colder by the day. Winter comes on strong. As you know…" The agent paused for a moment on the end of the line. "It is nearly time to decide if you will renew your contract with Constance for another year."

"Yes…I know. I'm not sure yet. We haven't talked about it."

"But you are still enjoying her services?"

"Yes, very much. But…" *But I'm in love with her, and she won't love me back. It's a nice little code-inflicted version of hell.*

"I had hoped to have a definite decision from you soon, Kai. If possible."

Kai frowned. "Well…why? Why do you need to know now? Is there someone else who wants her?"

Bastien paused. "I normally wouldn't divulge that kind of information, but in this case… I was going to contact you anyway for a personal reference. There has been an inquiry regarding Constance's availability. The interest comes from a gentleman of your acquaintance named Mason Cooke."

Kai almost dropped the phone. He fumbled with shaking fingers to put it back to his ear.

"Mason Cooke? *Mason Cooke?*" Kai pinched the bridge of his nose. "Here's a character reference for you. He's an asshole, a douchebag, and a selfish fucking prick."

Kai could have said more, but he was too livid. With the last shred of his control, he replaced the phone in the receiver. As soon as he found Mason, he would kill him. Wanted Constance for his odalisque, did he?

Ungrateful piece of shit excuse for a friend.

* * * * *

Constance woke at her usual late hour and stretched. Winter wasn't as fun as summer. In the summer she could have gone and jumped in the pool, or lay on Kai's deck under the crisp white awnings. In the winter all she could really do was some yoga. She could get dressed and go for a walk around Kai's property, down the trail he ran on sometimes.

But she didn't really feel like doing anything.

Instead she stared at the canopy fluttering over her head and worried about Kai. Since New Years, he was working longer hours than ever. He'd come home and go on lengthy runs, returning sweaty and taciturn. After he showered, he'd spend an hour at the piano, playing aggressively, and then he'd fuck her like he was trying to lose himself.

She knew Kai was worried about Mason, and Satya...they hadn't heard from her in two weeks. Constance knew she should use her talents to comfort him. That was her duty, according to the code. But so much of her energy was going to maintaining the required façade of detachment and serenity.

It has to be this way. Constance would always treasure her time with Kai. She would always love him and wonder what might have been, but she couldn't allow herself to daydream about happily-ever-after anymore. Kai needed a wife who could be a social butterfly, who could shoulder all his work-entertaining duties and pop him out a bunch of darling half-Indian kids to show off on his holiday photo cards.

It was ridiculous to think of herself as a wife...as anyone's wife, much less the wife of a gazillionaire. With her past—not just as a runaway, but as a sex worker—she wasn't society-wife material. Kai deserved better. He deserved a wife without a bunch of skeletons in her closet. He deserved a wife with a classy education and aching ovaries, and a respectable family and money of her own.

But you'll have money of your own...in a few years... Maybe they could meet again when Constance's years as an odalisque were over. When she could meet him as an independent woman. They could be friends, if nothing else. It would probably be better that way. The truth was... The truth was...

The truth was she was a fucking coward, and Kai Chandler scared her to death. Sure, he could make all her dreams happen with his money, but then her dreams would be his...and *she* would be his. Just like her mother, cowering under the protection of a man like there was no other way to live, no other way to be happy. And Constance would give him children, because she'd be afraid to do otherwise. Her whole life would be pleasing him, living up to his standards, while her own goals evaporated into distant echoes of intent...

A light in her bedroom flashed—the doorbell light. *Satya.* Constance threw on her robe, grabbed the notebook reserved for Kai's sister, and ran downstairs to answer the door.

But it wasn't Satya standing on the doorstep. It was Mason Cooke, looking like absolute hell. He clearly hadn't shaved in days. God, had he been living on the street or something?

"Constance," he said, his expression weary. "Can I come in?"

She drew him inside and led him to the kitchen. They sat at Kai's small table. Constance opened the notebook.

I was just going to have breakfast. Any chance of some omelets and burnt toast?

Mason smiled slightly, but he didn't seem himself at all. Maybe he was drunk. He was just....staring at her.

Kai's not here, she wrote. *But he's been worried about you. Are you okay?*

Mason looked down at her words and laughed.

"Well, not particularly okay, seeing as how my marriage disintegrated at a fucking scatter party. But I'm hanging in there."

I'm sorry it had to go down that way. I'm really sorry for my part in it. But at least now she knows how unhappy you were.

"Oh, yeah, everyone in the godforsaken universe knows now. The paparazzi are following me around, every guy I used to call a friend is making passes at Jessamine, and I'm living out of a fucking hotel."

Constance bit her lip, not used to seeing Mason in this kind of black mood. *You could stay here instead,* she wrote. *I don't think Kai would mind.*

"Oh, he would mind. In fact..." Mason paused and looked down. She had to shift to see his lips. "I think I did something that's going to make him really mad at me." He looked up at her with a strangely vulnerable gaze. "I contacted that guy, Gaudet, about getting an odalisque."

Constance smiled. *Oh, Mason. That won't make Kai mad. I think that's actually a wonderful idea. That's probably just what you need right now.*

His hand came down to stop her pen, and she looked up at him.

"I contacted him about you. About you becoming my odalisque."

Oh, Constance wrote after a moment. *Yeah, I'm not sure how he'll feel about that. Probably not great.*

"How would you feel about it? About being mine?"

Constance hesitated, trying to think of what to say. She knew Mason was feeling fragile. She didn't want to trample his ego when he was already down.

"I can learn to sign," Mason said. "If that's the issue. I can— Well. I'm not as brainy as Kai but I can do what I have to do. I'll try hard."

Constance rubbed her forehead. *You shouldn't have to do anything,* she wrote. *That's the thing. You shouldn't have to try hard.*

"But I would."

Constance looked away from him, down at her lap. She had to think.

Mason... she wrote. *Don't you think it would be too awkward? I mean, you're Kai's best friend. And me and him will have this history, and then I'll be out and about with you. And we'll run into him... It will be like Veronica showing up at the scatter party.*

"But...Veronica was his wife. You're just his odalisque. We can even keep sharing you, if he feels like it. But this time I'll pay, and you can stay with me."

Do you really think it would be that simple?

Mason shrugged. "I don't know. I don't see why Kai gets to have a say anyway. Your contract is up with him soon. And you make the choice of what to do next, don't you?"

She reached up to stroke the stubble on his face, then hunched over to write. *Forgive me, Mason, but I think you're not in the best state of mind right now. Maybe this isn't the best time to be making a big decision like taking on an odalisque.*

"A few minutes ago you said it was a wonderful idea!" Mason pointed indignantly at her actual words on the page.

Well, I think it's a wonderful idea to get an odalisque, but I'm just not sure it should be me! she wrote, adding a big exclamation point.

Mason scowled and leaned closer to look in her eyes. "Is it me? It's me, isn't it? I'm an asshole. I don't deserve to have anyone. To have anyone care about me."

Constance sighed. She was really over this conversation. *Mason, there's nothing wrong with you. You're very sweet. Very loving. You just need to find a deserving girl. Jessamine wasn't right for you. But it's okay. Life goes on, and you will find someone.*

He reached out to her. His physical presence was suffocating. He was so sexual, so masculine, even in his hangdog misery. He smoothed fingers down her cheek, cupping her jaw. "Wouldn't you like to be with me, Constance? Because the girl I really want right now is you. You make me feel comfortable. You're honest with me. Don't you want me? Am I so unlovable?"

She shook her head and wrote, *I'm not looking for someone to love! Besides that, there's a lot of tension between me and Kai right now. This is a really bad time to add yourself to the mix. I don't know what's going to happen, but you need to let us figure that out first.*

Mason leaned closer. Intoxicatingly close. Oh, God, he was going to kiss her, and Kai wasn't there, and it would feel wrong and unfaithful. When she turned her face away, he nuzzled her instead, snaking one hand inside her robe to fondle her breast. She grabbed his wrist and shook her head, pushing his hand away. She wrote, *Not now. Not when Kai isn't here.*

Mason narrowed his eyes, pouting like a child. "I thought you were the one person I could come to who wouldn't make me feel like shit. What about your code? You're supposed to serve men, and I'm a man. Are you a fucking cockslave or what?"

Constance slapped his face, a good hard whack. His blatant movie-star manipulation disgusted her, but the slap only seemed to inflame his passions further. He stood, pulling her with him, and this time he did kiss her, meanly, forcefully. She struggled, hating his rough stubble scratching her, and the scent of unwashed, drunken man.

His arm tightened around her waist and he trapped both her hands in his other hand. He gripped them so hard she whimpered. He tugged at her robe, his tongue forcing her mouth open again. She almost bit him, but then he released her and spun toward the door.

Kai was there, right in the kitchen with them. His shirt collar was undone, his briefcase still dangling from his fingers. He looked as dissolute and miserable as Mason.

"Well, well, well," he said with an accusing glare at both of them. "What have I interrupted here?"

* * * * *

In numb disbelief, Kai watched Constance shake her head, wiping her lips and pulling her robe closed. Why was she denying what he'd seen with his own fucking two eyes?

"How long has this little plan been in the works?" Kai asked. "And when were you two going to let me in on it?"

"What plan?" Constance signed.

"I got a call from our friend Sebastian today. He wanted a character reference for yours truly," he said, flicking a thumb at Mason. "So you could be his odalisque."

Constance shook her head again. "I only found out about all this today. He just came over and told me. I told him it was ridiculous."

Mason was silent, watching their conversation. Kai realized he'd been signing instead of talking. He turned to his friend. His *former* friend. "How long have you been coming over here without me knowing? You fucking bastard. Sneaking around on your wife *and* your best friend?"

"I haven't seen Constance since the scatter party," Mason snapped.

"That doesn't answer my question," Kai yelled back. "How many times?"

"Never, okay?" Mason grabbed his head, launching into the same weak, pathetic act he always used when he got caught being an ass. "Look, Kai, I'm just not myself right now. I wanted to talk to Constance. Things got out of hand."

Constance touched Kai's arm. "Things didn't get out of hand," she signed angrily. "*Mason* got out of hand. I told him to stop. That you weren't here, that it wasn't right. And I had nothing to do with him calling Bastien. I swear it."

At those words, Kai turned on Mason. He finally noticed the outline of fingers on his cheek. "Get the fuck out of my house, you fucking jackass. Don't ever so much as look at her again."

Mason started to the door, then turned back. "I don't get it. She's just an odalisque, right? She's available for hire. If she's something more, then fucking say so. But don't stand there and judge me like you're better than me. You bought her services. Why can't I?"

Kai lowered his voice to a near-growl, a second away from totally losing it. "One more time. Don't even think of touching her again. And you can forget about calling Gaudet about her, because Constance will be your odalisque over my dead body. Now go home to wherever you're living now, and forget we were ever friends."

"Wow, really, man? That's harsh." Mason turned and stalked to the door. "Fuck you," he yelled over his shoulder. "Fuck you both."

When Kai turned around, Constance was crying. Silent rivers of tears. Kai went to her, rubbing her back and pressing his forehead to hers. Constance held herself stiffly in his arms, like she didn't want to be touched.

Kai pulled back and searched her face. "What did he do to you? Did he hurt you?"

She made a curt sign. "No."

"I'll call the police."

Constance pulled away from him, shaking her head and signing again. "No, seriously. Nothing happened." She wiped away tears, trying to compose herself. Then she looked at him and started bawling again. "You believe me, don't you? I never snuck around on you. Not with Mason or anyone else."

Kai went to get her a tissue. "Yes, I believe you. I don't know why I even asked. It's just those…trust issues flaring up again. You know."

"It would be such a breach of the code," Constance signed, the white tissue fluttering from her fingertips. It put Kai in mind of a white flag. Surrender. *I give up.*

"Yeah, the code," he muttered, rolling his eyes. "We must follow the damn code or God knows what tragedy might befall us."

"Don't mock it!" she signed angrily. "I chose this lifestyle. You chose it." She swiped at her eyes, at the tears still squeezing through. "Why do you mock the code? Because when you do, you know you're mocking me too!" She turned and ran up the stairs to the odella, with audible, heart-wrenching sobs.

Well, so much for emotional distance. All of this was his fault, of course. She was perfectly happy sticking to the emotionless and static arrangement of "owner" and "odalisque." He wished he could be happy with that too. It would have made everything so easy. He could have shrugged off Mason's bid for Constance as an unfortunate faux pas, instead of going apeshit out of his mind with rage. He could have found any answers he needed about her in the code, instead of searching her light green eyes for something deeper.

Ten months ago he'd been dying for a faceless, emotionless sex slave, no strings attached. But now he wanted something else. He wanted Constance Flynn, with all her complexity, charm, and sensuality. He wanted to take her out to dinner. He wanted to romance her. He wanted to sleep next to her through an entire night and wake up with her in his arms. Hell, he wanted to put a fucking ring on her finger. He didn't want her distance, her censure each time he crossed some nebulous emotional line.

They had to talk.

He climbed the stairs to her odella and considered the closed door. That was a new thing. He could knock, but it wouldn't do much good. He cracked it open instead.

Constance was reading in bed. She gazed up at him with a completely blank look. No welcome, no anger. No emotion he could recognize.

No offer to serve him.

"Can I come in?" he signed.

She nodded, closing her book. Kai crossed to the saray. He beckoned her to join him with a jerk of his head. His odalisque came at once, without hesitation. Well, this was all in the code, unlike the messy scene downstairs.

She walked through the door in front of him, then turned, waiting for directions. Oh, God, even now he found her so sweet. So womanly and welcoming. He went to her and ran his fingers over the curve of her hips. He loved her softness, her femininity.

He undressed, waving her off when she would have helped him. One gesture and she was on her knees, stroking his balls, bringing his cock to life with her mouth. Such skill. No wonder Mason wanted her. No wonder Mason was fine with throwing away a lifetime of friendship to steal her from under his nose. Kai stopped Constance with a tug on the back of her hair. She looked up at him, sitting back on her heels.

"Could you really go to him?" he signed.

She didn't ask who Kai referred to. She shrugged and signed, "It doesn't matter, does it?"

"It matters to me. Yes. Could you have left me and gone to him without…without feeling anything?"

181

She blinked hard for a moment, her hands still in her lap. Then she said, "I'll miss you. So yes, I would feel something."

But what Kai heard was, *Yes, I would go to him.*

He pulled her toward the bed, then pushed her onto the white expanse of sheets on her back. He settled over her, between her legs, and pressed the length of his body to hers. He still remembered the first time he'd fucked her here in his house, when she was out of breath from jumping on the bed and he'd pushed her down and taken her so joyfully. It was almost a year ago now. That had been a hello fuck.

This was goodbye.

He just wanted her one last time. He kissed her hard and deep, rolling her nipples between his fingertips. She arched against him, responsive as ever. He slid his cock through the wetness of her arousal and pushed inside her, cradling her.

"Constance," he said, but she wasn't looking. Her eyes were closed, her arms stretched over her head. For one horrible moment, he thought he could be anyone. Any owner, any Master. Constance would serve anyone just as she served him. That was the code. He was the cock, she was the cockslave. He tapped her chin, distraught, until she opened her eyes. "Look at me while I'm fucking you."

She looked right at him, the obedient sex slave. Her lust-fueled grin would have thrilled him a few months ago, but now it made his heart ache. She ran her fingers up his arms to his shoulders, kneading, scratching like a kitten. She was so lovely. He loved her so much.

He pulled away, abruptly, roughly, and sat on the edge of the bed. Constance scrambled up beside him. Her eyes were wide and troubled. His erection was gone, like a dream interrupted.

"I just can't—" His signs were garbled and choppy. "Constance…do you feel anything at all for me?"

He hated that she pretended to be confused. "Like what?"

"Like anything. Any personal or emotional feeling."

"I thought you were paying me not to have feelings," Constance signed. "All I want is to be a good odalisque. I want to follow the code. You signed it—"

"I'm aware that I fucking signed it, Constance. I know! Why can't you—" Kai rubbed his mouth and shook his head. "Why can't you just step away from that fucking code for ten seconds and let me see who you really are? What you really feel about me? I see bits and pieces of you and I think I'll just die if I'm never allowed to see more. But I'm not."

He stood up and over her, a quivering pillar of frustration. He reached for her, the woman he loved, the woman who refused to love him. He pulled her up and held her close. He knew every contour, every curve of her. He'd memorized every gold fleck in her green eyes. He'd internalized her smell, her taste. "God damn you, Constance. I love you. Why are you doing this to me?"

Constance went stiff. "You're—you're not supposed to love me," she signed.

"No shit," said Kai. "But I don't know what the hell to do about it now."

He wanted her so badly. Out of all the things he had, all the things his money could buy, he just wanted this one thing. This one woman. Why this torment, this obsession? Then it hit him.

He'd been here before.

"You know," he said, looking down at her, "when I was growing up, I was an outcast. Tall and gangly. I was a total nerd, one hundred percent, and I had no friends. I acted too American to fit in with the Indians, and I looked too Indian to fit in with the American kids. School was...difficult.

"Then I met Mason. He got me through, you know. He always had it, the charisma, the personality. I rode his coattails. When we got older, I got women thanks to him. I gained a sense of self-worth. I used my nerd smarts to start a business, and when the success came I pretended I'd expected it all along." He shook his head. "But I hadn't. I was so shocked. It was like a dream I was afraid to wake up from. When I met Veronica, I was living in that dream haze. I was flush with success. I couldn't believe she wanted me, but part of me thought, well, this is what I get for working hard. For making it. *She wants me.*"

He stared off into the distance for a while, utterly still. Then he looked back at her so she could easily read his lips. "Well, you know the rest. She took me for millions. When she dumped me it was like being back in school again, huddled in the corner of the playground, getting kicked in the nuts and taunted with ethnic slurs. And I look at you and think you're too good to be true too. I wonder when you're going to kick me in the nuts like she did." He paused. "But I think maybe you've been doing it all along."

Constance shook her head, flushing. He could actually see the flush move across her skin. She shook her head again more intently.

"No?" asked Kai. "I mean, you knew how I felt about you. You knew it at the Maison, the night we swam in that pool."

She still shook her head, but it was empty denial.

"And the worst part...the worst part, Constance, is that I know you care for me too. Veronica never did. Somehow, you do. But there's something more important to you. I don't know what it is. Money. Security. Whatever it is women like you and my ex-wife want."

Constance shook her head and pushed at his chest. Her hands came up in a rush of signing. "No! Stop saying that. I'm nothing like her."

"I think you are."

"Yes, I want money. I want security. I need money to do the things I want in life. But it has nothing to do with using you—"

Kai shook his head with a bitter laugh. "I think it does. I think it has everything to do with using me."

"If I really wanted to use you, I'd marry you like Veronica did," she signed. "I'm trying to protect you! Do you think it's been easy for me?"

He held up a hand. "Spare me, please. I'm the one who's biting my tongue every night when I leave you, trying not to say how I feel about you because you might not approve. I'm the one who keeps trying to make you love me—which I've done before, Constance. I've lived through this once already, and it made me desperately unhappy."

Desperately unhappy. Is that what he'd gotten for his million bucks? He thought back on the past few months, the tension between them even when they were in each other's arms. But he had thought it was just part of the deal.

"Kai..." Constance signed, her eyes pleading. "I'm sorry. I'm sorry if I've made you believe— If I've made you feel—taken advantage of."

Kai put a hand over hers. "No, it's me," he signed. "It's not your fault. But here's the truth of it: I can't live like this anymore. I don't want an odalisque. I wish I'd never heard the word to begin with. I want someone who loves me."

"But, Kai—"

"Love me, Constance. Trust me. Or go. If I can't have you, the *real* you, with trust and love and emotion, then I want you to leave."

Constance threw up her hands in frustration. "Leave? Now? A month early?"

Kai pursed his lips and stared her down. "I want permission to love you. I want a relationship."

"But I'm your odalisque! The code—"

"Fuck the code! Choose! Your precious fucking code or me!"

Constance's signs were crisp and angry. "It's not fair of you to ask that. We signed a contract."

"Fuck the contract. You need to choose."

She signed, "Fine. If that's what you want."

Kai waited, his expression resolute, as she considered his ultimatum. Long seconds ticked by. *Every gold fleck*, he thought to himself. *I know those eyes like I know my own eyes. Come on, Constance. Take a chance.*

But she pulled away from him. "I'm not my mother," she signed, her nostrils flaring and her mouth pinched. "I won't beg to stay where I'm not wanted, where I don't measure up. Not in this lifetime. Not ever."

And with those parting words, she stalked out of the room, leaving him alone with his misery and suffocating regret.

Chapter Eighteen:
Mistakes and Truths

Constance fell into a kind of trance as she flew over the ocean. Memories crowded in, all the wretched occasions when her mother had been thrown out. Thank God Constance didn't have any kids forced to pack their bags, as she had, listening to her mother's tears, her pathetic pleas for another chance...

Constance had no intention of pleading. No fucking way.

She made it almost halfway across the Atlantic before her outraged bravado turned to tears. Her blind resolve to be immovable and unemotional melted away, leaving her to look back on the day's events in horror. What on earth had she done? How stupid and shortsighted was she? All the love she'd buried inside overwhelmed her, and for the first time, she let herself dwell on all she'd given up. She'd made such a huge mistake, not allowing herself to love Kai.

The staid Swedish businessman next to her hunched to the side, as if her unchecked grief might be contagious. Constance pulled a blanket over her face and cried with bitter regret until her chest ached and her eyes burned. Then she slept for a while. When she woke up, she found her armor had returned. She would not be her mother. Ever. She would not give a man power over her, especially the power of love. She wouldn't beg to stay where she wasn't wanted, where she wasn't accepted on her terms. She wouldn't compromise her long-sought goals for some ephemeral romantic illusion. She'd done *all* of this to gain security and independence, and she sure as hell wasn't sacrificing that now.

Kai would get over it. She'd get over it too. She let herself wonder about Kai only briefly, about how he was holding up. He hadn't even said goodbye, but instead called his driver to handle everything. He'd been so unlike himself at the end.

She hoped he wasn't having regrets. If he came after her, there would be a big fuss, and Bastien hated big fusses. Constance was already worried about how Bastien would react to her showing up in the middle of the night. She would have called ahead, but she'd left all her phones behind with Kai. They were his anyway. And she hadn't wanted Kai to be able to contact her and make her reconsider yet again.

In the taxi on the way to the Maison, she tried to pull herself together. She flicked bottled water into her eyes to combat the redness. She worked on her hair, and finally just pulled it back in a twist. Then she was on the doorstep of her old home, ringing the bell. The night butler let her in with an almost undetectable lift of his eyebrows. The cool, luxurious grandeur of the foyer looked different at night. Before she could ask the butler to send for Bastien, she saw him hurrying down the stairs.

"Constance!" He reached out to her in alarm. "What are you doing here? Where is Ms. Dresden? She didn't tell me to expect you."

Constance fumbled for a notebook in her bag. *Mr. Chandler asked me to leave.*

Bastien gaped at her words. "Asked you to leave? Ms. Dresden gave me glowing reports about you and your owner."

Constance shrugged and felt the tickle of tears at the back of her throat. She couldn't let Bastien see her cry.

She wrote some more. Enough, she hoped, to satisfy him. *Since New Years, things changed between us. He had a long time grievance with me that he was keeping hidden. He truly didn't want me anymore.*

Bastien searched her face. The tender concern in his features almost had her crying again. She gave him a wobbly smile and wrote, *It's okay. I understood how he felt.*

"But—" Bastien was still flabbergasted. "To turn you off this way. Putting you on a plane without so much as a—" He took her hand and marched her back to his office. She looked at his clock to find it was after one in the morning. Bastien gestured her toward a chair, then dialed

187

the phone. He turned back to her, scolding. "You at least ought to have called me. Let me know you were on your way, and when to expect you."

Constance wrote some words and held them up for him to see. *I was afraid you would tell me I couldn't come.*

He grimaced. "You will always be given refuge here at the Maison. No matter what. But this—this is not at all how things are done."

Bastien turned away from her, his attention back on his call. Constance saw him bark out Kai's name, and then Bastien turned his back to her so she couldn't see the rest of what he said. The conversation seemed to go on for hours. In fact, it lasted just under ten minutes according to the clock. Constance stared at Bastien's tense shoulders, watched the indignant gesticulations he made. Then Bastien would go still and listen, and Constance wondered what Kai was telling him. She was sure it was nothing good.

When Bastien hung up and turned back around, Constance couldn't tell anything from his expression. "We'll talk more about this in the morning. For now, I think it best if you get some sleep."

Constance nodded and stood to gather up her bag. Bastien touched her arm. "Are you okay? Was there an...ugly scene?"

Memories flitted through Constance's head, scenes from the scatter party, and from Mason's unnerving visit. Kai's accusations and the way he'd looked at her when he'd compared her to his ex-wife. She didn't have to say anything.

Bastien cupped her face and kissed her forehead softly, then looked into her eyes. "I am so sorry. I had a sneaking feeling. A misgiving about pairing you with him. I didn't trust my judgment, and now I'm afraid you've been caused a lot of pain. Come, let's find you a room where you can rest."

Bastien led her out of his office, but rather than taking her to the odalisque quarters, he took her to the guest wing, where the visitors and prospective owners stayed. She looked at him questioningly.

"You are staying here simply because you are not available for another placement yet. We have some legalities to tie up with your current owner first." Bastien paused and gave her a searching look. "Are you still planning to remain an odalisque? To find another Master?"

Constance nodded with much more enthusiasm than she felt. She did, of course, still want to be an odalisque. She was sure things wouldn't go so haywire with another Master.

No. There couldn't be another Kai anywhere in the world.

* * * * *

Kai lay awake in bed for the fifth night running. He'd gotten the legal papers from France today. Stupid papers. Like he cared about the contract or the money or any of it. All he really cared about was that Constance had arrived there okay after he'd kicked her out of his house onto the street.

Well, not exactly the street. He'd paid for her plane ticket, and the driver. He'd told her to take everything, but she'd left everything he'd given her. All the gowns from the New York trip, all the books and jewelry and naughty toys. Her odella remained as it was because he couldn't bear to go in there, not because he thought he might bring her back.

He wouldn't bring her back. Sebastien Gaudet wouldn't let him anyway. The odalisque agent had been furious, spewing the same nonsense as Constance about emotional detachment and the importance of adhering to the code. When he calmed, he'd offered Kai a replacement odalisque, and then it had been Kai's turn to rip into him. Ha! Kai needed another odalisque like he needed a hole in his head.

Kai rolled over with a groan, fearful of sleep but needing it badly. Since Constance had gone, he dreamed a whole new dream. It started the same, his children falling under the waves and calling out to him. Only now, Constance stood there beside him with that shuttered look on her face.

"Help me!" he would plead. "My children—"

And she would say, in her dream-Constance voice, "Relationships are dangerous. Just let them go." Instead of grief and helplessness, he'd wake feeling fury. Why was she that way? Why didn't she care?

Kai swung his legs over the side of the bed and sat hunched over, rubbing his eyes. There was no point lying there dreaming the same dream. With a sense of dread, he forced himself up the stairs and into her old rooms. He sat at her desk and sifted through the remaining notebooks for the tenth time. There was nothing to see. They were all empty. She'd taken all the others when she left, or destroyed them.

He turned to look over his shoulder, into the saray. How many hours had they spent there, her entire body laid open for him? No inhibitions, no limits except the limit of knowing her, really knowing who she was inside. *You bought my body. You own my sex. My ass, my pussy. Not this! Not my mind.* She had told him plain as day. Why hadn't he believed her? God, Bastien had warned him time and time again. No emotional attachment. He hadn't wanted the rules to apply to him. Typical rich prick.

Kai stood by the bed, staring down at the sheets, remembering their last moments together. After so much pleasure, to end things that way… He'd made her feel guilty, and compared her to his ex-wife just to make her hurt. He hadn't realized how angry he'd been at her inside. *I'm sorry, Constance.*

He was turning away from the bed when he noticed the notebook shuffled underneath. He bent down to pull it out, recognizing Constance's handwriting. The conversation was one-sided. She'd been writing to someone who was talking back to her. Jeremy Gray. He'd been alone in the saray with her the night of the scatter party. Kai knew he shouldn't read it, but what could it hurt now? She was gone.

It was painful, looking at the familiar messy writing. *Why are you asking? Are you in the market for an odalisque?* Kai's heart clenched. Had Jeremy been angling for her too? All these secrets he hadn't known. He'd thought Jeremy was happy with his wife. Kai almost put it down again, but his curiosity won out.

My year is up in February. So I don't know. Maybe. That fucking bastard. Next time he saw Jeremy, he was going to punch him in the nuts. He read on, compelled by some masochistic impulse. *I'm not sure I could survive another year.* Bitch. Bitch!

That doesn't matter. Love isn't part of the code. Anyway, we don't belong together. I'm deaf.

Kai paused. Huh? *What* didn't matter? *Love isn't part of the code?* Jeremy hadn't been trying to steal her at all. He must have been urging her to give a relationship with Kai a chance. Cancel the nut-punching. He owed Jeremy a drink.

And I have plans, her writing continued. *Dreams. Things I want to do. Kai wants children, and I don't. There are a lot of reasons it wouldn't work out.*

Kai dropped his head into his hands. Why hadn't she said any of this to him? He could have helped her with her dreams, helped her do anything she wanted. He could have told her that kids weren't important. But what else would she have thought, after the way Kai moped over the children he lost? Story of his life, finding the truths he needed when it was too late to do anything about them.

Wearily, he looked down at the last of the conversation, a series of scrawled lines. *Reasons it would work? Of course there are.*

He makes me laugh. He's kind and responsible.

He's the most generous person I know.

He touches me in ways no one else ever has, and he helps me hear music I can't hear.

He has this smile he gets when someone else is happy. I'll never forget that smile as long as I live.

I want him to be happy, Jeremy. He deserves it. He doesn't deserve someone like

The words cut off then. Kai remembered Jeremy and Constance appearing belatedly through the door at the top of the stairs, just as all the screeching and fighting began.

Kai ripped the page out of the notebook, fled back through the odella, and took off down the stairs.

* * * * *

Constance sat curled up on her bed, staring at nothing. Waiting. She tried to tell herself she wasn't waiting, but she was. Kai would have gotten the paperwork yesterday. Constance knew it was already essentially over, but when the papers of resignation were signed, their relationship would officially be through.

It was a good thing. Constance kept telling herself that. When the papers came back, she could take off her clothes and move back to the other side with her fellow odalisques. She could begin the process of forgetting about Kai and all the things she almost had in his arms. When she got back into the swing of things, everything would be okay.

She glanced up as one of the servants came to the door. "Miss Constance, there is a man here to see you. Downstairs. Would you care to come down?"

Kai. Just like that, she was petrified. What would she do? What would she say? She'd hoped against hope that he might care enough to come, but now that he had, she felt panicked. The formally dressed servant waited patiently, not reacting to the fact that she was sitting there like an idiot wringing her hands. She knew she ought to send the servant back with the message that she didn't want to see him...

But instead she was on her feet, out the door and down the hall, following behind the servant's swishing coattails. She almost stepped on the back of his heels, she was so anxious to walk faster, to get there—

The servant opened the door to Bastien's office. Her eyes swept the room in search of Kai only to discover...Mason Cooke.

"Constance, you have a visitor," Bastien said. "If you like, I'll send him away."

Mason raised his eyebrows just an iota. She read the plea there. He looked nothing like the last time she'd seen him. He was shaved, impeccably dressed in a button down shirt and khakis. Constance gave Bastien a nod of endorsement, and with one last look at the both of them, he left and closed the door.

Mason looked at her, relief clearly written on his face. "Thank you."

Constance went around the other side of Bastien's desk. She took a sheaf of his fussy linen paper and jotted down, *For what?*

"For not hating me, for one thing. You don't hate me, do you?"

Constance regarded him for a moment, remembering their last time together. *I don't hate you. But I meant what I said to you that day. I can't be your odalisque.*

"Constance, I'm so sorry. That day...the way I acted... It was inexcusable. And I know you can't be my odalisque. I was in a crazy place to even think about it. My marriage was over, I was lonely, I felt hounded, and I just..." He twisted his hands together. "I just wasn't thinking right. And Kai... Jesus."

Have you talked to him? Constance asked.

"No. But Satya says..."

Mason's voice drifted off, as if he didn't want to say more. *You talked to Satya?* Constance wrote to prompt him.

Mason shrugged. "I don't have many other friends right now. She wanted to know why you left, and Kai wouldn't tell her. Why did you leave?"

Constance shook her head. *I didn't leave. He sent me away.*

Mason looked horrified. "Because of me? God, Constance, I'm sorry."

It wasn't just you. It was a lot of stuff.

Mason fell silent, biting a finger. Constance finally wrote, *Is that the only reason you came? To apologize? To be forgiven?*

He took a deep breath and blew it out. "I came to make amends. I came because I did a really awful thing, and now I have to do a really good one. I came here to convince you to go back to my friend."

There's no point, she wrote. *He doesn't want me back. If he did, he would be here instead of you.*

"Satya told me he's really miserable. She's worried about him."

I'll only make things worse.

Mason narrowed his eyes at her. "In what way?" He tapped the paper. "Tell me."

Don't get snippy with me, she scrawled. *Whatever I write, you'll just argue with it.*

"Yes, I will. Because I happen to think the two of you belong together. He's in love with you, you know. And you're in love with him. Before you try to deny it," he warned, holding up a hand, "remember, I saw your face when you came to the door. When you thought I was Kai waiting in here."

Constance blinked, flicking at the edge of the paper. *He needs a hearing wife. Someone well-mannered and poised.*

"Bullshit."

To attend all those charities and things he does. Those parties.

"We don't have scatter parties that often," Mason protested. "And he wouldn't make you do them if you didn't want to."

She gave him a withering look. *I meant the business and charity parties.*

Mason shrugged. "He wouldn't make you do those either."

He wants children. He needs someone who would be a good mom.

"Now who's making excuses? You don't know any of that for sure. You don't know what he'd be willing to give up out of love for you, especially with all he'd be gaining. Listen, just come back with me. Talk to him."

There's nothing to talk about! she wrote angrily. *I'm the wrong person for him to be in love with.*

"Ah, but you know," said Mason, wagging his finger, "that's not your decision to make. Kai gets to decide who he loves. Not you. And you know who you love, Constance. You can deny what you're feeling, but that won't make it go away."

Oh God. It was so true. If she wasn't so chickenshit, she'd admit he was right. She'd go back with him to Los Angeles and at least take a stab at things with Kai. There had to be some slim chance things would work out between them. 1% chance? 5% chance? She was mentally calculating the odds when Mason jumped up out of his chair. A blur of bronze skin and dark hair passed by her, hands outstretched for Mason's throat.

Constance shook off her shock and tugged at Kai's arm. Bastien ran in, a couple of burly footmen behind him. They hauled Kai away from Mason. "He just stormed in, Constance, Mr. Cooke," said Bastien. "I'm sorry."

Kai was looking from Constance to Mason and back again like he couldn't decide who to murder first. "This isn't what it looks like," Mason said.

"Oh, really?" snapped Kai. "Because it looks like you're still trying to acquire my fucking odalisque."

Constance stepped in front of Kai to get his attention. "He's not here for that," she signed. "Mason came here to convince me to come back to you."

All the bluster seemed to go out of Kai then. The men let him go. Constance couldn't take her eyes off him, standing there, breathing hard and opening and closing his fists. He looked like some glorious avenger without a battle to fight. Or maybe he did have a battle to fight. Mason said something to him and then smiled at Constance. Bastien ushered everyone out until Kai and Constance were alone.

She waited to see what he was going to say, but instead he pulled a ragged sheet of paper out of his wallet. He unfolded it and slid it across the desk. "I found this in the saray."

She read the words, the truths she'd written about what she felt in her heart. Constance let the paper drop and gazed into his eyes. "I'm sorry. I only did what I thought was best. I never wanted to hurt you." Her hands dragged under the weight of all she had to explain. "I'm so afraid of upheaval," she signed slowly, begging him to understand. "Violent feelings. Dependence on someone. Love. I'm afraid of falling in love and having my heart broken. Or worse. That's a lot of the reason I became an odalisque."

Kai looked piqued. "Whether love is bad or forbidden by the code or whatever, it happened with us, damn you. It happened. Why do you think you can make it go away?"

"I thought it was for the best."

He came closer and took her hands. "Why? Why would you think that? Most women want a connection, a relationship. Most women want to be loved."

"Most of them want children too, but I don't. I won't. I just don't want the responsibility, and besides that, I'd make an awful mom. I can't hear. I can't talk. So even though I adore you, I can't do that to you."

Kai was staring at her like she'd grown two heads. "Do what to me?"

"Deprive you of children."

He shook his head. "Constance, I'm sad about the kids I lost. I'll always grieve for them, but that doesn't mean I expect them to be replaced, not by you or anyone else." She startled as she felt his hand on the side of her arm. His rough fingertips, his soft touch. He brushed back a stray lock of her hair. "It's not your responsibility to fix what my ex-wife did. I just... Constance. I just want you."

"Really?" Constance was skeptical. "You really don't want kids?"

"Did I ever say I did? I have three kids. Here." He tapped his chest. "Will I ever have more? I don't know. I don't care about that as much as I care about you. I love you. *I love you.* I wouldn't change a thing about you. Except that I would make you less stubborn and pigheaded."

Constance laughed weakly. "I might say the same about you," she signed. "But I love you anyway. I always did."

She loved him. God, she loved him so much. He tapped her chin, demanding her attention again. "Let's worry about kids some other time, okay? I don't believe for a second you wouldn't be a good mother, but if you don't want to be a mother, then don't be. If you want to be a speechwriter, or a fucking entomologist studying bugs..." He grinned down at her, a smile rife with possibilities. "This is your life. What do you want it to be?"

Constance's lower lip trembled. She squeezed her hands up between them and signed, "I hate bugs."

Kai chuckled, a little shudder against her. His lips were so close her eyes almost crossed trying to read them. "You know what our problem is, Constance? We're afraid to accept what's right here in front of us for fear everything will fuck up again. And I don't think that's any way to live. This is *your* life, not your mother's. What do you want? Point blank? Fears and anxieties aside?"

She made the three simple signs. "I want you."

Kai tightened his fingers on her arms, kneading the spot just above her elbows. "Then come back to me. I miss you. And Satya's come to love you too. If you don't come back she'll come over here and kick your ass, I guarantee it. You're the sister she never had."

Constance started to laugh but ended up in tears. Her hands shook as she signed. "I want someone to belong to. Someone who loves me just as I am, who wants me just as I am, unconditionally. Who doesn't use me like my mother, or despise me like my stepdads and stepsiblings, or pay for me like—"

Kai took her frantic hands and stilled them. "I'm not paying for you anymore. I resigned you on those damn papers. I don't want you as my odalisque. I want you as Constance, my beautiful, caring, sexy, slightly-messed-up woman."

"You left out stubborn and pigheaded," she signed.

Kai's kiss was searing, possessive. Unequivocal. "We tried living by the code," he said when he pulled away. "Now, how about we just try being in love?"

Chapter Nineteen: In Love

They left that evening with Bastien's blessing. Kai was sure the agent would never comprehend the depth of emotion Kai and Constance had come to feel for each other. But he understood the gist of it well enough to release Constance from her odalisque duties without prejudice, and embrace her by the door. "You will always have a home here," Bastien told her.

His farewell to Kai was a little less affectionate. "Keep my Constance happy. Or else."

Mason joined them on the flight home, and by the time they touched down at LAX, Kai and his longtime friend had made a fragile peace. Kai realized Mason was lost and hurting. He still remembered those black days and weeks after Veronica had left him, and how desperate he'd felt.

Those days were over though. Kai was starting to believe he'd found his way through, and he was sure Mason would find his way eventually. It would just take some time.

They dropped Mason off first, at the Hollywood hotel suite he was renting while his divorce was sorted out. Once they pulled away and got back on the highway, Kai turned to Constance and tilted up her chin.

"I think, when I get you home, I'll have to spend about five hours working you over. And I can't promise all of it will be activities you enjoy."

Constance swallowed. She signed, "Wow. It's so dark in the car. I couldn't see what you said just now."

Kai chuckled. This time he signed the words right in front of her face. "You. Me. Saray. Some of it will feel very, very good. But you were a bad girl too."

The side of Constance's mouth quirked up in a rueful smile. "Your signing is getting way too good. Far too good for my taste."

Back at Kai's house, there was no chatting, no preliminaries. He led her upstairs and they both undressed. He took her in his arms and they pressed close, skin to skin. She felt different to him already. More relaxed, less defensive. He drew back and grinned down at her.

"Do you want your spanking first, or last?"

"Never," Constance signed.

"Liar," Kai signed back. "You love spankings. You just added ten minutes in the corner with nipple clamps on."

Her look of protest was hilarious, but ineffective in softening his resolve. He knew she didn't want him soft anyway. Kai scrutinized her, tilting his head. "So, am I still your Master? Even if you aren't my odalisque?"

Constance thought a moment before she started signing. "If I believe you're my Master, that's all that counts."

"So I just have to work really hard to make you believe." He headed for the cabinet. "This should be fun." Kai didn't know if she caught his last words, but when he turned around with the cuffs in his hand, she looked beautifully apprehensive. He turned her and fastened her wrists behind her back, then led her over to the bed and pulled her over his lap. It was a turn on to put her on the bench, or over the footboard, but sometimes he just wanted the thrill of her squirming on his lap.

Kai started slow, teasing her. He squeezed and caressed her lovely ass as much as he spanked it. Then he increased the intensity slowly, drawing it out, making it last. He loved the feel of her trembling, trying to control herself, then giving up and pulling away. Any such attempts were answered with resounding smacks and a tighter grip on her arms. She was wailing by the end, tears falling on his leg. She didn't usually cry.

Kai stood her in front of him and reached to wipe away one of the glistening drops. *Emotions are dangerous.* He rubbed the liquid between his fingers and looked at her. "It's okay to cry, isn't it?" he signed. She held his gaze a long moment and nodded. "And you know I love you

198

very much. Don't you?" She nodded again and leaned forward. He held her, let her rub her tears on his cheek while her tousled hair fell against his face.

He kissed her, hard and deep, tasting the sweetness of her desire. He pulled back and asked, "Do you love me, Constance?"

She didn't hesitate, but nodded with a tremulous smile. Something in his chest turned over and clenched at the vulnerability in her eyes. He stroked her still-damp cheek. "That's okay too. Well, come on. Corner time."

Kai put on the clover clamps she hated and turned her to the wall. He sauntered back to the bed and lay down to watch her, basking in the sight of her feminine figure, her reddened bottom. The trembling in her knees. Her hands occasionally clenched and unclenched in the cuffs that held them fast. Every couple of minutes she looked back over her shoulder at him. He'd frown and sign for her to keep her eyes in the corner, but he adored her a little more each time her gaze sought him out. It was as if, like him, she was afraid of losing him again through some inattention or carelessness. But they were both too awakened now for that.

At ten minutes on the dot, he crossed to her and turned her around. "Are you feeling mastered yet?" he asked, with a sadistic little tug at the chain between her breasts. The bite of the clamps had her sporting a gorgeous woebegone look, a look that, unfortunately for her, made the dominant in him flare.

His cock pulsed, demanding relief. He pushed her to her knees, fisting his shaft and pressing it to her perfectly formed lips. The chain swung again, side to side, as she struggled for balance. She drew in a breath as he drove his cock into her hot, wet mouth. The warmth and pressure sent shock waves of sensation all the way to the base of his cock and down his inner thighs. It took all his control not to spurt right in the back of her throat.

Constance's hands strained in their bonds. Her mouth and tongue were all over him, fluttering, caressing, stroking his shaft and his balls. She sucked and licked him so blissfully. He was transported back in time to that first evening they'd met, when she'd fallen to her knees and serviced him without even knowing who he was. Perhaps she *had* known who he was, or had an inkling who he would become to her. Thinking back, he was certain he'd felt an instant connection too.

Kai drew her head back so she could see his face as he thrust into her throat. "Good girl," he crooned. "Such a good girl." He couldn't last any longer. He pulled out of her mouth and spurted over her chest, marking her for himself. He might share her again one day, might take a chance on another scatter party if they ever got over the trauma of the last one. But even so, she would be his, only his. He would make sure she knew it. He wasn't in a rental state of mind anymore. He wanted her for life.

Kai laid her down on the bed and rubbed his semen over her breasts, across her chest. Across her heart. She winced as his hand caught in the silver chain. He relented and took the clamps off, stroking and squeezing her breasts as she keened softly through the discomfort. He turned her over and unhooked the cuffs that held her hands behind her back. He kissed each delicate wrist before he turned her over again.

"Rest a moment," he said. He explored the recesses of the cabinet, returning with a sleek ebony glass plug and Constance's favorite brand of lube. She was already shaking her head.

"Oh, sweet girl," he said with tsk. "You don't have a choice. Did you think you'd seen the last of this lube?"

She signed, "I hoped I'd seen the last of it."

He took her hands in his and tsked again, and drew them over her head. "Ever the smartass. I think I have something for that." He nudged her over onto her stomach and placed her hands on either side of her head. He turned her face so she could see him. "Don't move them. Understand?"

She nodded, her eyes wide.

He toyed with her ass for a bit, forcing her open with his fingers and inserting and withdrawing the plug. Partly to assert his dominance, partly to tease her and turn her on. The trusty heating lube did its work. Constance squirmed and whined, and even disobeyed a few times and reached back to push at his hands in protest. Well, training was part of the process. A very fun part. He simply spanked her sore cheeks and returned her hands to where they belonged. Finally he drove the plug home, seating it deep in her ass.

Kai was rock solid again. He went to the bathroom to wash his hands and distract himself so she had a little time to lie there feeling naughty and punished. When he returned, he might have thought she was sleeping if not for the way she was curling and uncurling her toes.

Kai slipped a hand beneath her and lifted her onto her hands and knees. She'd been such a good girl. It was time for her to have her fun. He ran a hand up her back and kneaded her shoulders. She was pressing her ass against him, the delicious slut. He eased his cock into her cleft inch by inch, savoring the tight squeeze of her pussy. Once fully seated, he withdrew and thrust forward again forcefully, enjoying her little grunt.

He pounded her hard for a while, pressing the base of the plug at the same time to force it deeper in her ass. She was all limp and pliable, letting him have his way with her. He loved the way she trusted him, the way she accepted his dominance over her, answering it with her own sensual charms.

He softened his thrusts then, holding onto the alluring curve of her hips, grinding against her ass. He slipped his fingers down her front, between her smooth, slick pussy lips. He knew she was close to coming, but then he realized he really wanted to see her face. He pulled out, eliciting a moan of despair from her lips.

Kai turned her over with gentle hands. He spread his fingers against her belly, the tips of his pinkies at either hip. She was his. He ran his fingers up over her ribs to her breasts and stroked her nipples lightly. They were still sore and she gave a delightful squeak at the contact. She was thrusting her hips toward him, begging for his cock. He entered her a few centimeters, then pulled out again. In, out, teasing her. She gazed up at him with her patented pleading look.

"I love you," he said. Constance half beamed and half frowned, brimming with frustration. Kai laughed at the warring expressions on her face. "I know you want me to fuck you." He slid into her again, a little deeper each time. "I just want you to know I love you also. I should have told you that so many times before."

She smiled and signed that she loved him too. Her pussy was gripping him and her legs were splayed open, as if she craved more. He gathered her close and slipped his legs under the backs of her thighs, tilting her pelvis up. He drove in all the way, basking in her lustful moans. The toy in her ass rubbed his cock through her walls. From the noises and gyrations she was making, he guessed it felt exceptionally pleasurable to her too.

"Yes, yes," he murmured against her neck. *Yes, I want you. Yes, I want to try again, with someone worthy this time.* He leaned back to watch her climb to her apex, to see the intent concentration on her face. His own orgasm was shuddering to life, spurred on by her loveliness, the way she clasped him and arched her hips to perfectly match his thrusts. She threw her head back and he felt her pussy clamp around his cock in rhythmic, erotic completion. The pulses triggered a monumental climax within him. He felt it in his entire body, as if the nerve impulses had raced up his spine and sent the message to every fiber of his being. He collapsed against her, trying not to crush her.

After a few intense moments of spasming release, he came back to his senses and levered himself up on his elbows. He looked down with a smile at the woman in his arms. She was staring up at him in wonder.

"What?" he asked.

"I could hear your heartbeat," she signed weakly. "I could feel it pounding against my cheek."

Kai didn't doubt it—because she made his heart beat so strongly. She spread her fingers on his chest and nudged him. He fell onto his back, stretching in satisfaction, gazing at her in amusement as she knelt beside him and laid her head against his ribs. Her eyes were closed, concentrating, and he knew she was listening the only way she knew how. Through feeling. Through sensation. Her fingers trailed lazily across his skin, up to his shoulder and down his side. She made some little taps then, in time to his heartbeat.

It was so simple, he thought. All those years he'd listened to complex concertos, the crashing, banging, intricate noise. Constance was a new song in his life, a simple, honest song. *Tap tap. Tap tap.* His heart was hers. "Kai," she said softly, in her sweet, hesitant way. "Kai…"

God, what music on her lips.

* * * * *

Constance watched Kai warily as he finished the last of the knots. "All night?" she signed in the confines of her bonds.

"Yes, all night," Kai answered. "You're not my odalisque anymore, but you're still mine. I'll still like to keep you tied up now and again." He winked at her. "To deepen your sense of slavery, of course."

Constance squirmed. She had a sneaking feeling the plug, too, was going to stay in all night. If only he hadn't used that confounded lube, she might have actually enjoyed the feeling of fullness while she slept. Maybe if she asked him—

Damn. He was looking at her with that sadistic smirk.

"You are very, very mean to someone who is supposedly your treasured sex slave," she signed with a pout. "Really very cruel."

"Yes, I am very mean and cruel person," he agreed, rolling his eyes. "Now..." He lay beside her, fluffing the pillow under his head. "I would like you to tell me about all these plans you have. These things you want to do that I was apparently going to keep you from doing."

She flushed. "You're laughing at me."

"I most certainly am not. I'm slightly peeved you didn't tell me about the dreams in that pretty little head of yours. Just like those speeches you hid from me."

"Oh God," she signed. "It's embarrassing to write speeches when you don't talk. I have to leave the speeches to someone else."

He shook his head at her. "No. They're your speeches. Your dreams. Tell me your plans."

She shrugged. "There's nothing concrete I have planned. But I've always thought I would like to open some kind of home for kids who have nowhere else to go. Runaways. Smart, well-meaning kids who just caught a bad break in life. Kids who need a safe place. A family."

"Like, some kind of group home?"

"I don't know. I don't know anything about it. Maybe..."

She slid him a look. She wanted to ask his help, but she didn't want him to think she was using him for his money.

"Maybe what?" he prompted.

"Nothing. Well..." Her fingers collapsed, uncertain.

"*Maybe you can help me, Kai,*" he said, filling in what she couldn't bring herself to say. "*I know you like to help people, and that you have more money than you know what to do with—*"

Constance laughed and reached out to him. "Yes, I wanted to ask you for help. But I didn't want you to get the wrong idea. And I felt silly."

"Silly? Why?"

"Because." Constance squirmed again, feeling put on the spot. "Because..." Because now that she might actually have the means of putting her plans into action, she felt scared. "No one will listen to me," she signed. "I can't talk."

"You can talk. You're talking to me right now. You write spectacular speeches. Why don't you give some of them?"

Constance shook her head in horror. "No!"

"Why not? If you feel strongly about, say, runaway kids, put your voice out there in the world. I know it takes courage to try, but you've fallen in with a family of real crusaders. Once you see what you're capable of, you'll wish you'd tried sooner."

"What if I get up to give a speech in sign language and no one listens? I mean, signing isn't the same as speaking."

"Who says?" Kai stilled her hands. "You speak louder than anyone I've ever known in my life. Well"—he rolled his eyes—"except for Satya, maybe."

"Do you think Satya will ever recover?" Constance asked. "From crashing the scatter party that night?"

"She thinks we're all reprobates, but that's nothing new. She'll get over it. Don't try to change the subject," he said, tweaking a still-sore nipple. "From now on, I want to know all your dreams. Our contract days are over. Now I want it all, free of charge. Your body *and* your mind. And in exchange, I'll give you whatever you want. Whatever I can do to fulfill you."

"Take out the butt plug, and let me sleep untied tonight?" Constance signed hopefully.

Kai shook his head. "Anything but that."

Constance nuzzled her forehead against his chest in a kind of affectionate frustration. Or frustrated horniness. "Are you going to sleep in here with me?" she signed.

"Yes. Or we can sleep in my bedroom. I want to sleep with the woman I love. Is that okay? I don't think I snore."

Constance looked thoughtful. "It's going to feel strange, not being your odalisque anymore. No occlusion, no emotional distance." She caught his speculative gaze. "I mean, it's fine, but I really liked some parts of the code."

"What parts?"

"Being naked all the time. Playing in the saray. And serving you on command..."

The worry in his eyes turned to something warmer and a lot more seductive. "I liked everything about the code except the occlusion and the emotional distance. The cockslavery was a pretty fine thing."

Constance laughed softly. "Were you to untie me, Master, I could serve you. A willing cockslave. I think that will never change."

Constance saw Kai's jaw tense, and imagined he probably groaned. She snuggled closer to him, feeling his cock rise against her hip. He fumbled with the knots holding her wrists. As soon as she was free, she eased down the bed and took him in her mouth, savoring every inch. He twisted his fingers in her hair, urging her on.

He was her Master, her lover, her friend. He owned her heart now, not just her body. Constance was pretty sure she'd prefer it that way.

Chapter Twenty:
Eighteen Months Later

Kai smiled at Constance as she fussed with her hair and pulled at her stylish linen jacket. A late spring breeze rustled the flowers of the meticulously landscaped courtyard.

"You're more nervous today than you were at our wedding."

Constance shot him a look. "Our wedding was just a handful of close friends," she signed. "And I was really sure about what I was doing at our wedding."

Kai put a hand on her lower back, a gentle touch that steadied her. "You're not sure about what you're doing today?"

Constance scanned the large crowd gathered in front of her Center for Youth in Crisis. The new CYC spanned nearly half a city block, comprised of a series of dormitories, living spaces, medical and rehabilitation clinics, combined with recreational and educational facilities. First she and Kai had reclaimed the buildings, hiring contractors to remodel the ramshackle shells into useful spaces. Then they had worked together with experts to plan and staff the center, a mission that had taken nearly a year. The object wasn't just to give kids a safe place to stay, but to give them a new lease on life. Job training, rehabilitation for addictions. A sense of purpose to carry back out into the world.

Constance clutched at her stomach. It was her dream made reality, but she still quailed under the weight of the responsibility. "It's just...so many people are depending on me. Depending on this facility really working for kids."

Kai shrugged, strikingly dapper as always in his bespoke business attire. "Well, if the concept fails, you can always turn it into a training facility for odalisques."

Constance slapped him playfully. "Bastien wouldn't take kindly to the competition."

Kai grimaced. "That bonehead. I still feel the overwhelming urge, every time I see him, to plant my fist in his face."

Constance poked a finger at him. "Don't forget, Bastien brought you and me together."

"Yes, against his better judgment, he told me later. If you really want to thank someone for bringing us together, you'd do better to look over there."

A few yards away, Jeremy Gray and Mason Cooke were deep in conversation. Mason and Jeremy had both stood with Kai at the wedding, with Ms. Dresden and Satya on Constance's side. And Bastien, bless his bonehead heart, had walked her down the aisle like a proud father.

"Listen, love," Kai said, rubbing her shoulders, "everything is going to go fine. You've worked hard for this. I want you to enjoy it." He gave her a direct look. She gazed up into his insistent amber eyes.

"Yes, Master," she signed discreetly with a shiver of pleasure.

"Is your speech ready? All practiced and ready to go?"

Constance felt another frisson of sickening nerves. "Yes. Yes, I'm ready. I think."

"You look like you're going to be sick," said Satya, ducking her head into their private conversation. "Oh, Lord, did my brother already knock you up? You know, this center is proof there are too many kids in the world who need a home, so if you want to have a family you would do better to—"

"Adopt. Yes, we know." Kai held up a hand. "Satya, please. She's nervous, not pregnant."

Mason came charging over as soon as he saw Satya talking to them. "Constance is pregnant?"

Constance rolled her eyes. Mason nudged her and winked. "Married life suits you," he said. "You don't look pregnant. You look excited. Vivacious. Happy."

"Constance looks vivacious and happy because she's married to my brother and they're sickeningly in love," teased Satya, smiling between them. Like Mason, Satya had suffered a heartbreak in the previous year. Constance had a sudden thought, watching the two of them together— Satya's bright eyes and Mason's easy-going smile.

She turned to Kai and signed, "Why don't Mason and Satya get together? You can tell by the way they act around each other that they're halfway in love."

Kai raised an eyebrow and looked between Mason and his sister.

"What did she say?" asked Mason.

Kai brushed at a spot on the lapel of his suit jacket, smothering a smile. "She said she thinks you guys would make a great couple."

Mason and Satya both started making barfing, choking motions in a simultaneous show of disgust.

"Ugh," said Satya. "I grew up with Mason. Or should I say *Darwin*. It would be like hooking up with my brother."

"Incest," Mason agreed, pretending to barf again.

Constance turned to Kai with a daunted look that had him laughing out loud. He put an arm around her shoulder.

"Well, if your disastrous matchmaking attempt hasn't completely demoralized you, it's about two o'clock."

Panic clutched at her chest, but Constance pushed it down. "I'm ready."

"I'll be right there with you," Kai said. "But you'll be fine. You've been preparing for this your whole life."

Constance's knees shook as she climbed the five stairs to the temporary platform that had been erected for the Center's opening ceremonies. She looked out at the large, informally gathered group of charitable givers, child advocates, and various politicians and well-wishers. There were also a few young faces in the crowd, youth in need who were already starting to wander in off the street.

Constance felt a new surge of purpose. Familiar, supportive faces encouraged her. Satya, Mason, Jeremy and Nell. She looked behind her to see Kai arranging his notes at the podium.

Then her husband looked up at the crowd. His eyes seemed to catch for a moment at the back of the audience, his lips going tense in surprise, or perhaps recognition. Constance searched to see what—or who—he was looking at so intently, but then he seemed to recollect himself. He straightened the corners of his notes and smiled at her expectantly. There was nothing to do but begin.

Constance took a deep breath, focused on the faces before her, and launched into the act of giving her first speech. Her fingers felt stiff at the outset, her arms held tensely to her waist. But at the nods and smiles that met her words, she relaxed and began to sign with more confidence. Confidence turned to emotion and emotion to zeal.

"In this city most of all," she signed, "homeless youth need a place to find shelter. A place to feel safe. Young people come here seeking a dream career, only to find a harsh reality. Exploitation, abuse, a spiral of helplessness and addiction." She paused for effect. "But every life is worth saving. Inside every person is a spark that can be rekindled even when it's nearly extinguished. That's what we hope to do here."

She stopped as the people before her started clapping. She knew they only understood her words because Kai was reading them out behind her. She turned back to him and he gave her a furtive thumbs-up. She smiled and turned around to deliver the last of her speech.

"In closing, I want to thank you for being here today," she signed. "For sharing in my dream becoming a reality. Once I was a youth in crisis too. I had nowhere to go, but I found a place where I was welcomed and nurtured and it helped me arrive at this place I am today. With everything you give, with everything you share, with every dream you nurture, you help someone like me make a difference in the world. And when enough people make a difference, wonderful things can happen."

Her final "thank you" was met with another round of applause. She turned from the clapping guests in front of her to look at the magnificent complex behind her, and then her eyes fell on Kai. "Thank you," she signed softly, her fingers to her lips. "I can never thank you enough."

Kai gave a tiny shake of his head and signed, "You already have."

* * * * *

Their story had begun at a charity event, Kai remembered. A charity event for underprivileged children, no less. How unhappy he'd been then, slumped at his table in the back, listening to maudlin music. Smashing chocolate cake in mute fury.

This was so different. Constance's face was alight with happiness, and he—he was practically bursting with it. He was content to stand on the sidelines and let her enjoy her moment, the fruition of her long time dream. He'd hired a professional ASL translator to stay with her so conversation could come easily and so she, not Kai hovering over her, could take the credit for what she'd done.

After a half hour or so she made her way back to his side, glowing with excitement and pride. He gave her a crushing hug. She was wearing a smart little ivory business suit that begged to be ripped off. *Later. Let her savor all this first.*

He drew back to drop a kiss on her forehead. "My delicious little—" he began. But Constance's gaze was fixed on something over his shoulder. Kai turned to see a group of three teens. Fourteen, fifteen years old. Maybe younger. They were Indian, two boys and a girl. He had seen them earlier in the back of the crowd. For a moment, as he'd seen them buffeted in the squeeze of people around them, he'd thought of those three glossy heads bobbing under the waves.

"Hello," he blurted out. He reached out his hand. "Kai Chandler. This is my wife, Constance."

Only one of the kids, the oldest, reached out to shake it. The other two looked pretty bad. Drug addicted? Malnourished? He could see Constance looking over at him from his peripheral vision, but he couldn't take his eyes off the kids. They weren't the age his kids would have been, and they didn't look like Veronica at all, but...

"We need help," the oldest one, the brother, said quietly. "Can you help us?"

Help, help! The words in a shrill childish voice echoed in his subconscious. It was all he could do not to grab the three kids to stop them from scattering out of his reach. But they weren't running from him this time. They were here and they needed help. Constance stood beside him, looking at him encouragingly.

"Yes, we can help you," said Kai, finding his voice again. "Of course. Please..." He pointed toward the entrance to the center. The kids let themselves be guided, the second brother drawing his sister along when she looked like she might pull away.

Kai followed them inside, taking Constance's hand and squeezing it almost unconsciously. *This is your life. What do you want it to be?*

The door closed behind them in a whisper whirr of a slide that sounded almost like a dream come to life. Almost like a second chance.

A Final Note

In case any readers are wondering, the *Code d'Odalisque* actually exists and is now in its fifth edition, although Maison Odalisque and Agt. Sebastien Gaudet are products of my own imagination. I must express my deepest gratitude to Mr. Charles Molyneux, a tireless steward of the *Code d'Odalisque,* whose website http://codeodalisque.blogspot.com played a great part in inspiring this book.

While this book's version of the code borrowed heavily from the real thing, other aspects were completely made up. If you'd like to read the actual *Code d'Odalisque*, Mr. Molyneux and his group of volunteers have graciously offered to forward free PDF copies to any who are interested. They can be contacted at bedroomslaves@yahoo.com. Their mission is to spread the word about this lifestyle to provide an alternative to those attracted to a more sensual style of slavery.

As for the signing and lip-reading which takes place in this book, it is very difficult to do justice to a deaf person's true experience in communication. No disrespect was meant in trying to give Constance and Kai's sign language and lip-reading conversations a "spoken language" feel. This was merely done for the convenience of the reader.

Finally, if you enjoyed this book, I hope you will also read the first book set in this world, *Comfort Object*, which tells the story of Jeremy and Nell, and the second, *Caressa's Knees*, about Kyle and concert cellist Caressa.

Many thanks to all my readers for your continued support. Please subscribe to my website to keep up to date on coming stories, re-issues, contests and blog appearances: **http://annabeljoseph.wordpress.com**

A short excerpt from *Cirque du Minuit*, the first book in the Cirque du Monde series, by Annabel Joseph, coming in the spring of 2012

Kelsey was lost *again*. She couldn't believe it.

Four months at Cirque du Monde's Paris headquarters, and the mazelike corridors of its training facility still flabbergasted her sense of direction. The hallways met at strange angles and the numbers followed no system she could discern. Some walls were glass, while others were painted concrete. A small meeting room might be nestled next to a cavernous rehearsal space, a dressing room next to a director's office. She was looking for a trainer's office at the moment.

She was pretty sure she was in the "J" corridor, but she needed to be in the "I" corridor. She opened the next door she encountered, hoping to cut across, and found herself in a dimly lit, crowded storage room. The ceiling soared above her, dotted by skylights. She had just enough light to navigate through the densely stacked boxes, but she still managed to trip over a low-lying obstacle. Her gymnast's reflexes were the only thing that saved her from a total pratfall. She rolled and came to a stop with her back against the side of a crate, rubbing her aching shin. *Graceful, Kelsey. Thank God no one saw that.*

Then she heard voices, a man's deeper voice and a woman's soft one. The man sounded angry. She stood and peered around the crate in front of her in the semi-darkness. The couple was perhaps twenty yards away. Minya, a gorgeous Chinese trapeze artist, and *him*.

Theo Zamora, her soaring fantasy. Her gypsy king.

Kelsey had noticed Theo Zamora the first day of her auditions. He'd strolled through the studio around ten in the morning—she even

213

remembered the time. Just the way he walked, the casual flick of his wrist as he passed them, arrested her. She'd been unable to look away until he'd left through the other door. She'd seen him a couple other times that week, and each time his presence had affected her in the same visceral way. When she was hired a week later, her first thought was *Now I work in the same company as him.*

Kelsey was always watching for him, stealing peeks into practice gyms and company meetings in hopes of a glimpse of his tall strong body, his dark eyes. She stared at him each night backstage as they performed in the show *Tsilaosa*. Not once—not one time—had they exchanged words.

Exchanged words? Ha. Theo Zamora didn't even know she existed. He was unapproachable to her, a sleek and powerful idol to be admired from afar. Even now, her heart was racing to be in such close proximity to him. She pressed her hand to her mouth and stood perfectly still as she watched the couple in profile. He was scolding his trapeze partner. Kelsey couldn't hear his words, but she picked up the inflection of French, his native language. He towered over Minya, his face a menacing mask.

How would you feel if he looked at you that way?

Dark-haired Minya shrank away, fell to her knees. Theo pulled her up again, not roughly but not gently either, and pushed her face down over the edge of a box. Kelsey waited for Minya to pull away, but the quivering woman stayed still, her legs pressed together and her face buried in her arms.

Kelsey knew she shouldn't witness this private moment, but she couldn't look away. She watched with horrified fascination as Theo rummaged through his gym bag and then straightened. Some kind of belt or strap dangled from his hand. *Oh my God.* Kelsey felt traumatized and yet aroused by the menacing way he stood, his stern expression. She sucked in a silent breath as he put his hand on the small of Minya's back. The sound of the strap's impact made her jump.

Kelsey dug her nails into her palm, shocked that Minya didn't try to get away. But she didn't. She actually seemed to be enjoying it, squirming and pressing her hips against the edge of the box. Kelsey could hear her low, erotic moans each time he brought the strap down again. How did Minya stay so still? The only sign of any distress was a small kick of her feet—and those muffled moans.

Kelsey stared as Theo wielded the strap without mercy or hesitation. He was clearly enjoying himself too, from the aggressive pleasure written on his face. She'd read about people doing this kind of stuff, but to see it going on right in front of her eyes...to hear the cracking sounds of impact and Minya's intimate noises...

Kelsey's knees gave out. She huddled behind the crate and hugged herself, listening to the sound of the steady blows and Minya's whimpers. She slid her hand between her legs, trying to soothe the shocking, unexpected bloom of lust. Her stomach was in knots as the strapping continued, but her clit signaled something else altogether. *You like this. This violence against her.*

You want it yourself.

At last the sound of the blows stopped. Kelsey scrambled to her feet and peered over the top of the crate. Theo squeezed and patted Minya's ass cheeks through her leotard while she remained submissively draped over the box. A snap of his fingers, and she was down on the floor again. Kelsey's pussy seemed to pulse in time with the petite woman's movements. How would it feel to lie at his feet, conquered by him, her ass burning hot from his strap?

Kelsey held her breath as Theo thrust his hand down his gym pants and...*oh my God.* He fisted his engorged, jutting cock, beckoning his partner. His lover. Minya didn't resist him, even when he grabbed the back of her hair in his hand and... *Wow.* How could Minya take him so deep in her throat and still breathe?

Minya reached out to brace herself against his legs. He took her hands in his and pulled her closer. Minya gagged slightly, but she didn't fight, didn't resist, and he didn't back away from her. It was so carnal, so animalistic that Kelsey forgot herself and gasped aloud. His gaze flew to hers at once, over boxes and crates of equipment. Their eyes locked, and then his lips twisted into a grin.

"Hey you, girl, hiding there. Either join us or get out."

It was the first words he'd ever spoken to her. Kelsey ducked her head and ran for her life.

* * * * *

After that, Kelsey saw him constantly, no matter how much she went out of her way to avoid him. They were all working on *Tsilaosa* together, so it really couldn't be helped. She was in training, slated to replace one of the acrobats who was taking a break to start a family. Theo and Minya were a well-established act, one of the anchor acts for the production. With a cast of only fifty-odd people, Kelsey was pretty visible as a trainee, and there was no chance he hadn't recognized her. When he met her eyes the next day in the weekly production meeting, he made it abundantly clear that he remembered her and what she'd seen.

Minya, on the other hand, ignored her. The doe-eyed trapezist seemed lost in her own world. Kelsey had always interpreted her stand-offishness and dreamy quality as artistic affectation, but now she couldn't stop picturing her cowering at Theo's feet. She wondered what Minya had done to deserve that punishment—if it was even really punishment—and how often the two played out scenes like the one she'd spied on.

Damn. She had to stop thinking about them. It was after seven, and the troupe was assembling in the backstage area to prepare for the evening's show. Kelsey stretched on mats by the back wall while performers warmed up on tightropes, treadmills, and training bars in the center. She kept her back to the structure where Theo normally warmed up with a series of chin-ups. Kelsey had learned to resist the urge to sneak looks, because damn it, he always caught her. He'd pin her with those coal black eyes, and she would flush hot with embarrassment. But there was no reproach in his gaze, only an all-too-knowing assessment—that was the worst part of all.

Kelsey had a sick feeling he knew she hadn't been scandalized by what she'd seen. God, if he had any idea how many times she'd masturbated over it, hiding under her blankets in the company dorms... Even now, in the middle of the busy backstage, the scene replayed itself in her mind for the hundredth time. Minya's graceful submission and Theo's muscular arm rising and falling—

"Hey, Kels. How's it going?"

Kelsey swung around, hoping her train of thought wasn't written all over her face. "Oh. Hi."

Jason Beck was one of her coaches, a fellow Californian who made the unfamiliar French headquarters feel a little more like home. Like all the Cirque's employees, he was supremely fit and staunchly professional. He put a hand on her back. "Want me to help you stretch?"

She didn't take it as a come on even though, before Theo, Jason would have been her type—tall and muscular, with longish chestnut hair he tamed into a ponytail most days. Kelsey knew the countless times

Jason touched and manipulated her each day had nothing to do with sex or flirtation. It was just part of his job.

Jason had a reputation for being zealous about his new recruits, about getting them acclimated and involved in one of Cirque du Monde's fifteen currently operating shows, which is why she'd been glad to end up under his tutelage. Kelsey tolerated his poking, pushing, prodding, and general questioning as the practice space around them ratcheted up in motion and noise. Unfortunately, since she'd turned to talk to Jason, she saw Theo saunter past jugglers and a troupe of musclemen to lean against the pull-up bars. He scanned the room with haughty disinterest. Kelsey looked away before he caught her staring, but Jason noticed and turned to find the object of her scrutiny.

He turned back to her a moment later and pursed his lips, pushing her ankle back nearly to her shoulder. "I wouldn't recommend getting tangled up with the likes of him."

"'*The likes of him*?' You sound like my grandma."

"Grandma knows best," he said, releasing her. "Listen, all the new girls—and guys—get fascinated with him in the beginning. But he's not exactly relationship material."

"Minya likes him." Kelsey watched Theo's partner start warm ups on the practice trapeze. Theo glanced at Minya, then away. Kelsey studied them from behind Jason's back, trying to decode their body language. "So, are they a couple or what?"

Jason rolled his eyes. "I'll go with *or what*. You're probably better off not knowing."

"What does that mean?"

"I mean, they're weird. He's weird, she's weird. They belong together. You, on the other hand, are very normal and well-adjusted, and I'd hate to see that change."

"Well-adjusted? Really?" Kelsey frowned. "That basically means I'm boring." Since coming to train at the Cirque, Kelsey had the sinking feeling she was horribly dull compared to everyone around her. Being detail-oriented, focused, and responsible had worked great for her in the world of competitive gymnastics, but now...

"Kelsey, you are a breath of fresh air," Jason assured her. "Too many over-the-top personalities around here. It gets old." He finished with her other leg and chucked her under the chin. "What is this place, when two Californians are the most normal people to be found?" He started on her core, helping her twist and warm up her arms and shoulders. "While we're on the subject, I would also avoid the parties he and his cronies attend."

Kelsey frowned. "Drugs?"

"God, no. You know they test here. Therefore...they get their thrills in other ways. They call him the Rakehell, if that tells you anything. He's not a nice guy."

"He doesn't seem that nice."

"But he's good at what he does. One of the best in the business."

"So I should admire him professionally, but avoid him socially."

"Like the plague."

Kelsey laughed. "Okay, I'm sensing you feel strongly about this."

"I just think you should be concentrating on your training right now. This is a transitional time for you in the company. They have high hopes for your future, but you have to give them what they want."

"Do you think I *haven't* been concentrating on my training? I'm working damn hard. Ow!"

Jason ruthlessly worked at a knot in one of her back muscles. "I didn't say anything about you not concentrating. Let's keep it that way. New people come in sometimes and get caught up in the partying and backstage shenanigans. I call it the circus underbelly. I've seen more than one promising recruit go down."

"Really?"

"Yeah, way down."

Kelsey looked around at the assembled company as the stage manager called out "Ten minutes to animation!" None of the performers looked especially dissolute or seamy. Well, most of them didn't, she thought, with a sidelong glance at the object of her obsession.

"Don't worry," she said, shrugging away from her coach's prodding fingers. "I'm not taking chances with anything right now."

"Genevieve says you can take Marisol's place in just a few weeks, if you feel ready. How are things going with you and the other acrobats?"

Kelsey turned to take in the group of Argentinean tumblers she'd been rehearsing with. She was getting the routines okay. They were certainly within her physical skill set. The greater challenge was growing more natural as a performer, and tapping into the communal synergy. The Argentineans were a smooth, well-oiled machine while she was still a misfiring spark plug. She didn't even speak their language. She looked back at Jason and shrugged. "I just need practice. I don't feel ready yet, but I'll get it."

"Yes, you will." He was manipulating her feet now, paying careful attention to her joints. "You can do all the things Marisol does. Easily. It's just about getting into the rhythm of the group."

"And learning Spanish."

"*Sí, querida.* It will come. If you want to stay with Cirque du Monde, it wouldn't hurt to learn French and Russian too. Mandarin, if you're really ambitious." He winked and patted her thigh, then moved off to help some of his other charges.

Kelsey lay back with a sigh and stared up at the beams in the ceiling, and air conditioning ducts painted in red, orange, blue, and fuchsia. Kelsey had on a similarly multicolored leotard, and her puffy blue plastic wig with her light blonde hair tucked securely underneath. Her makeup was just as involved as the main performers, even though for now she was only an extra, cavorting during act changes and helping move equipment.

She was anxious to get involved in one of the actual acts, but in the circus, you paid your dues and worked your way up. In the world of gymnastics she'd been a luminary, making it as far as a U.S. Olympic team alternate. Now she was an alternate again, training to step in for someone else. But she was here. The Cirque du Monde. Isn't that what she'd wanted? She was tired of being the good girl, the disciplined Olympian. She was as creative and passionate as anyone else, and she was eager to let that side of her out into the light. That's what she'd said during her interview with Genevieve, the director of the show.

Now she just had to get it done.

Kelsey sat up and looked around the room at her colorful cast of co-workers. Only Theo and Minya weren't outfitted in rainbow hues. He was stark black from head to toe. No wig needed...his hair was black too. Minya was light to Theo's dark, in a shimmering white and yellow bodysuit studded with crystals and topped off by a wig of fiery orange hair. For performances, she streaked the wig with red and gold highlights, to stunning effect.

Theo took his partner's hand, and Minya looked up at him sideways. Kelsey couldn't see her expression. Was she smiling? Seductive? Or questioning? Theo looked at her so intently, so...possessively. What must that feel like? He cupped Minya's face in his hand and brushed a kiss against her cheek.

"Three minutes to animation!" The stage manager's voice boomed in the backstage area. Kelsey shook off her horny daydreams and leaned

219

to fish a red sugar straw out of her bag, tearing off the edge and upending it. A small, tart cascade of candy landed on her tongue. Across the room, Jason shook a finger at her, but she didn't care. It was her pre-show ritual. The tart sugar was the taste of her dreams coming true.

Kelsey pranced through her roles in the production, enjoying every moment of it. Bystander #3. Villager. Spotter. Minor roles, but each necessary, a small opportunity to shine. After she finished helping the juggler pull all her stuff off the stage, Kelsey settled down in the shadows of the wings to watch Theo and Minya's act at the top of the vast auditorium. The couple clasped the trapeze together and a cable pulled them up, so far up, at least sixty feet in the air to the bird's nest. They checked lines and the balance of the bar, and the act began.

Kelsey had watched them fly so many times, she knew every release, every trick. Minya catapulted from Theo's arms into a breathtaking somersault, and then back to his grasp. They flew side by side sometimes, in a sinuous dance of strength, and at other times, Minya hung from his hands, his knees, his shoulders. It amazed Kelsey, their strength and dexterity while swinging from a bar so many feet off the ground. There was no net, no spotters. For the final, most difficult trick, Minya wore a single safety line.

Kelsey could never have done it. *You can never have him, trapezist or no. He's not for you.* No, *they* belonged together, Theo and Minya, the gypsy king and his orange-gold shadow, flung and then caught up again in space. The beauty of their dance brought tears to Kelsey's eyes. Theo swung high, higher. It was time for the big finish. Minya flew upwards, her arms spread wide—

Kelsey knew right away something was wrong.

The angle was too great, the height was off. The audience didn't know. They gasped in awe at the way Minya soared. Kelsey watched Theo, her blood pounding in her ears. He swung back, a twist of his body, and tried to catch her on the way down. His legs strained and he arched, reaching for her. Even from sixty feet below, even petrified with horror, Kelsey noted the mortal concentration on his face. He caught his partner for a moment, grasped her by one hand. His grip arrested her arc and she jerked. She no longer looked graceful.

Now, with that jerk and break in formation, the audience knew something was wrong, and the gasps turned to silence and panicked sharp screams. Kelsey's own scream caught in her throat as the trapeze still swung and Theo lost his grip. Minya flew down, down, her yellow-red-orange-gold hair streaming behind as she dove head first toward the earth. It might almost be part of the act, it looked so graceful and dramatic. Kelsey waited for the safety to jerk Minya back, to halt her swan dive toward disaster. She saw the spotter pull the rope, faster and faster.

The safety never caught.

Look for *Cirque du Minuit,* a novel by Annabel Joseph, arriving in spring of 2012.

15454291R00118

Made in the USA
Lexington, KY
30 May 2012